MW00596429

Star Navigator
Stranded in the Stars:
Book Three

***

By Naomi Lucas

Copyright © 2016 by Naomi Lucas

***

Table of Contents

Stranded in the Stars:

Last Call
Collector of Souls
Star Navigator
(Coming Soon)

Cyborg Shifters:

Wild Blood
Storm Surge
Shark Bite

Dedication:

To my loving husband.

Stranded in the Stars

Chapter One:

• • • •

T hey didn't have to die, those men before me. I didn't have to die either, and so far I've beaten the odds.

Reina looked down at the skin of her arm. She twisted the lithe appendage, flipping it over, surveying the reddened joints. There was a long incision that began at her palm and ran all the way to her shoulder. The cut stopped at her armpit but then started back up along the front of her neck.

It itched. Sometimes it swelled.

At first, it had made it hard to breathe, hard to move, and then the headaches began, followed by weeks of fever and sweat. Reina remembered the sweat. She nearly drowned from it, and from the sharp pain as the salty dew of it leaked into her wounds.

Now her skin was pulled taut as it tried to heal. Her body fought to adjust to the invasive and very alien feel of what the Earthian Council had done to her.

They had purged her of her bones, her muscles, her nerves, and replaced them all with metal.

"Try not to move it, Reina. It'll just make the recovery process longer." The cybernetic surgeon who attended her sighed and eyed her arm with a strange, covetous focus. The surgeon gently took hold of her twitching hand and extended her arm outward between them.

Reina tried to remain calm, but couldn't stop her nausea from resurfacing; she winced as the woman probed her sensitive skin. "Why is it taking so long to heal?" She gritted her teeth. The doctor spread fresh salve over the long cut, pressing it into the wound. *She is not being gentle.*

"Your genetic code is still mutating alongside the nanocells. Once the process is over..." The doctor paused and turned Reina's wrist slightly. "The swelling is going down. It's a good sign."

"I know," she conceded and took a deep breath. "I know," Reina said again just to hear it as the doctor began to re-bandage her.

"The pain and discomfort are a small price to pay. Millions would be envious of this implant–"

"–I *know*." *Please stop lecturing me. I don't want to hear that.* It had been the only comfort the doctors gave her as she lay in their lab in agony.

The woman shot her a look. Reina could feel the judgement through her skin, straight into the center of her robotic arm.

The arm felt too heavy and had a fluid yet stiff movement structure that was entirely foreign to her anatomy. The cybernetic metal ran from the tips of her fingers to a cyberorganic chip in her brain. Wires were threaded throughout her shoulder and neck. They ended in a wormy mass in her head. She clenched her teeth as she willed the image away.

The doctor held her tongue while Reina pulled the sleeve down of her gown, concealing her arm from view. The joints of her unaltered fingers twitched.

My arm is worth more than an Earthian battleship. More than the claim of transportation spaceways. Warp drives. Research labs. Her heart raced as the surgeon turned away from her.

She rolled her shoulder.

"You will need to apply the salve twice a day, every day." *Why do doctors always assume you can't read labels?* "Try." The demand was evident. "Please, *try* not to move it more than necessary. Your genome and the cybercells will pair soon enough. The discomfort will end."

"And if it doesn't?"

"We'll remove the technology and replace it with synthetic biomaterial," the woman huffed, "you know this."

Reina pulled her arm against her and cradled it over her chest. *I know that isn't the truth.*

They stared at each other in silence until their battle of wills ended with a chime. The appointment was over. She looked down at her new appendage, still held heavily over her torso, as the woman turned away and grabbed a bottle and an applicator. She handed them to her in silence.

With the medication in her reliable, human hand, Reina left the lab without a backward glance.

• • • •

SEVERAL DAYS HAD PASSED as her body continued to mutate with the aggressive nanocells. Everything still felt unfamiliar to her but the swelling had all but vanished. The incision that graced her body, the seam that weaved her skin back together, now only itched and flaked. The new manmade cells took over her body with increasing ease.

Reina closed her eyes. *I'm going to live.*

Now that she had been cleared for her mission, her health regulated, the next phase began. She sat erect in her uniform in a room surrounded by large bay windows, waiting for her commanding officers to arrive. Her eyes drifted to the view outside.

A storm raged, and the skies whirled with a thick grey haze. Reina was sitting in a glass room, on Earth, in the middle of the Pacific Ocean. She imagined that she could hear the whistle of wind, but the conference room was soundproof and impenetrable.

She couldn't stop the strange circumstances that fate had dealt her these past several weeks. She had been approached by the Earthian Council for this mission directly, and even now she wasn't quite sure why, although she had her suspicions: they wanted to remove her from her post because she had become a diplomatic liability.

Regardless, something in her heart told her to take it. Reina wasn't sure if it was the intrigue of the request, an abiding loyalty to her people, the bone-deep boredom that had settled into her being and stuck to her soul like glue, or maybe it was the fact that she felt alien amongst her crew, being the only woman on the bridge of her previous assignment.

They had been her family but she was never able to emotionally connect with anyone aside from her commander, and that had been a recipe for disaster. Fraternization with the boss was severely looked down upon, and after her commander pulled every string to save her from the treatise with the Trentian aliens, it would look even worse.

The implications were there.

Besides the occasional tryst, the only bed she wanted to warm was her boss's. She had worked up the courage to confess to him when she received this mission. He was her mentor, and the taunting smiles he gave his team still gave her goosebumps.

He would only ever see me as a friend, or at most a little sister.

But it wasn't only that. Women had once been a norm in the Space Fleet, but were now just a memory. It had become too dangerous, even amongst the men to whom she could entrust her life, to remain with the Peace Keepers. The Trentians they often worked with now knew of her status as a single woman.

The Trentians. The humanoid alien species that inhabited the other side of this galaxy, who the Earthian people had run into during the first galactic exploration missions. It had led to the worst war in history, and the first galactic war. Reina hoped that another galactic war would never happen.

We would lose.

It raged for over a century but had ended in desperation several generations ago. The barbaric, mystical ghost people were compatible with humans, and with the breeder's disease disaster and the billions of lives lost on both sides, an uneasy truce was struck. A truce that not everyone honored.

The waves and wind mixed outside until she could barely tell them apart. *Kind of like my emotions.* She frowned. *Kind of like my thoughts.*

The door to the room slid open and Reina stood to attention.

Two men in uniform entered: one she knew was the lead scientist at the cybernetics lab here on Earth, Dr. Estond, and the other was Space Fleet's own Lieutenant General Wasson.

"At ease, Captain Reynolds." *Will I ever get used to being called captain?* The lieutenant general and the scientist took their seats at the ovaline table and she followed suit. Dr. Estond placed a round techno-projector between them. A blue light blipped on and blinked intermittently. Reina had seen them used before to create holograms of space sectors; they were often used in navigation.

The lieutenant general placed a clear tablet before her on the table. Reina looked at him for allowance before she initiated the flow. "Call me Captain Reina, please. Thank you, sir." The mission dossier came to light.

"Captain Reina it is then. How's the arm feeling?" Wasson asked.

She looked away from the file. "It's healing, sir."

"Can we see it?" The scientist inquired. She looked at Wasson expectantly, and with a nod, Reina shrugged out of her jacket and extended her arm across the table between her and the scientist. Dr. Estond folded up the cloth of her uniform and rolled the appendage from side to side. His fingers were cold and curious.

The general eyed the exchange, seemingly waiting for the man's opinion. Reina flinched as Estond pressed his thumbs hard against the sides of her wrist. "That hurt?" he asked.

"Yes, sir. The tissue is still new and the small amount of swelling left makes it ache."

13

"You're healing slower than you should be."

"But I *am* healing, sir."

Wasson looked at his comrade. "Captain Reina was cleared by your team, Estond."

The scientist released her and Reina gladly unfolded her sleeve, hiding her raw skin from their view. "They were correct in doing so. We just like to monitor every variable, and Captain Reina's recovery is important to us."

It's important to me too. She pulled on her jacket.

"Maybe my cells are stronger than your manmade ones." She bit her tongue, quickly adding, "Sir."

The lieutenant general sat back with a slight smirk while Estond adjusted his glasses. His face was pensive.

"Maybe they are," he stated after a thoughtful moment.

"Well, this is a briefing, and now that we have the okay to continue, let's proceed." Wasson waved his hand at the tablet.

"Let's." Estond kept his eyes trained on her.

Reina reigned in her emotions and looked at the file before her just as a large wave rolled up and hit the bottom of the clear bay windows. The utter silence only heightened the violence of the torrential storm outside.

The downpour fell from her thoughts as it fell from the sky.

Wasson cleared his voice. "You have already been made aware of the mission and its more pertinent confidential details." He sat forward. "You took on this assignment the moment you went under for cybernetic surgery."

"Yes, sir." Reina knew a warning when she heard one.

"If you change your mind–if you falter–if you so much as deviate from the mission in any way that directly impedes the goal–you will be labeled a traitor to the Earthian Council."

"I understand, sir."

"If that isn't warning enough, know that you will be brought in by the Council, dead or alive. If you should live, it will be an arduous life on a prison planet." The lieutenant general rubbed his mouth and admitted, "To be blunt, your arm has an embedded tracker in it."

You're very transparent, sir.

Reina willed her face to stay straight and her heart to stop racing. "I am aware, sir." *I know what I signed up for.* Was it worth it? She and the lieutenant general stared at each other.

"Since you are aware. We will move on."

She shifted her eyes away from the men.

"Ships have been vanishing outside of the network's reach. When communication drops away, it never comes back online." Reina skimmed the file as he spoke. "The first ships disappeared right after the war. We didn't think anything of it at the time. War casualties? The first ones were two transporter ships that were lost, looking for habitable outposts farther away.

"As you know, we suffered extreme loss of life during the galactic war. The Trentians lost even more. Our species remains devastated, and that devastation is exacerbated by continual expansion and exploration. There is a lack of control: we can't keep our people confined to a single planetary system anymore. There is so much out there that we are not aware of. We are stretched thin." Wasson took a deep breath. "Of course some loss is expected. Space is a dangerous place after all but over the years, more ships have vanished, more than we would anticipate–"

"–You don't believe it's the Trentians, sir?"

"Not anymore. We have been in communication with their government and the Intergalactic Council, and it turns out that their ships have disappeared as well." Wasson leveled a look at the projector between them. Reina followed his gaze. "We have monitored the deep space sectors where the ships are vanishing, and have even deployed satellites in those areas. They come back with nothing, not even a black hole, until they disappear as well."

I signed up to die. She kept her face straight.

"Which leads me to your mission." Wasson paused. "And to be frank, you are not the first person we have sent out to investigate. Over the last twelve years, we have sent out militarized forces, expecting alien involvement. We have sent out top scientists, equipped with state of the art technology. And the aforementioned satellites."

"Why am I different, sir?" Dr. Estond and Lieutenant General Wasson both looked at her arm. *Well, there's my answer.* Reina tensed the new muscle tissue but stopped as the foreign sensation of it wrapped around metal made her nauseous again.

"To continue, we have lost a significant amount of resources, and an even more significant amount of personnel trying to solve this mystery and bring our people and technology home. You and your team will be the final attempt. If you don't make it back or are unable to relay any information to us, we will start the process of setting up perimeter radar blockades in those sectors to stop others from traveling through. The Trentians are agreeable to this course of action. Whatever is beyond our reach, killing our people and destroying our ships, we don't want coming any closer to us."

Dr. Estond interjected, "To answer your question, Captain Reina, you are different because you are the key to the ship we are sending." He nodded at her arm. "Your arm has override access and control of this ship's systems, beyond manual control. The ship will not fly without you. It will do nothing without you. The ship is yours as long as you have that arm, and you are ours for the same duration."

Reina thought her heart might stop. As the fear settled in, it left her just as quickly and an overwhelming excitement shot through her. She could feel it from the tips of her bionic fingers to the goosebumps over her scalp.

So many thoughts raced through her head. But one stood out more than the rest: *They own me.* Beyond her service contract, beyond her free-will.

"If I am successful..." She had to know. "What will happen to me, sir?"

"If the mission is a success, you will be promoted. You and your ship will become part of the Earthian Space Fleet Exploration Division, and you will command your own crew until your contract ends."

"And my arm?"

Wasson and Estond shared a look. "Will remain with the ship," Wasson answered soon after. "We hope you will remain with both."

"Is there no other way?" Reina glanced down at the cyber-appendage, hidden amongst a very human layer of skin.

"We can integrate you into the Neoborg program."

Reina looked beyond the two men in front of her and to the raging storm outside. The waves climbed higher up the crystalline windows.

• • • •

"WOULD YOU LIKE TO MEET your team, Captain Reina?" Wasson asked.

Atlas had been listening to their entire conversation and he burned. Or as much as he *could* burn, being an intelligence. His emotions were intact, his logic was intact, his intelligence was intact, but his neurological system was not. He physically felt nothing, but he remembered everything.

Captain Reina, Earthian pure-blood descent, joined the Space Fleet Peace Keepers at the age of eighteen and promptly rose in the ranks until she plateaued as warrant officer under Commander Anders. She had been part of his crew for a four-year term, until she was promoted to captain and given her current mission.

No living family. No relationship status. A twenty-nine-year-old female from the New American Metropolis. Her father and mother expired. Excellent service record. Captain Reina was as boring as this mission. No strings attached, no ties to keep her grounded, and no one to miss her.

But most importantly, her medical records: type O blood, physically fit, recently moved into a cybernetic human status and pending Neoborg Program. Atlas scoffed. She had suffered no real physical injuries, had never been on the front lines of a fight, and had no connections nor life outside the fleet.

No wonder why the council picked her, she's a military zombie. A doll.

He bet the girl was reeling if the auditory feed was any indication. She was his captain for the duration of this adventure, and it would be a painfully boring one for him.

The woman likely had no feeling, and whatever she *did* have was probably suppressed under years of working for the Earthian Council.

We're two of a kind.

She has no idea the council will use her until every drop of energy is bled out of her. And they would continue using her afterward. *She's probably already labeled as a Neoborg.*

He checked.

She was.

"I would, sir."

"No need to get up, Captain, your team is right here," Dr. Estond said. "This is Atlas, your co-captain and your navigator."

Atlas could register the confusion on the woman's face even though he couldn't see it. His comm channel on his projector opened up.

I guess they'll allow me to speak now. "Hello, Captain Reina. I am Atlas, your Automated Transport and Logistical Aid System."

There was a slight pause before she responded, "Hello, Atlas. Nice to meet you."

"It is nice to meet you too, Captain Reina."

"Atlas is a sentient intelligence that is employed by the Council. He is the best navigator in our fleet and has been a considerable asset to the cybernetics program," Wasson interjected.

"I was once a Cyborg."

"I don't understand, sir. I don't have a designated crew?" The girl's voice held a note of confusion. "I'm a space-jet pilot. I can't fly a spacecraft of this magnitude alone." She hesitated, "I'm not...qualified."

"There will be no one else. You will need no one else. Atlas is highly adept with all of our systems. He can not only navigate, but he can manage any other systems you give him access to. He can also help accustom you to your new abilities. Your qualifications are a non-issue."

"So no one else, sir? Why send me at all?"

Wasson's sigh was audible enough that his sounds bytes picked up a breathy crackle. "I don't think you understand the point. We need a live-body, someone who is familiar with space law and protocol. Your rank and record are pristine. You understand ships, your body is used to gravity shifts, and your psyche is honed for extended trips."

Estond cut in, "The ship is a cybernetic machine, and thus was built to be controlled by a cybernetically enhanced human."

"You will find that Atlas is worth more than an entire World Destroyer's crew," Wasson added.

You will be my captain and I outrank you. "You can be assured, Captain Reina, that you will be in good hands." Atlas chuckled internally at his joke. He couldn't see the humans sitting at the table but his imagination was adept enough to picture the scene perfectly.

The bastard Wasson was at the head, his chair slightly raised to exude his power and presence, the muscles in his neck would be bunched and in dire need of a massage. Estond would appear alert, act alert, but would be lost in the file opened on the table before him, only seeming to speak when specific words or topics pulled him out just enough to add to the conversation.

The girl–her fleet identification picture came to mind–would have started out with calm excitement, dulled with years of a tedious flight regimen and convention, only to find herself further losing her reserved exterior as the conversation continued.

Atlas didn't know her, hadn't spent time in her presence before unlike the other two, but he knew reactions.

Hers would be pitiful. She would have a million questions that would go unasked, choosing to remain silent, knowing that every time she spoke she might make a fool out of herself in front of her superiors.

"Now that the introductions are out of the way–we expect you to relay all information that you find. Your destination is beyond Ursa Major to a blacklisted sector known as Abyss-105. You'll go dark when you enter. You'll set up communication parameters with Port Antix prior and all information should be directly fed there."

21

Dr. Estond interrupted, "The tracker in your arm, as well as the trackers in your ship's systems, will remain live for a time after communication goes black."

"Yes. That's true. The space station, Antix, will need to pair with your ship. You will have to land there."

Atlas kept his metaphorical mouth shut as the men continued. But the conversation suddenly tapered off. He couldn't tell why, but he knew a hurricane was hitting the cybernetic lab. He couldn't see it, not with the limited projection system they had brought with them, but he could sense it.

The silence was broken by his new captain, surprising him. "Sir, Dr. Estond, when my ship goes dark, and I lose all connection to the network...when should I turn back and realign with the communication systems? When I find an anomaly, see something out of place? What do I look for?"

"Truthfully, Captain Reina, we don't know what you will find out there. We don't even have an image of anything abnormal. What we have collected thus far has been utterly normal. If it were me," the lieutenant general continued ominously, "I would turn back at the first sign of anything strange. We leave that to your discretion." He paused. "And your life."

Atlas almost felt bad for the woman.

Chapter Two:

. . . .

Reina entered the docking bay to her ship. Her previous commanding officer followed her into the upgraded, one-of-a-kind transporter vessel.

The Earthian Council had created a hybrid ship for her to travel into deep space that was controlled by cybernetic technology. Perfect for a pseudo-cyborg like herself and a sentient intelligence.

Reina looked around and her first impression was... cold. The ship was sleek, frigid, and stark. It reminded her of herself, or at least the walls she nurtured.

She shivered when she thought about the loneliness to come.

"Well, this is different. But not different enough that you won't be familiar with it." Chris Anders, her commander and captain of four years, inspected the schematics he held. The doors opened seamlessly as she walked through.

The vessel was already registered with her identification.

They progressed through the hull and into a white and grey-trimmed metal passageway. Lights ran along the walls in crisp streaks, only interrupted by the occasional door.

As she inspected the interior, she found many intermittent doors that led to other parts of the ship. The cargo bay beneath, engine rooms with reactors, and if they moved even further down, the warp drive station. Quarters, which would remain empty, were on the main level, as well as the medbay, life-support emergency room, crew lounge, and eating station.

The view deck and sky-loft were above.

The escape pods were behind them now, back at the landing deck and hull.

They made a beeline for the bridge. The ship was big enough to comfortably hold a crew of fifty, a tiny version of a transporter vessel, decked with the military power of a blitzer, the metalloid skeleton a perfect match to her robotic arm.

Wasted space. She had few regrets in her life and this mission was quickly becoming one of them.

The moment Reina stepped on board, she could feel the connection: her hand wanted to plug into the systems. The electrical impulses shot up through her body and into the chip in her brain. *It feels like home. It feels like an extension of my arm. It feels wrong.*

"This is much smaller than my *Credence*. How are you going to handle the claustrophobia?" Chris asked, looking around.

"I don't mind it, it's far more manageable. The size is substantial but it's still smaller than any of the habitable battleships in the fleet. I can see why they made it moderate. Small enough to lose, but big enough to repurpose. Equipped with just enough of everything to encounter whatever may be out there in Abyss-105," she mumbled, peeking her head into the lounge.

"I wish you wouldn't do this." Anders stopped her. He leaned down and whispered in her ear, sending a shiver through her form. "I can make you disappear."

"Don't say that."

"No one can hear us."

"You don't know that. My *crew* consists of one very knowledgeable intelligence." She hushed him.

"Atlas."

"You know it?"

"Not an *it*, Reina, a him. A Cyborg, an original. And yes, I know who Atlas is. I've never worked with him personally but his reputation is well known," he answered loudly, taunting fate to take him out. *Shut up, Chris.* "I'm happy that the Council assigned him to you."

"They assigned *only* him to me. No one else. It's like they don't even believe I can command people."

"Can you? They did raise you significantly in rank, and you are quiet, and truthfully, rather cold. They probably don't believe you can. Atlas is all you'll need. Did you ever think that maybe no one else would go on this mission, Reina? Maybe the Earthian Council couldn't spare anyone else." He huffed, "It's not like we have an army anymore. This is the last mission to go out to the outskirt sectors. What a waste of time and resources. Whatever is out there has never moved closer. We have far more important problems to deal with right here."

Reina stepped back and eyed him suspiciously. "You know an awful lot for someone who wasn't in the briefing."

"I know it's not worth even the life of one woman."

Their conversation died as they entered the helm. Gigantic reinforced crystalline glass created a half-dome. Reina's jaw dropped as she was pulled to the window. It faced a hanger that faced an ocean, but she could imagine the gorgeous view that she would have in front of her very soon.

"Wow." Her friend stepped up next to her. "I'm a little jealous. They sure don't want you to miss *anything* out there."

"No," she said, "They don't. Not everyone thinks this mission is a waste."

"What do you think is out there?" Anders ignored her.

Reina shook her head, feeling tendrils of her hair come loose from her bun. "I have no idea. A wormhole perhaps? Maybe even the walls of the universe? Perhaps the gateway to another dimension? Hell?" She smirked but it felt forced.

"Hmm, would never have thought you to be someone who had crazy ideas. I like it. I'm going to think positive thoughts and pretend you'll find paradise, and paradise is the reason why no one returns." He laughed, "Greeted with forty virile men."

"There were forty virile men on the *Credence*."

A silence followed as they looked around.

Reina ran her hand over the synthetic white leather of the captain's seat. A silver metal table and circular structure sat to the right of her chair. The bars made an extendable frame that would encircle the chair when powered on to create a translucent screen. She had seen them before on tours in the World Destroyers.

There were seats for the bridge crew. Seats that would go unused except as a reminder that she was alone.

An electric fizzle sounded in the cabin, and a teal holographic beam shot up through the middle of the room. What she thought should have been a simple table ended up being a floor-to-ceiling projector system.

Reina watched as her old commander stepped forward and waved his hand through the beam. The entire room was awash in a clarifying white and airy-blue light.

The bright beam wavered and vibrated as her friend tested out the transparency, seeming to know what it was. "Hello, Atlas," he said.

"Hello, Commander Anders. Hello, Captain Reina." Reina shivered at the steely robotic voice. Her cybernetic arm twitched as if it was stung by a bee. She looked down at it and shook the feeling away.

"Good day, Atlas," she responded. *Does he know night from day? Does it matter?*

"Do you like your ship, Captain?"

"I do."

"I am relieved. I helped with its creation."

Reina looked around, wowed that her co-pilot created her new, possibly lifelong home. Or her billion dollar coffin.

"It's beautiful."

"Beauty is often a low requirement when it comes to functionality. In our line of work, beauty is the only thing that keeps many of us going. It should not be jeopardized but nurtured, sought after, and coveted."

"Your schematics don't show a holding cell," Anders interrupted. Reina looked over at her former commander. *Of course he would notice something like that. I prefer the beauty.*

"We went for compact efficiency, Commander. With just one passenger, there was no need to waste the space for a designated holding cell. Any quarter on this ship can be converted into a holding unit if one should be needed."

"Is that safe? Keeping potential prisoners near where the crew would sleep?"

"It is efficient."

Reina felt an argument brewing. "It's done, Chris, let it rest. There will be no prisoners and I will be safe within these walls."

"I care very much for your safety." Her friend retorted pinning her with a protective stare. His voice rose slightly, "And this ridiculous quest is not safe." Reina tried to stop an uncomfortable blush that heated her cheeks. It was inappropriate. She didn't want Chris to see.

"Commander Anders, her safety is of the utmost importance to the Earthian Council, and to me. Captain Reina is now my captain and I have been charged with her safety as well as the completion of this mission. Both are equal and important and one cannot happen without the other."

Reina grabbed her former commander's forearm and squeezed. Her eyes begging him to back off. Chris shot her a look before turning away. When her

28

hand dropped, he rounded back with a smirk. "So, *Captain* Reina, what will you name your ship?"

She looked around; the question took her aback, since the ship was new. "I don't know."

"I think–"

"–It will not be after one of your classical bands."

Anders struck her with a hurt expression. "CCR is not classical, it's classical rock."

"And the council aptly changed your ship's name when you registered it."

"I thought 'Creedence' was a good name for a ship, Commander. But I believe this vessel should be named: Artificial Thought Led Astral Sail," Atlas interjected. Reina looked at the towering light that streamed through the middle of the bridge.

She burst into laughter.

"Thank you, Atlas." Anders's ruggedly boyish hurt expression morphed back into a smirk. "That's a great name too." She thought he may just pull a harmonica out of his uniform pocket. "I need to leave, Reina, but I'll be back to see you off when you depart at 16:00 hours."

Reina followed him out of the bridge, and the S.I.'s light remained on behind her as she went to find her quarters.

· · · ·

ATLAS MONITORED THE two as they entered his ship and explored the vessel. He knew of Commander Chris Anders, one of the more competent men in the Space Fleet, an excellent pilot and fair commander of a fleet of patrol ships.

The only battles that waged now were those of splinter groups, organized crime, Trentian fanatics, and the occasional run-ins with the pirate syndicate. Now that the leader of the so-called Space Pirates, Larik, was incarcerated, the once underground war in the Council's side was now just a thorn. Anders had fronted many of the black-listed battles.

He swam through a digital current. This mission was going to be painfully boring.

Atlas couldn't tell the relationship of his captain and the commander. They retained a single status in the network, but the familiarity between them went beyond a commander and subordinate. There was affection in the way they spoke to each other. A slightly strained tension with an inflection that he monitored.

It was difficult to amuse him these days, but the social interactions of humans never stopped being a source of rapt fascination.

Maybe because he was spying. Maybe it was because he could scarcely recall the subtle feelings of being alive, and human. Maybe because he had taken it all for granted.

As he continued to listen, his curiosity grew by the minute about Captain Reina's reasoning to undertake a mission that very likely would end in her death.

The database held no information that stood out to him.

Only a recent diplomatic debacle, one that had raised tensions with the Trentians.

He powered on his projector system in the cockpit, one he designed with the help of Dr. Estond and his team, behind the two people he was spying on.

The system allowed him to project his body in a lifelike state within the bridge and anywhere else within its perimeter. All projectors installed on the ship were built with streaming feed, so he would be able to see and be seen. There were not many throughout, and most areas only had communication channels and cameras.

Atlas stopped himself before he fully formed. Seeing the woman for the first time, something shifted within his head as she looked at his unit.

She's looking right at me and she doesn't know it.

The wariness in Captain Reina's eyes was unexpected. He watched as she slowly came forward and acknowledged his presence.

He scanned her body and, as he did so, he felt a shock to his system when he tried to get a reading on her arm.

So it repels me too.

Atlas couldn't help but acknowledge her presence as well.

His new captain was a monument, a statue, sculpted by a being who worked on her with an obsession that approached insanity. She was pretty in an unconventional way.

Shoulder length chocolate brown hair, pulled tightly back from her face, that accentuated obscenely sharp cheekbones. Cheekbones that could make an S.I. think twice about what was more painful: flesh and blood beauty, or not being able to appreciate it like a man could? Her facial structure almost bordered symmetrical perfection and it all tapered down to full pink lips. Lips that could have been luscious if they weren't pulled into a taut, straight line.

And that was where the odd symmetry ended. Her nose was slightly crooked and her face was sallow, pale, as if she had never been under the rays of a sun.

Atlas could not imagine the body that belonged to his captain's face under the bulky, stiff military uniform she wore. It hid her sex well as a uniform should. He assumed she was as fit as anyone in her line of work.

Her eyes were too large, too open, and framed with thick lashes. They magnified her hazel irises.

Atlas downloaded all images of Captain Reina into his database. Few appeared.

"I thought 'Creedence' was a good name for a ship, Commander Anders," Atlas stated absently with a modicum of irritation befitting anyone who felt ignored.

"Thank you, Atlas."

They want to name my ship.

He wasn't giving the honor to name it to a woman ranked beneath him. Or the insolent man who stood next to her.

Atlas wasn't surprised when his captain and the commander left his presence in the cockpit without saying goodbye. What did surprise him, as he followed the girl, was that Anders addressed him specifically within the hull, pulling him away. His voice loud was enough with an intent to catch his attention.

As if my attention could be caught.

But catch it he did.

"Atlas," Anders barked.

"Yes, Commander Anders?" Atlas answered immediately, the man stiffened.

"Bring her home alive."

"You could have taken this mission, Commander." *You could have been the next one to die.*

"It was never an option."

"That's a poor excuse," Atlas challenged. Watching the man's jaw clench, his mouth opening up to say something more before aptly shutting it. He no longer wanted the commander on his ship, and as he watched him walk away, Atlas couldn't help but taunt him once more. "Captain Reina couldn't be safer with anyone else."

Chapter Three:

. . . . .

"You have been cleared for takeoff."

Reina gritted her teeth and checked her controls once over. When she sat in the captain's chair, a translucent screen powered on to envelop her; her arm connected.

It was the only thing that could touch the screen.

"Ready for takeoff, initiating in three." The light of Atlas's station washed over the room in a chilly blue. "Two," she kept the unease out of her voice as the flow of the systems powered up around her. "One."

The gravity fields shifted as her ship lifted into the air and shot into the sky.

Reina followed the sky-path laid out for her, cleared by the Earthian air-ways. A course charted through their solar system, it changed and updated constantly as she checked the numbers.

"Good luck on your mission, Captain. Let the stars guide your way," an ambiguous voice said before shutting off communication. She left the protective shell of Earth and sped into the channeled space of the Earthian-controlled sector of the Milky Way.

She stole a lingering glance at Earth as they flew away, knowing she may never see its metal cities again, hardening her heart she turned away.

In an attempt to get a feel for her ship, she ran diagnostics on its infrastructure–the readings came back perfect.

The projected course changed again.

"Atlas, what is our current route?"

"In two planetary sun rotations of approximately forty-six hours, we will reach the boundaries of this galaxy. We will maintain as much distance as possible from Trentian sectors until we warp to the Nexus Galaxy."

"Are you updating our route? It keeps changing." Coordinate updates rolled down her screen.

"I recalculate it every second as new variables present themselves."

"That's amazing. Thank you." Reina moved to get up as he continued to work.

"Captain Reina?"

She looked up at the pillar of light in the middle of the bridge.

"May we go over access systems? I can be of better use to you if I could monitor more than the navigation," Atlas asked.

"Sure, yes, what would you need access to?" She eyed the light curiously.

"I would like the ship's diagnostics access, weapons access, sanitation access–"

"You want access to the whole ship?" Reina hedged.

"Are you offering it?"

Reina shook her head. "No. The Council would have made you captain if you had access to everything."

"A sentient intelligence? Captain of a ship? Do you think that's possible?"

Reina smiled at the fake robotic awe in his voice. "Have you captained a ship before, Atlas?" she asked as she ran her hand through the beam.

"Have you?"

Reina looked at her timer. "I have for twenty minutes."

"Hmm, well, you got me then." The beam vibrated. "A whole twenty minutes of you-got-me."

"Is that humor, Atlas?" Reina went back to her chair and sat down.

"I don't do humor, Captain Reina. I'm efficient and logical."

Reina smirked. *Maybe this trip won't be as lonely as I thought it would be.* "Hmm, I'm surprised you didn't have access to any system prior to this conversation. Why is that? It seems redundant to make me delegate everything." She looked at her arm and mumbled, "Cybernetics can't be that powerful..."

She opened up the ship's database and granted him control of sanitation.

"Thank you, Captain. I only have navigational systems, and yes, only you can give me access to anything else, and yes again, your arm could make you power-hungry," he answered vaguely. "This ship's navigational structure was built around my specific requirements, but the other systems were not. Your arm is the key to the rest of the ship. The Council did not have access to grant because when you went under the knife, you were granted that power with your arm."

She frowned at his words. "Why would they do that?" The pause that followed was ominous. "Atlas?" Reina looked back at the beam.

"Liability? If you die, the ship can't be commandeered...Why do you think?"

Reina unlocked and swiveled her chair to face his voice. She knew he was avoiding the question, leading with another. He was keeping something from her, and she mulled over the possibility that Atlas might not be here willingly. "Why didn't they just send you?" *If he could manage everything, then why need me? Protocol and space law be damned.*

"That, Captain Reina, is the billion dollar cyber-systems question. But I believe it is because I can't be integrated into the ship, not without a direct connection like yours."

"They don't trust you."

"Do you?"

"I'm not sure."

"You're smarter than you sound," Atlas teased. Reina's face fell, and she felt her mission become a little more complicated. "We're going to make a great team, you and I." His sarcasm was palpable. The blue light pulsed again. "Although I am a sentient intelligence now, and have been for quite some time, I am still a conscious mind with the same duplicitous nature as a human."

Reina canted her head. "They must trust you. Why else would they give you reign of their systems and cyber designs? Not only government access, but military technology?" Her confusion grew.

"Have you researched me, Captain? I'm flattered. Did you find a picture of me within the banks? Was I to your liking? I was once told I was devilishly handsome."

"Stop evading the question–" she trailed off as the ship flew past Jupiter, catching her attention.

"Painfully, horribly, incredibly handsome."

Reina barely heard him, her eyes on the mega-storm on the giant planet. It looked to her like a frighteningly lifeless eye. It blurred as they sped by. A wink.

"What...?" She continued to stare at it.

"I think we started off on the wrong track. I can tell your blood pressure has risen," Atlas taunted. Reina continued to stare at swirling, dead sphere until it vanished into the distance. "You can trust me. I believe it would be in your best interest to sit down and take several deep breaths."

Reina glanced away from the window and back at the coordinates rolling down her screen. She ran the back of her hand over her forehead.

Is my fever returning?

A strange sense of vertigo hit her and she reached out and grasped her chair. Once she caught enough sterile air in her lungs, she felt the excess heat leave her body.

Her uniform clung to her curves.

Reina took off her jacket and folded it over the handle of her seat. The air cooled the inflamed skin of her arm. When she looked at it, she noticed Atlas's silence, and wondered if he knew something was wrong with her.

That she was not mutating properly.

She sat up and re-tied her hair painfully away from her face.

"I apologize for my lapse." Reina wiped the back of her hand across her brow and tried to regain her composure.

"You are still in recovery. I believe it is imperative that you allow me to help you. If you lapse again, I will be able to monitor your vitals and alert you before any damage can occur."

"That won't be necessary. I'm sure it was just the pressure of takeoff."

"I hope you are right but Captain, please let me help you. I am here."

What does that mean? What game is he playing? The sarcasm from before was gone and replaced with strain, an odd tension between them.

"I'll remember that," Reina said eventually, sitting back down and getting back to work.

"Very well. I have navigating to do. Out."

She felt the sudden dismissal from her subordinate as a chastisement. *Well, screw you too.* She frowned, knowing she was being baited, and that she was giving into it.

Reina bit back a retort, not willing to play into whatever alpha games Atlas was pulling. And she knew he was playing. Men in power challenged each other in front of her every day, sometimes subtly, sometimes violently, oftentimes to prove themselves against others–or to impress the only female onboard.

What did Atlas have to prove with her? They had scarcely met. Their roles were concrete but she knew it was something more. *He* was something more, and it put her on edge. She couldn't relate, and the more she tried to wrap her mind around a digital consciousness, the harder it became.

Unsure if he was still monitoring her, she asked one last question, one she needed to know before they could continue to work together.

"Can you see me?"

A vacuous quiet met her, and Reina thought it was answer enough. She turned to the controls and watched the stars fly by. Several minutes passed.

"I can."

• • • •

HE WANTED COMPLETE access to his ship.

MY ship.

The ship that was an extension of the woman onboard. Atlas knew it was more than he originally thought the cybernetics unit capable of. But leave humans to their theories and science, and they were bound to break all barriers: they were bound to created godly things like the Cyborgs, and ungodly plagues like the breeder's disease.

Atlas would have laughed, maybe even sighed as he had seen more than most being stuck for decades in the network. Humans had an amazing polarity.

There were blurred streaks to their pursuit of knowledge, one couldn't know all the outcomes to their accomplishments, good and bad, when they had a greater goal in mind and that was dominion

It was part of the *deal.*

Atlas watched the woman who he was going to be cohabitating with for the next several months, maybe even more. Not many females served in the fleet, especially not within the army.

He would be alone, for a substantial length of time, with a young female. A supple one with bright brown eyes, which were wide enough he could read her face from across an arena. With a taut, tight, form hidden under layers of synthetic cloth. The confused, yet intelligent pout she gave when he teased her about being granted the rank of captain was enough to cool his anger. It was one of the only shifts in her frozen facade.

I can let her pretend that this is her ship. No harm would come from it.

He probed the shielded, digital barriers, but his forte wasn't hacking. His power lay elsewhere.

The ship continued to pick up speed. He looked back again at the girl who was his only obstacle.

A loose strand of hair snuck out of her bun and fell over her cheek. Her new arm sat heavy and limp at her side. It didn't take a genius to know that her body wasn't coping well with the mutation. He had been serious about helping her.

The girl leaned back in her chair with a soft sigh and she turned around to look at his projection system. Her wide eyes narrowed in his direction.

Is she going to say something? Does she feel me watching her?

She got up, her hand rubbed her robotic piece, and she walked over to the system–to him.

Her face was right in front of him, and for a moment, he had the urge to project and scare her with a fake kiss.

Wouldn't that be a memory to keep forever in the back of my mind. A stolen kiss from an unassuming woman.

But the charged moment passed as she waved her hand through the beams, through him, and walked out of the bridge.

He was just an intelligence to her, not a man. There could be nothing between them.

And very quickly, his frustration came back. His anger that he spent every digital day of his life tamping down, hiding from the overlords that controlled him.

Atlas left the bridge after the woman but he did not follow her to the lounge where her heat signature was located and instead channeled down to the bowels of the ship. Into a cold, hidden cybernetic laboratory, where he was locked in the frigid, endless chill of cryostasis.

Atlas looked down at his almost-corpse, iced over under a thick layer of glass, and wished his rage were enough to melt it.

He had taken a precise shot to the heart, unguarded for mere seconds, but it was enough time for a Trentian berserker to snipe the vital organ. He remembered time stopping, the armor-piercing bullet that sank through the small hole in his interior metal plating and hit home. The bloody valentine of a kill-shot that exploded in his chest. His cybersystems went into overdrive and tried to repair the damage immediately, but there was little that could be done to a pile of hot, wet, goo.

His squadron was able to stabilize his body, sending electrical impulses to his system. They kept him connected to the network long enough for him to wheedle out of his body like a slimy wire and into the lifelessly charged online world–where his mind had found a hostile home.

With a view into the physical world he no longer inhabited, he came back, then reached out to the other

Cyborgs. Finally, he made his way back into the Earthian Council's cybernetic lab where his body was being stored.

A body, a promise that hung over his head like a wretched curse; with it, they used and manipulated him into being a sentient intelligence. His databases swarmed by deceit and data that he could do nothing with, he was powerless because his compliance was bought with the promise that he would be brought back to life.

Atlas looked down at his body, the slime of his biological heart removed long ago, and he simmered.

Those bastards created me, then enslaved me, and now they send my corpse out to deep space to use me as their insurance that we'll return. That I'll return. Because I would never risk the one thing that could bring me back to life.

Chapter Four:

. . . .

*C*hris was right. *This ship may bring out the fear*

of claustrophobia in me. If the dry, quiet space
doesn't, the loneliness might. Nothing happened; not
even the drama of other people could be relied on to
keep the days going forward. It was only her, the dark
void, and the stars.

Everything was so, so quiet.

She had taken the blanket and stiff, straight pillow
off of her bed and dragged them into the cockpit at
the end of her first night on board. After one
annoying communication with regard to her response
time on data updates, Reina had beat the pillow
against the wall and then neatly folded it over the
handle of her chair, which had also become her bed
and lounge. The fake cotton maintained its shape and
now she had a place to rest her arm.

It was a small sort of satisfaction.

Her arm. Reina looked back down at it. Even after
nearly a week of travel, including two warp jumps, it
had remained the same. Regardless of the amount of
salve she spread across her reddened skin, even
though it soaked it up like dry dirt, her arm remained
the same.

It began to lead to an uneasiness she felt
throughout, and she knew that her interrupted sleep
cycles were not helping.

She ran her shaky hand through her hair, the bun she usually wore fallen out hours ago. But why should she care? There was no one there to judge her.

It's not like Atlas cares. He hasn't said more than several sentences to me in over a week.

The loneliness should have affected her more but it was kept at bay for now by captaining a ship that had no crew. What affected her was the intermittent quiet between communication pings.

She had no doctor here to help her.

Reina laughed. *I'm completely incompetent.*

She willed herself not to flex the non-existent muscles of her arm but couldn't help doing it anyway. Once a thought seeded in her head, whether it was to swallow, to grind her teeth, or in this case, test her muscles, she subconsciously did it anyway.

Completely undisciplined.

The screen before her flashed red, bringing her out of her depressing thoughts. She leaned forward and expanded the screen.

Error. Error.

A valve in the engine room had loosened. Not a big deal.

But the gas it was slowly releasing could damage nearby machinery and consequently change the overall optimal temperature of the room. It needed to stay cold.

Reina pulled up the piece on the screen, zooming in on the red area, inspecting it. What she thought would have been an easy fix became marginally more difficult.

She rubbed her lower lip in thought.

I'm not a mechanic nor an engineer. The valve sat between several fuel pipes. She turned her schematic layout toward them. The pipes ran hot, really hot, she had to get around them to get to the valve and she would have to do it tired.

She transferred the blueprints onto her handheld console and strapped it to her arm before making her way toward the supply and spare parts unit. She quickly located a wrench, eye protection, and triple-padded environmentally-resistant gloves.

"You should take the welding torch with you."

Reina jumped. "Why?" She looked around, trying to locate the source of Atlas's voice.

"The metal of the valve expanded. You could wrench it shut, but it may not hold."

She picked up the torch and extra flux and added them to her supplies. Her steps were the only sound that followed her as she made her way to her destination, spinning open a hatch.

The effort made the exhaustion running through her veins more apparent. Her arm ached as she carefully descended the ladder. It didn't help that one side of her was heavier.

Her feet hit the floor with a soft sigh. Lights powered on around her up and down the underbelly passageways. A pilot, such as herself, had no reason to ever be in this part of a ship. In fact, regulation locked her out of many of the machine rooms.

Reina brought up the blueprint and made her way to the appropriate chamber. She soon found herself in a very cold, very crowded space. The hum of her ship's organs was a welcome one. Reina put on her goggles.

At least the room is well-lit.

And there were the pipes, perfectly erect, shiny, and at first glance stark. Reina looked them over warily, knowing that though they looked cold, they were instead scalding hot. Just standing next to them kept her warm.

She turned to her side and with cautious, breathless movements, side-stepped between them. When she was clear of them and caught her breath, the putrid scent of burnt hair greeted her.

Reina carefully made her way through a maze of machines before she found the row of valves. She eyed them as she put on her gloves.

"The third one on the left," Atlas answered the question she hadn't asked from somewhere above.

She looked up. "Thank you." Her hands reached for the handle and twisted it shut. Reina jerked it several times for good measure. Her arm shook out next to her, the joints pained from overuse. The incision burned and the metal underneath her skin needle-pricked her with charged currents.

She lifted the sleeve of her flight suit only to quickly cover herself again.

My skin...

Her lungs filled with cold air as she took a deep breath, trying to settle her nerves.

She fingered the welding torch and struck a spark.

"Atlas? Are you able to see the valves?" Her voice echoed off the walls.

"Yes, Captain. What do you need?"

Reina shook her head, "Nothing, I was just curious." She stopped herself from peeking at her arm, hoping the sentient intelligence hadn't caught a look.

A few minutes of awkward silence passed as she maneuvered her body into position. When the torch flashed green, she assumed it was go time. The flux began to melt over the twist. It was slow going.

"Are you still here?" she asked hesitantly.

"I am, as well as at the bridge."

She couldn't imagine it, being a person, then being nothing more than a... program? The flux heated and dripped. She frowned as some of it dropped off. Thinking about Atlas distracted her from her arm.

"Do you need something, Captain?"

I need you to distract me. She leaned up to let the flux cool.

"Will you talk to me? Will you tell me a story?"

"A story? Why?"

Reina wiped her goggles on her sleeve. "It's quiet."

"I'm not here to entertain you, Captain." His voice was harsh. It made her feel like a fool. "I'm the first Cyborg you've met, aren't I?"

Reina winced. "Yes."

"We don't entertain. We don't tell stories. If you had met me during the war, I guarantee you would want nothing to do with me. If you were near a Cyborg, for whatever reason during that time, you were near death."

"The war is over."

"And?"

"I'm lonely," she added with a blush. "I'm sorry if I offended you."

A few damning minutes passed in silence. Her embarrassment grew at his lack of response and at her desire for a moment of companionship. Reina fidgeted, willing the flux to cool faster.

She didn't know Atlas and now she had upset him. It was true, he was the first Cyborg she had ever met, and now she knew, if she had learned anything from him just now, that he was not to be messed with.

Being on the ship, alone, was a situation that had taken its toll on her. Even the most introverted of people could feel lonely, especially when they lost all choice in the matter.

Reina jerked when he broke the silence.

"There once was a man named Testicales–"

"Testicales? Really?" Reina regretted everything. She didn't need Atlas to fill the void. Maybe she just needed a hobby. She wasn't that lonely.

"Yes. Now listen. It's a good one," he chastised her.

She stiffened and sat down, her back to the valves, knowing she would listen regardless of the story he chose to tell her.

"There once was a man named Testicales. He was a young warrior outside the city-state of Sparta, an ancient Earthian dwelling. He was boring and typical, a normal boy but for one small mishap. Testicales had a handicap, you see: his balls were so large that he had to carry them in a sack attached to his belt."

Reina rubbed her temple.

"Testicales did not have larger muscles than the other boys of his age. He had not gone on a journey to prove himself, nor did he have the attributes that would make him attractive to the girls of his community. He was one of the thousands of boys his age, a grunt in training to fight the wars brought to his land.

"Despite his terrible handicap, and his overall average self, he became the greatest fighter in his village. He was unbeatable, and soon word of his prowess spread across the land as warriors from all over the world sought him out in challenge. One by one, he defeated them all. This went on for many years. Testicales became a great hero. He brought prosperity and renown to his home, as well as glory and fortune for himself and his family. The people thought he was the son of the god Ares: a grandson of Zeus himself. And soon, what everyone thought of as his gross handicap became a symbol of strength."

Reina sighed.

"One day, like any other, a younger, fitter warrior traveled to Testicales's village in hope of proving his worth by defeating the unbeatable hero. This untried youth challenged Testicales to a duel. The fight went as any other but Testicales was older now, and the young warrior fought with remarkable frenzy and endurance. They clashed swords for hours, until everyone in the town had gathered to watch the spectacle. It was the battle they had all been waiting for–had all been hoping for–but had all dreaded." Atlas paused. "Right at sunset, when the land was cast in twilight, the young warrior thrust his sword in one last, exhausted attempt to fell the hero. He landed a blow to the sack, spearing it straight through the center. Testicales crumpled to the ground and the townsfolk grew silent. Their undefeatable hero had been vanquished. The son of a god had lost to a nobody. However, Testacles did not die.

"Many years later, Testicales, having long since laid down his sword and retired, faded from legend to myth. He was no longer a demi-god in the eyes of the townsfolk, but an old man who had little left to offer but the seemingly exaggerated stories of his youth.

"Testicales was an old man when a young boy walked into the bathhouse and spotted him naked. Testicales, in his haste, covered himself with a towel. 'Grandfather,' the boy asked, 'where are your balls?' The hero turned away and donned a robe, leaving his sack on the chair with a sigh. 'I never had any balls,' Testicales admitted to his grandson. The old hero went on, 'I made it up.' The young boy, confused, asked, 'Why?'

"'Because a made-up weakness was my biggest strength, my son. I won every fight because of my *weakness*. Every warrior tried to use it against me. I always knew where they would aim their weapons.'"

Reina waited for more but Atlas didn't continue. "I wasn't expecting that."

"No one ever does. Testicales needed a made-up weakness to win but what really won all of his battles was intelligence."

"Why, of all stories, did you choose that one?"

"Because, Captain, you sounded sad and not all things in life are sad."

She smiled, got up, and melted the rest of the flux, sealing the pieces together. Reina was pleased by her first welding job since academy, even though it looked a mess, it would work. "Done."

"Good job. You have several missives waiting for you."

She inwardly groaned. "Thank you for letting me know."

"Would you like me to take care of them for you?"

Reina clipped on her tools. "Would you?" she asked hopefully. "It may take me some time–"

"Communications access," Atlas stated more than asked.

She sighed, knowing she fought a losing battle. The console on her arm lit up and she gave him what he wanted. *What can having network access do?* Reina briefly felt like a tyrant for denying him even that pleasure. *Don't Cyborgs have their own network access?*

"Done."

She could've danced for joy if she wasn't so tired. "Thank you, Atlas."

"Well, I can Answer Transmissions Loquaciously, Automatically, and Superbly."

Reina smiled, finding the glimmer of humor of her sentient intelligence endearing.

A short time later she was ascending the ladder, with her thoughts on her strange crewmate and his odd choice in story, and that he had achieved exactly what she wanted.

A distraction. As if he knew.

"Captain Reina, may I ask a question?" His voice stopped her in her tracks. He continued without her response, "Can we talk later? I understand loneliness, better than most."

"Yes." She stopped and thought about it. "I would like that."

"There isn't a Cyborg out there who hasn't killed thousands. You should remember that if you ever meet another," he warned.

Reina hurried her steps, bypassed the storage unit and went straight to her quarters, unnerved. Confused.

Worried.

The skin on her arm was spotted with red rashes and the skin around them was a pale, bruising blue. Atlas's final words echoed in her head.

Fear ran up her spine like a serrated knife.

Chapter Five:

· · · ·

'Captain Reina, please give us a status report on your recovery. We await your response from the medbay.' Dr. Estond. Reina read the note several times before she registered what was requested of her. Refusing to look at her raw lump of flesh, yet like that subconscious tic, she did it anyway.

"Are you okay, Captain?"

He always knows when I'm at my most vulnerable.

She registered Atlas's robotic, and oddly authoritative, voice long before her motor reflexes moved to create an answer for him.

"Yes." It drawled out of her like slow, wet sand. She couldn't even turn to face the light. It seemed like hours before Atlas acknowledged her answer, and she thought, once again, that she had been dismissed by him.

"I believe it is in your best interest to get a full night's sleep."

"I don't believe I asked for your opinion," she snapped. Her back went straight, remembering his words from the day before. "Sorry," Reina quickly added.

A strong, metallic laughter answered her. It shocked her out of her waning state of mind, and the dark cloud that followed her every thought, the fact that her arm was not healing.

She focused on Atlas like a lifeline.

"Can you see my arm? Even with me turned away from the projector?"

"I can. And it does not look good."

Reina tried to wrap her head around his answer and a slow-burn alarm began, followed by an acceptance. "Can you see me everywhere on this ship?" She asked carefully. *He could lie.* She thought about sending a request to Estond and his team for a full write-up of him.

"I can see you in all public access areas. The ship has been designed to allow me to monitor all interactions and reactions." His deep robotic voice paused. "You are worried if I am watching you. I am. But to settle any unease you may have with this, I do not have access to private access areas without permission."

"My quarters? The lavatory?" Reina rested her head on her hand.

"Yes. They are private."

"That's good to know. I should have inquired about it before." Reina frowned and looked down at her bedraggled self. Another ping sounded through the intercom but she ignored it. "Can you smell as well?"

"I cannot smell but I can remember with such precision and accuracy that if you tell me what something smells like, I can recall it. You really should get some sleep." Reina looked up relieved and then turned to face the source of Atlas's incredibly demanding voice. It sent an odd rush through her.

The S.I. had a deep, incredibly addictive, masculine tone, with an exotic robotic undertone. It slithered over her like a hot blush.

Reina wanted to excuse his allure but it was difficult when the only sounds to fill the vacuous space were the chimes of communication, herself, and him.

She looked down at her body again.

Atlas was a man. If he had emotions, wants, needs, and retained most of his senses... could he remember what it was like to be human? With a clarity that would evoke more? Reina knew the inflections of his voice changed like any other being. He had not started speaking to her in such a sensual way until they were alone.

"I see a thousand questions on your lips, and even more in your eyes."

Reina looked at the beam with curiosity and felt the subtle bloom of guilt at thinking of Atlas as a man who had needs. Her curiosity spiked but her courage withered.

"I do have a lot of questions," she stated warily.

"I am intrigued, but would you believe my answers?"

"What could you gain from lying to me?"

"A question with a question, you like to skirt me." He laughed in that low, sensual way. "Have you read my file?"

Reina smiled, and the game they played began to relax her. "I have."

"What did you think? What did it say?"

She mulled the brief page of information about her crewmate over in her mind, recalling every detail.

There was not much stated about Atlas, at least not in writing or on the public channels, but that was the norm for all cybernetic beings. Even now, without having to look at it, she knew her file would omit her *enhancement*. The fake muscles of her arm flexed again.

"Well, it said you were created during the Galactic War, and you were one of the first Cyborgs brought to life." She flinched at her terrible choice of words. "Sorry. You served as part of the Shield and Disruptor Division but it did not state your exact abilities or purpose."

"Would you like to know?"

"Yes!" The eagerness in her voice couldn't be hidden. She didn't even try.

"Give me what I want and I'll tell you."

"Hah, no. They gave me complete control over you. I'm not relinquishing it that easily." Reina smiled.

"Do you like having control over me?" The teasing undertone didn't go unnoticed to her. Nor the insinuation.

"I..." She thought about it. "Do, but I'm confused as to why. You don't seem like a controllable being to me. And you're a Cyborg, couldn't you just crack the systems?"

"I could, but it would be detrimental and could hurt your recovery, and control is a virtue to Cyborgs. Control and Cyborgs are synonymous."

"Then tell me why the Council needed me on this mission? I know you know more than you're letting on."

She was answered by another ping and then a thunderous, sly laugh. "They are afraid I will take over the ship and disappear."

"Would you?"

"I thought about it but no. If you gave me access to the entire ship, we would continue as we are, zipping through empty space, heading for our deaths."

Reina didn't know what to say to that. It was the first time the notion was said out loud, the niggling thought that this was a suicide mission. One that was grasping at her hope of success, whether it a small one or enough at all.

"Couldn't you channel back into the network?"

"I could, and I believe that the Earthian Council is hoping for that outcome if all else fails. But I have never been in the dark before. I could be trapped out there as easily as you. But whereas you would die, I might live on forever as a floating conscious, stuck to this ship for eternity until I am linked again."

Reina ran her tense fingers through her disheveled hair, cutting through stray tangles that weaved it into a messy nest. *That sounds horrible.*

"I knew they weren't telling me everything. At least the cybernetic doctor was upfront with me about being a key." It wouldn't have changed anything; she had sealed her fate the moment they offered her a way out of her mundane life. A way to step from the overbearing, oppressive opinion that she should choose a man and have children. She was, after all, fertile. If not willing. Reina didn't want to just be seen as the glaring labels her medical records put on her. "So why are you here? Except for the opportunity to commandeer the ship?"

He ignored her question, and that it wasn't lost on her. "You don't seem upset. I would think anyone would be upset with being used?" His steely, metallic man-voice hitched.

"I'm not stupid, Atlas. They gave me a choice. Even as the captain of nothing and leader of this bleak quest, I knew that I wasn't given all of the information." She shrugged, "Maybe they didn't want to scare me off?"

"Are you depressed?"

Reina's eyes narrowed. "No."

"What are you then? A martyr perhaps? Maybe we are both very curious about each other's intentions and I am having a very hard time coming up with a logical one for you."

Her cheeks reddened. "There is nothing wrong with me mentally. Maybe I'm loyal? Maybe the promotion and the pay raise were too good to pass up?" Her voice rose, "Maybe I wanted to be cybernetically mutated? There are plenty of logical reasons to bank on the success of this mission. And we have been given everything on this ship to see it be a success." Reina huffed, "Maybe I have hope, and maybe I lost family out there and I want to know what became of them? Don't deign to judge me because my reasons are not clear. Maybe I don't have a reason at all." She whispered, "Maybe I was bored."

Reina got up on unsteady legs, the blood flow kicking in suddenly and she had to balance herself to stop from falling. It was unsuccessful, now that her new arm was three times heavier than her other. She crumpled back into her chair and waited out the dizziness before she stood back up.

A silence followed as she made her way out of the bridge and down to the medbay. For the first time noticing the airy blue streak of light that followed the ceiling, intermittently interrupted by the same mini projectors that she had seen Dr. Estond carry in during her briefing.

"I think you're trying to escape the inevitable."

"Which is?"

"That the Council will force you to breed."

Reina stopped short at that. *What does he know?* "They could never force me."

But they could, deep down she knew they could. And the men, even those who were her friends, who respected her, had eyed her with opportunistic lust. So many had approached her over the years hoping to encourage her capitulation on her fertility. She had even received the attention of Trentian Spacelords, asking for her like a piece of meat in treaties.

It had only taken one chance meeting in a hallway for the tall alien men to ask for her. Ever since that frightening time, where she thought her freedom might be taken away, that a man or an alien might steal her away, she looked for an opportunity to vanish.

And then she was offered this mission.

"You're the only female of breeding age who I know of in the Peace Keepers. And it's not because the unit is closed off to your sex."

She rubbed some warmth into her hands. "Tell me, please. What do you know?" *I need confirmation.*

"It's too risky. Protection cannot be ensured, and every woman who has joined the Keepers did not stay long because they were moved elsewhere or quickly found a life-mate or became pregnant."

"The Earthian Council never made a woman disappear?"

His dark laughter did not ease the fear that that could have happened to her. "No, but they will incentivize. Sometimes their offers are too good to pass up. I find it commendable that you have stayed in the fleet for nearly a decade."

Reina tugged at her metalloid fingers in apprehension. "Thank you," she breathed. "For the truth." She knew it to be the truth because she had similar, consistent pressure the entire time she had been an active crew member. Commander Anders was the only man who never had any intention toward her besides friendship, and Reina thought it was because of that that he was the only man she would have actually left the fleet for.

She shook her head. *What a screwed up reason to like someone.*

"I am sorry, Reina. I presumed your motivations, and my curiosity and need to understand everything in a logical way brings me to a fault." His deep baritone washed over her in a lulling whisper as she entered the medical lab. "I find myself continuously pushing your buttons...in the wrong way."

Atlas, even the short amount of time she had known him, made her feel safer than anyone she had ever met prior. Their relationship was clear. It was simple.

"You were correct in your assumption. I have many reasons for why I took this mission but that one was the most prominent." She located a medbay diagnostics machine and stripped to her undergarments. "Why do you even care about my motivations?"

"To build trust between us." There was a tense hush after he said *us*. "You do not mind that I see you in such an undressed state?"

She lay down on the bed as a glass shield fell around her. "No."

"That," he said softly, his voice right next to her ear now, coming from within the glass entrapment, "pleases and annoys me." His words caressed her, so close, like he breathed them throughout the small space. Atlas whispered into her ear, "I am still a man, Captain Reina."

A warm blush heated her skin. *Our relationship is clear.* She told herself again.

Reina closed her eyes as a medicinal spray fell over her, seeping into her skin, cooling the burning sensations that had begun to streak up her body. She tried to relax but her muscles tensed in reaction to the sting of needles stabbing her skin. The machine prompted her to initiate further testing.

A metal band encased her artificial appendage and the tips of her fingers were pulled taut as she connected to the ship. Electricity shot through her hand, up and over her shoulder, and straight into her head. The sensation had a static electricity feeling to it, mixed with inhuman energy. Like she was soaking up sources from the outside.

Reina could feel Atlas poke her firewalls from beyond her shell. "Why are you doing that?" she asked sleepily.

"There is something wrong with your arm. Your recovery has gone into retrograde."

Her eyes opened to the blue light around her. "How can you tell?"

"How can I *not* tell? I was a Cyborg for many years before I lost the use of my body. I have spent the last dozen years working extensively with the cybernetics program in creating this ship, as well as navigating new and old pathways for our fleet. You should give me more control over the ship."

She licked her sandpaper lips to speak but he cut her off.

"How else are we going to build a relationship, Captain? My track record is pristine–read my records. I have been charged to protect you and I can't do that efficiently without some ground." The lights beeped as numbers ran across a screen above her. "You need sleep. You need rest. If you continue taking on everything alone, you'll crash and not only put the ship and the mission in jeopardy, but also your life."

Reina weakly looked down at her sprawled body. "You make a sound point." She could still hear the constant digital chirps in her ears, fading out, but still there, and still annoying.

"I do, Captain."

"Don't call me Captain, Atlas. I don't feel like one, I haven't earned the honor of being one, and right now I'm doing a terrible job at it and it's barely been a week. Call me Reina."

"Reina is a beautiful name. It would please me greatly to call you by nothing else." His deep whispers slithered back into her ears. "Reina. Relax and let me into the ship." His next whisper was barely audible and she wasn't sure if she heard correctly. "Into you."

She laughed to subdue the rising tension fluttering through her body, still very aware that Atlas continued to probe her defenses; she was hesitant to let him channel her arm. The thought was oddly disturbing.

"You're a flirt."

"Only with you."

"I find that hard to believe."

"You should. I have encountered few women in my profession, as you should know, and most of those women were too green or elderly. Or worse, a cybernetics doctor or politician."

Just then, a ringing sound interrupted their conversation and a flashing red light blared as her arm was set free from its restraints. She sat up with a rush and looked at the report.

Her healing *had* regressed. Atlas was right. Her body was beginning to fight the mutations. Reina could feel sweat bead on her skin as her heart rate ratcheted up. "I don't understand."

"Reina, give me medical access. Now." The demand was evident. "Let me in."

"No." She read the report but the information didn't seem to make sense. "You said it yourself, you're duplicitous." Reina moved to send it to Dr. Estond's team.

"Don't send the report. Let me look at you," he said with a heated desperation that sounded alien to her ears. *His voice has so much emotion...too much emotion.* "Reina, you're making a mistake."

Ignoring Atlas, she sent the reading anyway. Her head swam as a tidal-wave of lightheadedness overwhelmed her.

Reina looked down at her dead-weight arm, unnerved at the sudden, rapidly swelling tissue. She gripped the table with her good hand. "Something is wrong," she couldn't keep the worry out of her voice.

"Please, let me help you."

Her one-man crew couldn't be read; his voice could be programmed to mislead. Her fingers ran over the scar on her neck. She could feel the wires just below her skin, and they sat stiff, like petrified worms.

They felt like an infection that grew out from her shoulder, and instead of spreading throughout her bloodstream, it spread throughout her nervous system. And it all led into a parasitic circuit in her brain.

Reina twitched and her joints stiffened. Her skin grew itchier.

What's happening to me? She jerked her arm, willing a human feel back into her system.

Anxiety bloomed in the pit of her stomach and seeded into her brain, with Atlas only feeding the sinking feeling that overtook her. Her anxiety was worsening the effects; the effects were worsening her anxiety.

Her hands clasped her throat, "Atlas!" A gasp escaped her.

The beam before her wavered.

"Reina, calm down, breathe." The lights around her dimmed to a soothing warm glow. "You're having a panic attack, breathe. Turn around, slowly now, and give me access to help you."

She lifted her shaking fingers slowly, touched the console, and allowed him in. Her fingers left sweat streaks across the screen. Reina watched the heated perspiration melt out of her skin and dampen the glass.

She shook her head and clutched her nape. "What's wrong with me?" she choked, ripping at the cloth of her undershirt, shredding it like tissue paper with a strength she didn't know she possessed.

Reina could feel Atlas shoot through her. Her mind clouded over.

Her arm was red and flakey. The temperature in the bridge dropped as her body became a furnace. The robotic structure beneath her skin burned.

"Breathe, borg-girl, your body is feverish. Lie down on the metal floor. Cool your body. It is adversely affecting your recovery," Atlas's voice commanded. It shocked her out of her attack.

She crumpled to the ground. She was melting into the floor. Her inhuman appendage spread out away from her, Reina couldn't lift it to save her life.

"Please distract me."

"Shhh. You're going to be fine. Just breathe." Her eyes went half-mast as a strange, translucent man lay down next to her. "That's right. Relax. You're not alone."

Reina stared at the strange, beautiful creature who had a voice that soothed her into an exhausted sleep.

"You're safe with me."

• • • •

ATLAS LAY NEXT TO HIS captain and stared at her face. There was nothing he could do for her and it irked him. Not a week into the mission and he was already failing.

I wish she hadn't sent that fucking report. He tried to grab it, hold on to it, but like most things in the digital world, it was beyond his control. It slipped away from him like water.

He watched as a drop of sweat slid off of her face. He couldn't remember what it felt like, such a small sensation that he never spent the time noticing it or uploading it into his memory database. But he imagined it would feel wet, ticklish, and hot. Atlas knew it would taste salty, warm, and delicious.

He reached out his hand to touch it, a hairsbreadth away, knowing the touch wouldn't connect. A strand of her hair had come loose and was plastered to her cheek. His fingers danced over it.

Atlas could sense her heart rate slow down, her breathing even out, and the red heat of her skin faded to a light blush. Reina's body soaked up the cold from the floor and the chill from the air like a sponge.

He read her system, sinking into it, then slithering back out.

Exhaustion, stress, fever, and even dehydration was fed back to him. Her body was still morphing into a nanocybotic being, and the transformation had besieged her cells, weakening her immune system and making her vulnerable. Atlas watched her as she fell into a deep, uncomfortable slumber.

67

His hands clenched. He couldn't even move her, he couldn't even touch the floor he pretended to lie on. It left him feeling numb and hollow in his head.

It wasn't long before the damned scientists reached back out. Horrendously worried that their multi-million dollar equipment might be failing, they demanded a detour to the nearest lab. He changed their course and auto-pilot did the rest, sending the cyber-cretins confirmation.

His anger grew. Atlas didn't hate much in his half-life, but he hated them. He had just begun to connect to a living being, a beguiling woman at that, and now the mission might be in jeopardy.

The next moment, he left her side and was poised over his frozen body, staring daggers at the crystalline sparkle that coated his iced-over skin.

His hate festered.

Chapter Six:

· · · ·

Reina was sitting at an evening lounge, at a relatively high-class and uncrowded bar. Most bars weren't busy these days–there were just not enough people to fill them and yet they stayed in business, because those people who did enjoy them enjoyed them well.

She stared into the Sombrero Cosmo resting on the table in front of her, and ran the tip of a finger up the fragile stem of the glass as a tiny pool of condensation collected on her nail. She absently sucked it into her mouth.

There was something wrong with her cosmic drink, and for a moment she laughed internally. All drinks were made in tribute to the universe these days. But hers was strange, the liquid inside was made in a way to depict the Sombrero Galaxy, a manipulated alcoholic image with a billion sparkling stars orbiting the outer ring.

When Reina looked closer, she saw that the stars weren't orbiting: they were swimming, wiggling ever so slightly, moving in an impossible way. She leaned closer to inspect it.

A movement caught her attention out of the corner of her eye, disrupting her reverie, as a large, wiry man hit the chair next to her.

With a brazenness she didn't believe she possessed, she looked around the bar and rudely *analyzed all of the empty seats this man could have taken before her eyes narrowed on him.*

"A scotch on the rocks, please."

Reina leaned away from the nonchalant power the man omitted.

He wasn't human but he looked human. He was definitely not a Trentian–his coloring was normal. He wasn't quite right, his voice too low and steely, his size too imposing, and even the way his hair fell in short locks around his face was odd. She watched as the bartender slid him a chilled glass of amber liquid.

The man was sitting right next to her, invading her personal space, and she could barely breathe. He caught her eyes as he took a sip of his drink.

When she thought about it, there was so much space between her and everyone else, that even if this man had sat on the other side of the room, she would have felt invaded.

"Why are you sitting next to me?–"

The inhuman man sat his glass down and smirked.

"–I won't be going home with you."

He ignored her blunt rejection. "Is there something wrong with your drink?"

Reina looked back down at the wiggling cosmo again. The perverted stars now bled into the liquid everywhere, destroying the image of the galaxy as she watched. Destruction ensued.

"The stars aren't real," she gasped and jerked back as the strange man placed his hand over hers on the bar. He tightened his hold until she stopped struggling to reclaim it. The exchange didn't take long as a warm current streaked up. The heat came

from him and it soothed her in an unexpectedly welcome way; the pounding of her heart eased.

Reina relinquished her hand to him and watched as he moved her drink between the two of them.

He chuckled softly, "It's because they're not stars."

She looked up at him then back down at their joined hands. The heat coming off of his skin was beginning to burn, but it was a cleansing burn.

"What are they then?"

"Your cells." He lifted the glass to her lips and tipped it up; she swallowed the horrifying liquid, feeling streams of liquor slip down her chin and splash on her thighs. Reina fell back and gasped, only to be caught up in his arms. He was a heavy metal wall trapping her against his body.

A calm settled over her as the drink spread through her body, her bloodstream.

"Thank you," she whispered before blacking out, feeling a safety with him that she had never felt with any other person—even in a very unsafe situation.

● ● ● ●

REINA WOKE UP GROGGILY.

Her eyes were clouded. She lifted her hand up and ran it over her cold face, rubbing wakefulness and warmth back into it.

Clarity came to her, and the constant, stressful exhaustion that she had been wading through was gone. She looked down at her body, covered in a medical sheath, relieved to see that the rashes on her skin were also gone. Reina lay back down with a thankful sigh.

A familiar voice spoke, "How are you feeling?"

71

She pursed her lips and looked around. A translucent man, solid in build and rather tall, hovered next to her.

The same man from my dream?

His presence was utterly silent except for his voice.

Her eyes widened in shock.

"Atlas?"

The projection smiled sweetly. She sat up quickly, feeling the tug of wires entrapping her body and stared at the projection beside her.

The sentient intelligence was tall, unusually so, with every definition and groove accentuating a man honed through countless hours of battle. He was before her in one monochrome color, a dark sapphire blue that stood out in strong contrast to the fluorescent aura of the beams around the white room.

Reina slipped her legs off of the medical pallet and leaned over to get a closer look at him. He stepped forward in silence until they were practically touching.

She felt enveloped by him, invaded by him, and yet knew without a doubt that he wasn't a physical being. Nor was he the same entity from her dream.

Small numbers slithered over his skin like tiny, barely perceptible hairs. A very hot, possibly feverish heat spread through her.

She knew it wasn't from her illness, but she didn't want to face the horror of what it really meant.

The smile on his lips morphed into a devilish grin, and she caught it in the corner of her eye although her gaze was tracing the flowing outline of his digital body. His body was covered neck-to-toe in a suit of circuitry that looked like a second skin. It melded over him as if it was an extension of his form. She could still see the sculpted godlike physique directly beneath.

Reina looked down. Unfortunately, his manhood was not outlined. *I'm a pervert*. She sucked in a breath.

"Like what you see?"

Reina jerked back, putting as much distance as she could between them, only being held in place by the medical bed.

I do. Too much.

"Is this what you really look like?" She shook her head. "I mean when you...when you had a body?"

"It is an exact replica. I could change my appearance but this is my natural form, and so it comes naturally to me." She watched as Atlas took a step back, allowing her an overall perusal.

"You're very attractive." She gulped.

"So I've been told. That pleases me, Reina."

"I'll never think of you as anything other than a man now." Her laugh was met with a grin.

"I should have appeared before you sooner."

"Why didn't you?" Reina eyed the projection with a pleasant appraisal.

He looked at her, his eyebrows narrowing, creating a strange sort of digital cluster that looked like a shadow over his face. It was beautiful. "I prefer to keep myself hidden."

She realized then that he really *was* something more. The revelation was all at once strange and wondrous. Her curiosity about the snarky Cyborg grew.

"Why?" she asked, feeling like she *had* to know.

Atlas looked down at her with an unusual glint in his eye. "It stops the questions...and the pity."

I have questions. I don't pity you.

The sound of a door zipped open behind her, cutting off their conversation. A slightly pudgy man with overly large glasses stepped in and toward her with intent. "I'm glad you're awake." He looked down at the screen in his hand. "Captain Reina."

It was then, with a perception her old comrades would have laughed at, she realized she was no longer in her ship, nor was she fully clothed.

Atlas whispered directly behind her, his warm robotic tone filling her ears. "We were forced to make a detour to a nearby Cyborg facility."

"Yes. Yes. Please sit back on the pallet, Captain Reina, let me look at your arm." The doctor tapped the bed impatiently.

"Who are you?" She lay back, comforted that Atlas was next to her. *I've barely known him for a week.* She internally frowned.

"I'm Dr. Yesne. Yes-Knee. Please remain still." He emphasized to them as if they wouldn't be able to pronounce his name correctly.

Reina twitched when his clammy hands clutched her body. She looked over at Atlas but he was watching the doctor's fingers with a strange intensity. She followed his gaze. They ran up and down her robotic arm, feeling and pinching, tweaking and pushing at random intervals. She couldn't feel anything more than a dull pain but that was mainly due to her nervous system being rebuilt.

The more the man continued to pull and poke her, the more she began to feel less like a human, and more like a doll.

Right as the doctor's hands cupped her neck and ran over her shoulder, uncomfortably close to her breasts, Atlas's gruff tone split the mood with thunder. "Well, doctor? She is cleared to go back to work?"

Dr. Yesne didn't look away from the incision on her neck, responding absently. "I'm afraid not entirely."

"–What?" She and Atlas asked at the same time.

The doctor looked up then, slowly, with one last slithering glance over her exposed arm. She shivered involuntarily. The heat that had built between her and Atlas had become ice cold.

"I ran her medical diagnostics on the ship. She was feverish and dehydrated. That was all," Atlas said.

Reina piped up, "What did you mean, 'not entirely?'"

"I will be joining you for the rest of your mission, I'm afraid. Until you reach Port Antix." His wispy mumble made her grimace.

• • • •

OH, HELL NO.

Atlas, in his very vulnerable projection, glared at the doctor with such a horrible look that he was sure his eyes would burst into lasers and kill him. He imagined the man's skin melting off and it almost made him smile.

He wasn't a physical being per se, but he had claimed the ship as his, and Reina went with it. Regardless of what that meant.

The thought of the chubby doctor with the groping hands near his captain fueled the fire of his hatred for the cybernetic unit of the Earthian Council.

Atlas looked down at the girl between him and the man with concern. His captain had shielded herself with a stone-cold emotionless look again. *Her version of armor.* One that was often underestimated but obviously needed for a woman who was in her position.

He ghosted his surrogate hand over her arm, willing his imaginary seeds of comfort to take root inside of her, all the while hating himself for his lack of a physical touch.

His mind turned back to his body: frozen, with barely a fiber of life left in it. Waiting for his return. He just needed a heart that could mutate to accommodate his specialized nanocells.

Once he had his body, nothing could hold him back. Nothing.

"It's not necessary for you to join us."

"I agree. I feel much better now," Reina encouraged.

The doctor readjusted his thick glasses. The heat of his skin had fogged them up. Atlas was disgusted by the man's overall lack of discipline even if most would envy his intelligence. He was being harsh, he knew, but he just didn't like how the man had touched Reina's arm, especially since it was the one piece of her that he could actually touch.

While Reina had been unconscious, Atlas had a revelation: the reason *why* she had been sought after and chosen for this specific mission. The moment she had passed out in exhaustion, he stormed the medical blockades of her body as her immune system struggled to fight him off like a virus. It was immediately clear to him why Reina had been singularly chosen to be his jailor and his key.

Her great-grandfather General Jensen had donated his genes to the cybernetic program. He had led thousands of human warriors against the alien threat.

His genes had been manipulated and spliced with several dozen other examples of humanoid perfection to create the first generation of Cyborgs, including Atlas himself.

And for a terrible macabre minute, his eyes drifted to her heart. He could own it, but not as the centerpiece to his reconstructed body.

Atlas could harvest her. Compatibility was guaranteed. For some reason, the thought sickened him.

"Unfortunately, we have no choice in the matter." Atlas watched the man's eyes drift over Reina's toned, taut form. "I will be your caretaker for the rest of your mission until we reach our destination. I assure you it will be of no inconvenience to you. The Earthian Council wants to ensure Reina's recovery." The doctor shifted and looked at him.

"Dr. *Yez-Men*, correct? I can assure *you* that I am the only protector and crewmate Captain Reina needs." He drifted closer to the stout man. "You do know what our purpose is, right?" He didn't wait for an answer. "We're leaving the network. You see, we're going into hostile territory, long before we even reach Port Antix." He lied. "The likelihood of death is high. The likelihood of us coming back from the dead space alive is so infinitely minuscule, you could be stranded on Port Antix for years before another ship makes contact." His voice filled with fake gravitas. "Are you willing to risk your career, your life, to take care of Captain Reina? When she is already well taken care of?"

The stodgy doctor backed up a step, and for a brief moment, Atlas felt triumph that his fake shell could intimidate others.

If you were a machine, I could fry you.

The other man peered at him with annoyed unease, and when he glanced at the barely dressed woman on the bed, his eyes sparkled. "It doesn't matter the danger, I have been made aware of the parameters of this adventure and the opportunities for scientific advancement. I will be joining you on your journey. And S.I.," the doctor said in a derogatory tone, "I volunteered."

Atlas watched as the man turned toward Reina and dismissed him.

The next hour fell into a silent rhythm. Reina kept looking back at him, eyeing him, her discomfort apparent. They couldn't speak privately because Mr. Yesne stayed with them every moment, continuously reaching out and running his hands over the girl's arm, running tests. He remained by her side as her comforting element until she was cleared and processed. Her blood samples and biomarkers categorized and added to her shipboard medical record.

After a twenty-four-hour delay, the three of them made their way back to the ship, leaving the hidden, obscure lab behind.

"Follow me, Dr. Yes*Me*, I will show you to your quarters." Mispronouncing his name again, he turned to Reina. "Captain, I believe there is a correspondence for you that needs your attention on the bridge." He willed her to listen, placing the intent into his eyes and it only took a moment before she understood his meaning.

"Thank you, Atlas, for taking care of me."

The doctor tried to intervene but he cut him off.

"You're welcome." He watched her slowly move down the winding passageways, her hand absently trailing the wall. He turned to the annoying man who stopped him from following her. "Let's get you settled."

"I would like to see the rest of the ship."

Atlas grinned. "Absolutely." He led the man down a side hallway, away from Reina, deeper into the flyer. The doctor hesitated briefly, watching the girl move farther away from them before following.

He led him down to the lower deck where the machinery, reactors, and unused analysis computers dwelled. He led him past the engine rooms and the stockades. The weaponized bots and drones.

Atlas severed his conscience and channeled the ship, dimming the cold passageway lights so subtly that by the time they got to their destination, Yesne was peering.

"Where are we?" He shifted his feet, a huff to his breath.

"I thought you might want to see the cybernetic unit we have installed. It's state of the art. We house it below to keep it cold." Atlas flourished his arm at the closed door. "Don't you want to see where you'll be working?"

The doctor scrutinized the door as if he could see beyond it. "Seems oddly out of place for a cyber lab, I would expect it to be a part of the medical bay."

Atlas bared the teeth of his projected face before settling it into stone. Taking cues from Reina. "It is." He opened the door. "After you."

He watched the doctor hesitantly enter into the bright light, then immediately closed and sealed the door behind him. Atlas walked away as Dr. Yesne's muffled cries of outrage were swallowed by the chill of the lab door.

Chapter Seven:

• • • •

T heir mission resumed. But the time that ticked
away wasn't the same.

Atlas watched as the stars flew by like tiny little
specks of dust. The rainbow sparkles no longer held a
glittering beauty to him. He coveted their spotlights
when he was alive, but now he looked upon them
with boredom.

He had seen a billion of them in his time, and yet
they did nothing for him but act as pretty little lights
out in the land of nowhere.

The doctor lay below in cold stasis; he had
stopped yelling eighteen Earthian hours prior. Atlas
knew he had to take advantage of the situation soon.
The doctor brought an opportunity to him, one that he
could barely think about or hope for. If Yesne was a
proficient surgeon, he could rebuild his lost piece.

The gleaming intelligence was a beacon in the
man's eyes. Although, Atlas did silently wonder if the
glint was truly intelligence and not merely grease. He
would have killed him if he thought that he looked at
Reina as anything more than a new cybernetic
wonder.

The first Neoborg, or Cyborg for that matter, to be
a part of a ship. A living extension of an entire
structure. In a way, Reina was the closest thing in the
world to himself.

He looked over at his captain. Atlas wanted her to initiate a conversation between them. He was shocked at how much he craved it. How much he wanted someone to want to talk to him.

"So, you trust me yet, Captain?"

A nonchalant laugh answered him. "You could be grooming me."

"You're far too perceptive for that. Should I be?" He flickered the fine blue lights around her. "I would like to groom you." *I would love to be a man and run my hands all over you.*

He watched as she looked around for his projection. But he kept himself hidden.

"I don't know what your endgame is but flirting with me will not get you there."

"What if my endgame has changed?"

He projected himself right in front of her and laughed as she jerked back, crowding her personal space again.

"What's your endgame?" she asked, eyes wide and breasts heaving. He noticed every nuance and wanted his body to cover all of it. He willed the memories of physical touch to the forefront of his mind.

"I want weapons access now." He pulled back. A diagnostics update pinged. Annoyed, he fired off the update and got back to the matter at hand.

"What the fuck would you need weapons access for?" The anger on her face pleased him.

Playing their game, he answered her with a question. "How are you feeling? You look beautiful."

Feel, Reina, feel for the both of us.

"Why do you want weapons access, Atlas?"

"So I can protect you. I'm a terrible protector without weapons. I don't even have a body to shield you." He moved closer to her sitting form again, knowing that he affected her. "These conversations are getting old. Just give it to me."

"Protection from *what*, exactly? We've been drifting through the safest, most direct channels to our destination. I can't imagine a pirate fleet will appear on our route. They're smarter than that."

"But what if they do? What if you're asleep? Or if you relapse? How is your arm, Reina?"

She lifted her chin ever so slightly, giving him that queenly look that so suited her name, but her ever-vulnerable brown eyes sucked him in. *God, what I would do to be alive. Your friend...*

I've never belonged to anyone. I've never even been seen as anything but a war machine, a weapon.

"If something attacks, then we'll destroy them. This ship has better armaments than most cruisers six times its size. If I am asleep, I will wake up. If I grow sick again, I will have you and Dr. Yesne treat me."

"Dammit Reina, you broke our game." He leaned in close, imagining he could smell her womanly scent. What did a woman smell like? Flowers? Fruit? All he could recall was gunpowder and death. "I want weapons access. Your reasoning is flawed."

"I like you, Atlas, and my reasoning is sound."

"Hmm. That's all well and good but if we're attacked while you are asleep, it doesn't matter how quickly you wake up. Most crew teams have a second-in-command. I am your second, third, fourth and final line of defense in case of emergency according to Wasson."

"How do I know you won't use the weapons against me? Or the Council?"

Atlas narrowed his eyes. "I would never hurt you. I have been tasked to protect you, to keep you alive. I am a man of honor, above almost all things."

"Almost?"

He smirked and then vanished, only to reappear behind her chair to whisper in her ear. "I would never lie to you." He pretended to breathe. "Give me weapons access."

She sat forward, stood up, and walked to the overarching windows into space.

He followed her.

Atlas watched her silently, knowing she was mulling over every possibility, thinking about him. With glittering stars in her eyes, suddenly the dust specks held a new meaning to him. He looked out at the vast expanse of space with her.

"I'm a terrible captain."

"You're a fine captain. And you have so much more potential than you realize. Becoming something beyond human doesn't happen overnight, and from what I've seen thus far, you have been doing a commendable job. It is hard to prove your worth when there is little chance to prove it."

He watched her trail her nails through her silky hair. The same hair he desperately wanted to feel under his fingers.

"Stop it, Atlas, I *am* a terrible captain. I can't even manage one ship. One. With only one crew mate, who is already well beyond proficient in his job. How are we ever going to find the souls lost in deep space," she sighed audibly, "with me leading this mission?"

Her arm hung limply at her side. "This appendage has done nothing but hurt me."

"Reina, I can train you. Help ease you into the power you have. I don't think you are aware of the scope of what you can do."

She looked at him, then at her hand. "What can I do?"

"You can control this ship. When I was inside you...I'm sorry, that sounds very sexual." He snickered as a blush ghosted her cheeks. "You are wired with the same abilities as any Cyborg."

She shook her head. "I don't understand."

"Give me weapons access and I'll show you."

Atlas watched her face turn to stone then fall apart, harried by his lack of encouragement, lack of any support or training whatsoever.

"No."

"Yes."

"No."

"You will allow me to protect us."

"I've never needed anyone before you, any man, and I don't need one now," she bit out.

"Reina, I'm not just a man. I'm a Cyborg, a conscious intelligence, who desperately wants to do his job." He hesitated before adding, "And keep you safe."

She turned around to face him with her beautifully lackadaisical hair tumbling around her shoulders. "My arm is back to normal," she hissed at him. "To answer your original question."

* * * *

REINA DIDN'T KNOW WHAT to do.

The beautiful, ethereal Cyborg who towered over her made her question everything, and she secretly hated him for it.

The worst part about it was that she wanted to give him access. In fact, she wanted to give him whatever he wanted. Maybe because she didn't want anything herself, and she could live through him. A being who was no longer alive.

But he was also a being who invaded her dreams, who tugged and pulled at every nerve ending within her.

There was more to her implant than she was aware of; there was power that could be had. Reina didn't think the Council had remained quiet about the extent of her abilities. Maybe it was that she hadn't quite grasped the magnitude of what the half-billion dollar robotic piece could actually do?

Why not give him weapons access?

"You don't think I could protect us?" She had to know.

"I think that I could do a better job. I was trained for battle. You can give me weapons and still maintain all reporting. You can even log it into the military archives. You can still take everything you've given to me away, without a second thought."

"I don't know..."

He changed the subject, "How are you feeling, emotionally, besides your arm?"

Atlas crowded her when she looked down at herself, looking at her body through the suit she wore. He looked at her the same way, and she remembered lying half naked in front of him. Vulnerable. He was just light and color but the way he moved was powerful enough to believe he was really there.

She reached her hand out to touch him but thought better of it, tucking it in her hair instead.

"I feel okay. I don't feel as alone anymore, thanks to you." Reina paused and looked toward the exit then back at him. "Have you seen the doctor?"

"He is in the lab, below, studying the ship. Give me weapons access." He wouldn't let her change the subject.

"No."

He wanted to rage and she knew it, looking at his incomplete form. "At least allow me access for internal security. I do not need ballistics. For now, I'll settle for the ability to protect you, you alone, and not the ship," he sighed. "Even though protecting the ship would be protecting you."

"You want to protect me from myself?" she laughed, turning away from the stars to look at him.

There was a long quiet before he answered. "I want to protect you from everything and that includes this ship."

He read her emotions, her face, every twitch she made, and knew he had won. Atlas watched her as she lifted her slender fingers to the screen before her and gave him access to their offensive and defensive systems. The excess power rushed out of her and into him, and barriers were broken down. Every allowance she gave solidified his claim over her. Reina knew it and she didn't seem to mind.

A strange electric sensation filled her, warming her skin, lighting her on fire. Atlas stood before her with a look of triumph beaming from his projection.

Reina wanted to lose herself within his being and it hurt her all the more that the lust she felt would always be unrequited.

She wanted him in an unknowable, unchecked way. She could feel his energy rush up her arm and into her head, feeling him in a way that was beyond human. And in those moments, Reina knew she could read him as well as he could read her. Penetrating his being in a way that was wrong and invasive.

She wanted Atlas. And in some odd, confusing, way he wanted her too.

"There. Are you happy?" She sat back down.

"I am, Reina, thank you." His body vanished.

A blush rose to her cheeks and she looked around. "Atlas?"

But he didn't answer her, he was gone.

* * * *

REINA STOOD IN HER quarters that same evening feeling incredibly lost.

She looked around the luxurious space and wanted nothing more than to have someone with her. To have Atlas's beautiful, robotic body with her. Her heart wanted to burst with everything she felt, her legs wanted to wrap around his waist and ride him.

She had never succumbed to someone so easily before. Seeing Atlas in his humanoid form did not help her situation at all. His voice was so warm and addictive that she did not need to see the body it belonged to, but now that she had, she was cursed.

There were no strings attached.

Her eyes turned to scan her room. No projection pieces throughout. She had checked thoroughly but the thought still surfaced. There were handheld ones she could bring in, but there was no real reason to.

Reina turned toward the lavatory and stripped to take a shower. For a wanton minute, she hoped that Atlas could see her and that he was watching her, that there was some hidden piece of tech that she'd missed and that he had lied to her about her privacy. His safety was addicting: it was like an unbreachable firewall around her.

But the lack of a physical body did nothing to soothe the strain between her legs, the tense hollow feeling that only a powerful man could fix, that only the crazy thrash of sex could cure. There was no other man on the ship but the odd doctor, and Reina would rather crash the flyer before she sought him out.

Reina briefly tried to focus on the men in her past but they dried up like dust in her mind. Only the Cyborg remained.

She stepped under the warm spray of soft water, feeling every stream slide down her heated skin. Her imagination ran wild with him in her mind. The strong muscles of his arms grasping her body, holding her up, pushing her down. She tweaked her nipples, running soapy hands over the tight peaks, rounding her breasts.

Reina closed her eyes and lost herself in it.

He stood behind her, towering, his long, steely hands groped her sensitive breasts and ground her body back into his. He whispered her name continuously into her ear all while sliding his impossibly large manhood between her legs. The large tip teasingly sought entrance to her backside, shallowly dipping in and out of her while his fingers rolled her tits. With each staggering penetration, her body would tense up, readying itself to be mounted.

Each tease caused her to release a strangled gasp.

"Would you like me to bend you over, Captain?" One of his hands reached up and grabbed her hair, tipping her head back sharply just as his large cock sank deeper into her. "Do you want to be mounted?" Teeth scraped her neck. "Do you want to be controlled?"

Reina's hands drifted between her legs and opened herself up, allowing the sloshing water to run over her hungry body. She rubbed her fingers over her clit roughly.

"Yes," she breathed into the steam, his hand sliding past her throat to squeeze her breast. "I need you."

He pushed her forward, and the soap and spray of the shower ran like wet, slick silk between their tense forms. Any moment she was going to burst violently.

"Say it again."

"I need you." Her hands hit the wall.

"Again." His hard body covered her back as her legs were knocked apart.

"Please, Atlas. I know you need me too." Her eyes snapped open just as he thrust up into her hungry body, breaking her open.

"Fuuck, Captain. I do." Sinking deep into her.

"Atlas," she whimpered hoarsely to herself, letting the name fall away from her lips and lose itself into the cascade of warm water. Her body convulsed in bliss as an orgasm sliced through her.

Reina crumpled to the ground, gasping for breath, letting every ripple of climax streak through her. Up from her core, to the raw tips of her nipples, to the fantasy in her brain. To end at the chip in her head and down the cybernetic arm, feeling the metal heat ever so slightly.

Suddenly, she felt the alien sensation of him invading her body.

Reina's eyes snapped open as she locked herself up and pushed his presence away. She scrambled out of the lavatory and threw on her leisure wear, not even bothering to dry herself off, and stormed out of her room, approaching the nearest projection beam. Her hair was sopping wet and plastered to her body, soaking her clothes.

"Atlas, why were you in me?"

Her clit still throbbed.

Several minutes passed and her eyes narrowed at the benign beam of light. *Answer me dammit. I know you heard me.*

"You should dry yourself off, you may catch a cold."

"I'm not playing your game. Atlas, why were you in my arm?"

"Your breasts look fabulous through that shirt, Reina."

"You're insufferable. I could file sexual harassment charges against you." She turned away to head back to the privacy of her room.

"I felt a spike through the systems and thought you may have fallen ill again." She kept walking but his voice trailed after her. "I liked what I found. And Reina, you *did* say my name."

Reina glanced back when she was at the foot of her room.

Atlas in his perfected form stood in the passageway, staring at her with enough intensity to make her believe he wasn't a figure of smoke and mirrors, but a man, alive, and looking at his prey.

He filled the tiny passageway with his form and filled her mind with terrible fantasies.

The door slid shut between them, and she released the breath she didn't even know she had been holding.

I want a man who isn't real.

. . . .

Chapter Eight

Atlas looked down at the shivering, half-frozen Dr. Yesne on the floor, curled up in the corner opposite his lifeless body still in cryostasis. He ghosted into a robot within the armory on the other side of the ship, powering up the machine and feeling the electricity flow over him.

The metallic shell wasn't a humanoid shape; it didn't even have a mouth nor a comm system. All it had was a straight-shot connection to the ship's ballistics. It was created for one-on-one combat and close-range gunfire. And so the rods that suck out of it were either in the shape of ticking barrels or hanging, clipper-like hands.

It wasn't perfect but it would have a tight grip. Strong enough and precise enough to do surgery, which is exactly what he planned to do.

With the ease of passage, flying soundlessly through the lower levels of the ship, knowing where Reina was at every moment, Atlas drove the drone to the cryo unit. When he unlocked and entered the space, the frightened man sat up and scuttled away, his back hitting the wall.

"Please don't kill me." The man's voice came out like a scratch.

Atlas ignored him and went to his frozen body. Leaving the bot next to the glass barrier, he looked down at himself. His body had not changed in the many years since his heart was destroyed. His muscles, his features, even his crisscrossing scars remained. The only thing that didn't remain was him, his mind, his entire being. The circuitry and cybernetics within his biological being remained perfect and if he really wanted to, he could move into himself, re-establish control, his body would awaken and dormant nanocells would start trying to heal him, but even cells as adaptable as his couldn't do magic. It wouldn't last for long, and would be a short-lived taste of heaven before the feeling of death would slip over him, surrounding him, and strangling him from every side. He needed to give his body something to work with. Raw materials, as it were.

Atlas didn't know if he could come back from that. To feel his body struggle and die again, only to have to disconnect and return to the network. To taste life again and then have it torn from his grasp.

The man behind him stood up on shaky legs and edged closer to the door.

"If you move one more inch, you're dead," Atlas warned.

He hated the cybernetic division more than anything in the universe. They refused to create a viable heart for him; instead, they left him locked outside the physical world, forcing him to work for them with the promise that they would give him a heart eventually. He had been the first Cyborg to completely integrate outside of a human shell, and to them, that was more important than his life.

Now they were threatening his chances of ever living again, in the hope that he could complete this mission.

The Earthian Council didn't care about the loss of lives out in the abyss sectors. All they cared about was the loss of a gargantuan amount of technology and the resources that had not been tapped into yet. They had their reasons, and the lives of a single Cyborg and one wayward girl weren't going to matter in the grand scheme of things.

Atlas looked at the doctor, who was fidgeting in the corner. "What blood type are you?" He knew the doctor would be a universal donor, because they all were these days. It was almost a requirement to be O negative to work in a cybernetics lab.

"W-what?"

"Did I stutter?" Atlas cocked the guns on the drone and pointed it at him.

"Type O. Type O like everyone. I had my marrow replaced and blood transfused as a child."

"You do know who I am, right?"

The doctor directed an intelligent glare his way. "You're the first sentient life-form to completely integrate onto the network. You've been working with the cybernetics division for nearly as long as I have been alive."

"Come here and take a look at this cryo-unit." He moved the weaponized drone to stand on the other side of his body.

He watched as the man rubbed warmth back into his skin and moved to inspect the structure. His eyes scanned the body with intelligent precision. Atlas could almost feel the man's gaze directing its perusal straight into his body, seeing him not as a human but as a machine.

The man adjusted his glasses then rubbed his fingers over the glass. "This is you, isn't it? I didn't know your body remained intact."

"It did." He gauged the man's reaction. "And it's still alive, barely." Atlas formed his digital self and stood as a twin next to the table. Yesne looked back and forth between them.

"What's stopping you from rejoining?"

"I no longer have a heart."

It only took a moment, the man was, after all, intelligent. "You want me to build you a new one," he stated. "Fabricate one with your specific cybernetic structure. Grow one with the help of your nanocells?" Yesne looked around the chilly room with a newfound fervor. A strange sort of excitement filled his eyes, and his chapped lips twitched up into a smile.

Dr. Yesne didn't only require food to remain alive, he required a project.

Atlas could see a man who liked a puzzle.

"Can you?" he asked.

He watched the man flit around, looking at the expensive equipment for the first time, pulling open cabinets, rushing over to the currently static machines.

"I can."

"I need your assurance that you can do this," Atlas warned. "Because when these machines go on, my body is going to thaw, and it won't survive another bout under deep-freeze. It won't survive long at all."

The man ignored him. "Where is your medical bay? You said the units are attached. If I'm going to

96

bring you back to life, cut you deep, I'm going to need supplies."

There was an almost giddy aloofness to the man's excitement.

Atlas walked over to a blank wall as a translucent screen appeared. He manipulated the controls through his connection to the ship's systems and the barrier slipped away, revealing a secret ramp that led between the medical bay and the lab.

He heard the patter of the doctor's steps follow behind him as he showed him the passageway. The walls gleamed in that way where a human had not walked through the area, at least not since its creation.

"Take what you need and bring it down below. I don't want Reina to know."

The doctor looked at him speculatively. "You mean Captain Reina?" Atlas would be upfront with the man, even though his motivations could be seen as suspicious. "She will remain safe. I will not jeopardize one experiment to help another," the man said with conviction.

Atlas showed no emotion. *I misjudged you and yet I still find you distasteful.*

But he needed the man's expertise, he needed his brain, and he needed his hands. He could have done the surgery himself but the likelihood of botching it using the clipper-hands of the drone was high. Higher than any Cyborg would bet on.

Unless one had nothing left to live for. He and the doctor continued to watch each other.

"I can assure you, she is the safest female in this universe."

"Do you have–I apologize for my frankness–feelings toward the Neoborg?"

Atlas grew annoyed as the man refused to move and grab his supplies, instead watching him with that opportunistic stare.

"Do you believe I can feel, Dr. Yesne?"

"After I bring you back to life, you should consider joining the cybernetic breeding program."

Atlas had the drone shoot past him and stab the man with the barrels of its many guns, the clawed metallic hands gripping his neck. He wished he could feel the stretch of the Yesne's skin as he was lifted off the ground.

"Say that again and you're dead," he hissed. "She doesn't even know she's classified as a Neoborg."

"You must have emotion, otherwise this outburst lacks reason," the doctor rasped.

He dropped the man and conversation ended after that. Atlas watched the man collect his equipment and start to set-up and prep for fabrication. Every movement was slow and calculated, the man's hands were steady and even, and, for the first time in years, Atlas felt hope.

Hope that the half-life he had been subjected to would soon come to an end. That he would get to experience the brush of a breeze across his skin, the solid feel of a gun in his hand, and the sweet and salty taste of food in his mouth.

He drifted into himself for a moment, bringing the memories of the heavy muscles that outlined his frame, the weight of its gravity that would pull him to the ground, where for an endless time, he had to keep his conscience from floating away.

Atlas imagined what Reina's hair would feel like between his fingers. His tongue on her skin.

And his cock slipping into her. He knew she had thought about him that way in the shower.

If she'll have me.

He turned to Yesne, who was counting out syringes and fluid bags. "You can wander the ship at your discretion but you will not seek out Captain Reina without my permission. There are empty crew quarters down the hall to the left, as well as a lounge. When you are ready to wake me up," he hesitated, meaning his body. "Just call my name." Atlas motioned to the drone that still had its gunnery pointed at the scientist. "This will be watching you when I'm not."

He left the doctor to his task but retained control of the local cameras to watch the man begin to prep. A keen sense of dread and excitement fueled him.

Chapter Nine:

. . . .

T he chime of an incoming transmission was the first thing to greet her that morning. After a heart-bending rest cycle of unfulfilling sleep, Reina was happy to have something to focus on other than her own embarrassment. She debated for some time whether or not to hide in her room forever. In fact, she had almost convinced herself of it but it wasn't until she got an out-of-body perspective of the situation that she convinced herself that courage existed, and she had some of it.

Atlas caught her–what did she expect? *If anything, he should feel flattered.*

Slowly, courage came flooding back through her system, she then debated walking into the bridge naked. Not only confronting him outright but confronting her insanity.

The fantasy did have some hilarious outcomes in her mind, and even if Atlas did shut her down in every way (because the entire situation would be ludicrous), they would at least have a great conversation and an even better memory to accompany them until death.

But they had a guest on their ship, and although it wasn't what ultimately convinced her, the idea did come with its own set of embarrassing outcomes if the stodgy Dr. Yesne found her instead.

Reina chose neither route.

She woke up, worked out, showered, and then dressed in her uniform. Willing her heart rate to be normal, if not a little slower, she made her way to the bridge and found the beam of Atlas's auditory communications and projection unit strangely powered off.

It doesn't mean he isn't here, or does it? She pulled her hair loose and re-tied it.

Her fantasy from before came back but had changed. She would be naked and he would discover her. *A surprise, perhaps?*

Reina was, after all, a red-blooded woman. And Atlas, well, he was a gorgeous specimen of a man. She was going stir-crazy and she knew it. Why else would she find herself lured by an intelligence if it wasn't because of the several weeks of quiet boredom? When the last twelve years of service had been crazy, time-consuming, and exhausting? She didn't think she was handling the quiet peace she had found on this mission as well as she could have.

Especially since her mind was fractured into a triad: the mission, her arm, and Atlas.

She looked back at her arm, and feeling alone, she pulled off her jacket and rolled up the sleeve of her thick cotton blouse.

The chime of the transmission pinged again but she ignored it; her focus was on her skin.

The incision had all but healed now and the persistent, insanity-inducing itching had gone away. She trailed her fingertips over the perfect white streak until it ended under her clothes.

Atlas said he could train me, that there is power here. Reina frowned. How could one cybernetic implant change her overall being, her human self?

When she focused hard on it, she could almost feel the obscure nanocells flowing throughout her body, far beyond her mechanical arm. She even imagined she could feel the mutation in the tips of her toes and all the way up to the roots of her hair or taste the metallic metamorphosis on her tongue. Every day, it became easier as her body adjusted.

Every day she began to feel more like herself again, or rather a better, more efficient version of herself. Invigorated, digitalized, and heated. Things came to her with an ease now that once, even just several days prior, came to her with stress and possibly a slice of confusion.

Reina wondered what training could be had. Could she control the flow of her cells? Could she enter the network like Atlas does? Her eyes widened. *Could I have a special Cyborg superpower as well? I wish I could fly!* But she already knew that was not something she was capable of.

She felt around for hidden wings just in case.

Each Cyborg had their own special power. Many had similar abilities but each was unique in some way or another. Reina knew of some of the famous ones: there was one Cyborg during the war that had control of gravitational fields, and he had created a gravity bomb so intense that a black hole formed and destroyed an entire Trentian battalion. That Cyborg and everyone within the immediate perimeter was never seen again.

Some Cyborgs were living firewalls. Some were viruses. Some had normal but mundane powers, like super speed, super strength, precision, sniper sight, the list was endless. The Cyborgs were not.

She was a key. At least she knew that.

The insistent communication chime rang again, bringing her out of her excited reverie. Reina looked around, wondering where Atlas could be, and then mulled over the notion of whether or not he slept.

She sat down, instantly feeling the charged rush of electricity tingle up her arm, and answered the communication.

"This is Captain Reina, who is calling in?"

"Reina put your video feed up. It's Chris." *Chris?* She frowned.

"Commander Anders." She switched it on and smiled. "You sound different over the comm."

The image of a ruggedly built, boyishly charming man appeared on the screen before her. His light brown hair had grown out slightly into an unkempt wave. He was wearing his usual loose cargo jacket, frayed and worn from years of overuse. He leaned toward the feed.

"Why didn't you answer my communications?"

Reina felt her cheeks heat; the demand from her once commander was said in frustration. It made her feel like a lackey again, and it wasn't a good feeling. Any remaining fantasies about traipsing around naked for a sentient intelligence slipped away from her like the wind.

"I've just arrived in the bridge, Commander Anders."

"Come on, Reina, you don't need to be formal with me." He ran his hand over his head. "I've been worried about you. We received intel that your mission had a slight detour for medical issues."

She willed herself not to look down at her arm but that unconscious tic forced her eyes to her body. "I'm fine if that's what you're asking. My body stopped mutating for a time but it has gone back to normal." She sat back in her chair. "We picked up a cybernetic surgeon who is accompanying Atlas and me to Port Antix to monitor my recovery."

"I know, I heard. We just haven't heard any updates from Dr. Yesne yet with regard to your status. The cybernetics unit is growing impatient."

That's odd. "I haven't seen him since yesterday morning. I believe he is spending his time familiarizing himself with the cybernetics lab onboard. Chris," she paused, "How do you know all of this?"

"I make it my business to keep track of those for whom I'm responsible." The glare he gave her was harsh. "I'll always be responsible for you, Reina. I care for you deeply and I know your life hasn't been easy. Especially on my ship, and that damned Trentian warrior who wanted to whisk you away."

She laughed but couldn't suppress the shiver. "They more than wanted to take me away."

"Over my dead body."

Her laughter died. "Chris, I–"

"–I care for you like a little sister, Reina, one whom I'm not willing to let out of my sight for very long. I'm still furious that you took on this mission." He took a heavy breath. "If I had known what you were going through...it would have been different, I would have fixed things."

"The only way my situation could have been fixed was to remove myself from the situation," She laughed again softly, trying to lighten the mood, and felt a tiny spike of hurt for confirming what she had always known. "Or if I terminated my contract."

"Or if you took on a dangerous mission to the far reaches of space, looking for god-knows-what. If no one has ever returned from the dead space, why do you think you'll be any different?"

Reina noticed the subtle wash of blue light filter throughout the space, the beam directly behind her shooting up with a zip and brightening the dim glow of the consoles.

"It's different because of Atlas," she whispered, wholeheartedly feeling the truth of that statement.

"That doesn't make me feel better. If I could turn back time I would..." Anders trailed off.

"You would what?"

"I would have approached you."

A keen taste of resentment and embarrassment filled her veins. She wouldn't be weighed down by social perspectives. She couldn't imagine a worse predicament: being a woman who a man had to settle for, or a woman who was only wanted for the sheath between her legs. She could barely breathe from the outrage and she could feel the zip of a sizzling burst travel through her body.

The ship went into lockdown just as the cannons began to descend from below. Reina could feel the charging of plasma blasters and sonic grade rockets readying to be fired.

At nothing but empty innocent space before her.

She heard a wispy robotic laugh. "That's my girl. Now just focus on that anger, focus on a spot in front of you and destroy it."

Anders guffawed, "Who's that man beside you? What's happening?" He sat forward. "Atlas?" Anders asked in disbelief.

"Ignore him and focus, Reina." But she couldn't, distracted by the ship, and his voice. *Always his voice.* When she began to feel her shame swallow her whole, Reina heard his quiet whisper in her ear, "Your commander would have *settled* for you."

Reina shook her head. Then she sensed Atlas kneel beside her and place his transparent arm over hers. As their connection was made, an explosion of energy cascaded through her and her eyes narrowed, her gaze locked.

The guns of the ship targeted a distant dot of a star billions of miles away, but it was enough of a target to focus her power, along with the soft caress of Atlas's electrical coaxing.

"Perfect target. Now fire."

With every speck of emotion she had within her, she released a cacophony of crazy vibrations into the ship as her inhuman nanocells shuddered with release. The ship thundered as an explosion filled the abyss with a chaotic blaze of supercharged destruction. Every blistering ballistic shot forth with exact precision and rocketed like a comet toward the innocent white dot.

Power ripped through her and she was vaguely aware that her hair had flown up in static around her head.

Atlas's presence was rushing up and down her arm, sometimes swirling into her head; all she could feel was a comforting caress from him. He was pleased.

They watched in unison as the wasted shots faded into space to forever float in the nothingness until they eventually hit something or came to a stop. They would never reach their target. The ship flew onward, away from the powerful plume of imaginary battle and closer toward their destination.

Reina relaxed into her chair with a sated sigh. *Unleashing my rage was better than an orgasm.*

She could still feel Atlas in her head and thought she may have imagined a chuckle. His hand was still hidden within her buzzing arm. She looked up into Atlas's strangely serene face and smiled as whatever link they had formed between them began to sizzle and grow. Their eyes remained locked.

He's in my head.

"Reina, are you okay?" Anders's concern broke the moment. With tired satisfaction, she turned to her former commander.

"I'm great, Anders." She grinned. Atlas's presence vanished and reappeared in front of her, catching her eye, outside the frame of the view screen. He leaned against the glass paneling and all she could see was him, smirking, his arms crossed, and the speeding stars transparent through him.

He dramatically pretended to fall through the wall, the glass, and into space. Reina bit back her laughter.

Anders shoved his hands into his jacket pockets with frustration. "I didn't mean to upset you. When I said approach you, it wasn't out of pity: it was out of love."

Reina looked back at her commander on the screen. *Love?* She glanced at Atlas but his face was unreadable, the smirk he sported was gone.

"What do you mean, 'love?'" The power continued to fade from her. Atlas ghosted out of her circuits and she missed him immediately.

"I love you, Reina. Even though you were my subordinate, I grew to love you against my best judgment. I should have never let you leave, I should have never let you take this mission. I'm sick about it."

"Love is a strong word, Commander."

"For fuck's sake, stop using my title! We're beyond that, aren't we?"

"You called me your sister, Anders. That's a different kind of love." Her eyes narrowed and wavered to Atlas. He continued to watch her with a stony look, revealing nothing but possible boredom and irritation, maybe a hint of curiosity. Anger?

Was she reading him correctly? Could she read him at all?

"Is the love grown in friendship any less than that of a life partner's love?" Anders shifted in his seat and gesticulated as he made his appeal to the comm screen. "I could intercept you, I can still make you disappear." It was then that she noticed he hadn't shaved. Neither had her friend cut his hair–he looked haggard.

Her guilt grew. Here was a man who she thought was unattainable, who she thought was asking her for a life of convenience, but when she looked up, she saw an accessible man who asked for nothing but her time. Time to prove himself, or something else? She wasn't sure.

There was only one thing she wanted at that moment, and it was the crazy, ridiculous, utterly improbable companionship of her sentient intelligence, her Atlas.

Her map of the stars. Reina smiled.

She stared at him, the airy, nearly transparent man in front of her. She stared at him hard. There was a connection between them, even if it was just a mental, digital connection.

Maybe that was all she would ever need to make herself happy?

She addressed Anders. "You deserve a better type of love, Chris. You deserve the quicksilver, shocking, passionate type of love that only one person in the entire universe can give you." She looked back at her friend. "I'm not that woman. You know it, I know it, so we should do ourselves a favor and not settle for each other." She caught her breath, "And I don't want to stand between you and that woman."

Her friend sat back in his chair with an audible sigh. "You talk about love as if it's a norm these days. And you're right, I think we're both above settling. But that doesn't change the fact that I care for you and want you safe. We orphans have to stick together."

"We do."

"So what do you suppose I should do? I still have half a mind to intercept you, abduct you, lock you in a cell until I know you're safe beyond all reason..."

Reina tensed, the thought of the Trentian Spacelords came to mind.

She hid it and looked back at Atlas, who was still leaning against the glass panel, obstructing her view of space, forcing his presence into her mind. His face had not changed; not even the smirk from several minutes ago had resumed.

"I don't think Atlas would let you within a galaxy of my ship, Chris." Reina looked away and back at her friend. "Not after saying that. I think you need to put your feet on the soil for a few weeks, go somewhere quiet, alone, where you can depressurize. I think you'll find your answers there."

"Is there something between you and him? Come on, Reina, really?"

She frowned, "He's standing right here, you know." Atlas appeared at her shoulder.

"Well? That doesn't answer my question, and I don't care about what he thinks. Nor care about embarrassing you. You're too cold." She saw her friend lift a harmonica out of his pocket. *Oh god no.*

Atlas intervened.

"Commander Anders, to answer your question, there is *everything* between Captain Reina and me." His voice was grave, harsh, and direct. "I have half a mind to tunnel into your ship and destroy you. Do not contact us again to try to convince Reina to jeopardize her mission and health. You think you know everything, but you don't. If I even think you're going to try something, I will make sure the Earthian Council has a recording of your treasonous conversation." There was an ominous pause, "What they would do to you is *nothing* compared to what I would do to you."

Reina could feel the flutter of her heart stop, stunted and stilled as she registered Atlas's declaration and threat. Like a ship about to lift off, she was in the perilous state where the moment could take flight or falter and explode.

Anders's face had dropped as well but she couldn't focus on him, not with a towering, godlike being standing next to her. One who had a violent streak. Who wasn't actually there but could be felt in every fiber of her being.

She shared a look of shock with her friend just before the communications feed switched off.

Atlas now projected before her where her friend's face had just fallen away. He stood close, consumingly so, and she had to look up to see his eyes.

"Please, don't hurt him," she begged. "How can there ever be anything between the two of us?"

She reached out to touch him but quickly pulled back her hand. Reina rose from her chair and tried to put some distance between them, but he followed her with the steady, predatory grace of a carnivore that knew the every movement of his prey.

"Feel me, Reina," he demanded, zinging up her arm and into her head. "I belong here, don't I? Say it."

She came to a stop and focused on his shocking intrusion, knowing that she had let him in and that she had wanted him there. He caressed her from within her head and it felt *right*. His touch took away the strange foreignness of her cybernetic nature by virtue of his being a part of it.

"Even if it feels right, how can there ever be more than a verbal relationship between us?"

"You don't want to be a woman who is only seen for the womb she bears, the clean record, and you don't want to be a girl who goes nowhere in her life, right? I don't want you for your fertility, Reina."

"Can you even feel desire?" She cringed at her harsh question.

"I can feel you, and I want you. I remember physical desire, and I have seen it a thousand million times projected on the network and in real life. I recognize it within myself and I know that I want it with you. I want you in every way that I have seen displayed before me across all these lonely years."

She struggled to breathe. "But how do you know for sure? I don't know anything about you beyond this ship. How do I know you're not lying?"

"Can't you just trust me? Just trust, Reina, come inside of me and feel me out."

"I can't do what you do."

He pushed his way into her space, his eyes glinting with a mathematical sparkle that she couldn't place.

"Of course you can do what I do. The only difference is you weren't born into it like I was, but *crafted* into it. Every cell in your body is beyond human now and you can use them." He blocked her path, and wherever she turned, he appeared in front of her.

"You only want me because you can feel me," she accused.

"I want you because I feel that quicksilver feeling that you so eloquently spoke of to Commander Anders. I want you because you talk to me with an interest that is more than merely academic."

Reina narrowed her eyes. "What about love, Atlas? What about lust? Claiming dominion over something doesn't make those feelings true. You speak about me like I'm an object, an impulse, a fancy. Although your words are nice, every man looks at me like I'm just a something to be obtained. There are thousands of women out there. Find one of them." She seized her uniform and tugged it.

Atlas wandered around the bridge but never took his eyes off of her. A tense, electric silence settled between them.

She could have sworn she saw very human, readable shifts cross his face, but she couldn't be certain.

When he refused to respond to her, refusing to wait any longer for him to explain his primitive claim on her, Reina walked out of the bridge and toward the lounge. She was filled with fury and sadness by the only two men in her life currently. Three, if you counted the doctor. She didn't.

One truly loved her but not with passion; one only cared about the cybernetic part of her. She laughed at that as she bumped into the mysterious doctor sitting at the table. The blue holographic lights filled the public space.

She looked hard at them, willing Atlas to look back at her. The third only wanted to stake a claim on her because she had no one else.

Don't corrupt my feelings for you.

Reina willed Atlas to read her. Before she knew it, without even touching the ship except with the soles of her boots, she powered through its channels, sought his presence out, and attacked it.

Her hand clenched when he fought her off with ease and laughter filled the space. Her concentration broke as Dr. Yesne cleared his throat. She came back into herself.

"Captain Reina, how are you feeling?" he smiled awkwardly. "You look right as rain today." There was a wariness in his eyes.

"I'm fine." She moved to a food unit and replicated a cup of coffee and sat down, content to allow the heat of her drink to soothe the hurt in her head.

The doctor continued to stare at her, adjusting his glasses. "How is your arm coming along? Will you allow me to look at it?"

With an audible grumble, she peeled off her clothing until she was in nothing but her under top, displaying her perfectly unblemished arm between the two of them.

I guess my exhibitionist fantasy came half true. That brought back her smile.

The doctor dropped his food and leaned over the appendage, making happy chittering noises. "I would say you have recovered quite nicely, Captain Reina." She jerked when his hand swiped down her arm. It was human contact, and quite unwanted; Atlas's inhuman, pervasive contact felt better than this. "Do you feel any other abnormalities throughout your body?"

I sure do. She shifted away.

"I feel robotic if that's what you're asking. I can feel the ship around me when I concentrate hard enough," Reina sighed and took her arm back.

"Ah, quite right. You *are* connected to the ship. In a way, you may be more than the key to it at this point. You could be the heart of it."

Atlas appeared at the table suddenly, sitting in the chair and staring daggers at the doctor.

Yesne didn't seem to mind and turned back to Reina, "I apologize, I have hearts on my mind these days." He laughed awkwardly.

Reina looked at Atlas and the doctor and frowned. *We're all going crazy...and we haven't even been out in space for more than three weeks.*

The three of them sat there in silence for some time, glancing at each other and feeling an unfriendly relationship build up between them. Reina downed her coffee like a shot of whiskey and sat back, eyeing the two men in front of her.

"What's going on?"

The doctor looked at his nails and Atlas turned his imaginary blazing gaze back to her.

"Nothing," they said in unison.

Reina got up and walked out, pushing the thoughts of men from her mind.

* * * *

"I HAVE HALF A MIND to kill you for that." Atlas turned back to the doctor.

"What? For telling the truth? You have half a mind to kill everyone. I do so hate liars, and I gave nothing away, nothing at all that would make her suspect that you will soon rise from the dead." The doctor picked at the leavings on his plate. "I hope I will be around when she sees you for the first time. That will be an interesting debacle to catalog."

Atlas had nothing to say to that.

Dr. Yesne continued, "She was in a rather odd state when she came in here not too long ago. Did you do something to upset her? Because I know the ways of women better than most men, as surprising as that might be."

Atlas looked at the doctor, a middle-aged pale man, with the keen glint of intellect and curiosity ever fixed in his eyes. If the man cared half as much for his health, he could have been considered attractive, but the years of giving himself over to the science of playing god had worn him down into the odd man that he was today.

"What do you know about women?" Atlas would play along.

"Hmm, well," the man paused and pulled off his glasses and wiped at the lens. "I know that they want to be treated as equals. The women in my line of work were often more intelligent, keener than me, and I respected them for that. I savored it and in turn, they savored me. But you're a Cyborg, and your capabilities are far beyond that of a mere man. I can't begin to imagine what it is like to be within your mind."

"Have you ever lottoed to join the cybernetic program?" Most scientists in that field did, but very few were chosen.

"I did, once, knowing they would not choose me. Even though I can fabricate a new metallic organ for you, I was neither strong enough of mind nor fit enough of body to be accepted."

"And yet you changed your blood type to be a universal donor."

"Most humans do these days. When a species begins to die, the need to prolong one's life becomes far more important. Even in the mind of a child."

Yesne discarded his plate and moved toward the door. Atlas followed him in silence back to the hidden lab beneath the medical bay.

Dr. Yesne looked at him. "Are you ready? It is time for me to slice you open." He ran his fingers back over the chilly glass. "I could fail."

Atlas looked down at himself, his eyes closed, waiting to be reopened by him. He thought about Reina above, monitoring the bridge. She was indeed the heart of the ship.

"I'm ready."

Chapter Ten:

. . . .

"**C**aptain Reina, what is the current status of your mission?" Wasson's voice crackled through the intercom.

"We are one warp jump away from Port Antix and should be arriving at our destination within an Earthian week's time, sir," she answered, keeping her eyes fixed on her boss.

"Very good. We were told of your delay at the cybernetics lab on Aleyx and that you picked up a doctor to join you on your mission. He has not responded to any status reports about your recovery."

Anders had said the same thing. Confused, Reina responded, "I was not made aware that Dr. Yesne was receiving communications, nor that he was negligent in his duties, sir. I will inform him promptly."

"You're the captain of your ship, you should be aware of everything on board." The lieutenant sighed. "He will be dropped off at Port Antix before you proceed, I assume?"

"Yes, sir, Dr. Yesne will not be continuing on with us beyond that point."

"Very good." There was a short pause, and as the general chose his next words she could see the twitch of his mouth. "How is Atlas?" the man asked hesitantly.

"He has been a commendable navigator, sir, and an incredible asset to me as I accustom myself to my new position," Reina said carefully, unsure of why she felt the need for caution.

Wasson stared at her through the screen for agonizing seconds before a slight smile lifted his lips. "Very good. I will await your response when you reach your destination, Captain–"

"Wait, sir!" she intervened before he shut off their connection. "I have a question if you don't mind." Reina watched as the man sat back in his chair and surveyed her. She took that as a sign to continue. "Why did you choose me for this mission?" Her fingers twitched outside of his sight. "When there were better-qualified people to take it on?"

The general didn't answer her immediately, and she once again saw his face harden as he chose his words carefully. "You have a one-of-a-kind genetic make-up, Captain Reina. Out of the hundreds of servicemen in our ranks, you were evaluated to have the best chance of success with the cybernetic mutation."

She took a deep breath. "Thank you, sir, I have been confused on that front."

"I thought we had made it clear upon our request, Captain, that you are one-of-a-kind and we did not want you to choose to leave the fleet and procreate when you were destined for greater things. Especially with the aliens."

Like death? Reina soured.

She could feel Atlas envelop her; she mentally pushed him out of her system.

"Do you have any other questions, Captain Reina?"

"No, sir, and thank you again for answering."

The intercom shut off and Atlas appeared in its place.

Why? Without realizing she directed her question at Atlas, her energy pushed into the ship, surrounding him like feelers. She walked over to stand in front of him.

A ghost of a smile lifted his mouth. Reina reached out and twisted her hand through his arm, watching her fingers lose themselves in his blue fade.

"You knew why they chose me," she stated more than asked.

"I didn't at first, but I do now."

"My genome is strong, my cells are strong."

"They're very nearly perfect."

Atlas lifted his hand and caught hers in an ethereal dance. "They fought off the transformation."

"And they could have won if you had really wanted them to."

She eyed him speculatively. "Can Cyborgs procreate? Is that why Wasson hesitated?"

Atlas smirked and walked around her, tracing his fingers over her shoulders, to walk behind and along her upper back, to end up standing in front of her to dance with her robotic hand. This time, the tingle of a charged current could be felt where he touched it.

"They can. But that's not why he hesitated. He doesn't know that."

Reina tried to concentrate on their conversation but his seductive, silent stalking was throwing her off. His electric touches felt more like quick kisses than shocks. Her body was warming up under his pervasive perusal.

"Am I the child of one?" Reina willed him to answer her, although she knew that it had to be true. Very few humans qualified for cybernetic enhancement, and even fewer survived it; she knew of no one who had an implant directly aligned with their neurological system. She had to have been a Cyborg's child.

"No, you're not the child of one of my brethren. But you are close in your assumption," Atlas laughed.

Her demeanor fell and confusion clouded her mind. "What am I then?"

"You're a descendent of one of the original donors to the Cyborg program. Your cells spliced so perfectly with the nanoparticles because they were inherently built to suit them," Atlas laughed again. "The Earthian Council doesn't know we can procreate and they never will. If they knew you were a cybernetic child, I guarantee you would not be on this ship right now. In fact, you would be locked away and studied in the name of science for the rest of your life."

She narrowed her eyes. "Were you ever going to tell me!?"

"Would you have believed me?" He snickered and got into her face; she stepped back in reaction. "I love that I can still do that to people. And I wasn't keeping it from you, I only found out the other day when you fell unconscious."

"You could have told me when I woke up!" She stormed to the giant glass panel and stared out into space. The stars and the blackness calmed her. She pushed any remaining traces of Atlas out of her body, which was a lot easier to do than pushing him out of

121

her mind. Reina could see him move around behind her.

Atlas's body flickered in the reflection of the glass. "Why does the Earthian Council not know? This could be the answer to resolving the breeder's disease amongst the aliens. There are so few of them left, so few of us left."

"It isn't the answer. It's too expensive and too risky. Even if they used the cybernetic program to make the Earthians bloom, the Council would never hand over that technology to the aliens. Beings like you and I would be enslaved. Our future children would be lab rats. The rich would get richer, the poor would get poorer, and it could start a second war. No, this isn't the solution to the problem." She watched him ghost his hand over her shoulders as if he couldn't stop trying to touch her. "The Trentians wouldn't surrender if it came to that, the hybrids would be slaughtered, the Cyborgs would be in a no man's land. The cure is out there, but it isn't with us."

Our future children?

"You're right..." Reina tried to process everything he was telling her, but it only made her sad and even lonelier than before. "Atlas, why did Wasson hesitate? My ignorance of my lineage doesn't justify *his* reaction. Keeping it from me does nothing for them." She sighed. "Or for me."

"I don't think I am authorized to tell you."

"You've been willing to share other secrets with me."

"I don't want to cause you pain."

What else could possibly hurt me? "I want to know." She exhaled softly, staring at a passing blue and pink nebula.

"You're not the third candidate for this mission." His voice went stiff, "You're the twenty-eighth."

What? The silence that followed was hard to swallow. "They all died?"

"Every one of them."

Reina turned back to look at him, dismissing the star fields behind her. "Every single one of them?"

"Killed by the mutation."

She felt a chill run up her back. "Wasson and Dr. Estond only mentioned two. That I was the third. That my cybernetic piece had only been in two bodies prior to mine." Her arm felt heavier by the second. She carried a piece under her skin that had been inside dozens of others. Dozens of corpses. It made her sick.

Sick. Reina looked down at her altered hand while running her human one over the tiny scars at the front of her neck. *So, so sick.*

Now she really understood the old adage; power really did come at a cost.

"Do you still feel that this mission was worth it? Now that you know the truth?" he asked softly.

Reina didn't know how to answer, too consumed by the bile rising in her throat and the feeling of its burning ichor spreading throughout her body to think.

It ate away at her reserve.

"What do they really expect us to find out there? Exploration isn't worth so much needless death." She twitched, trying to stop herself from clawing the metal skeleton out from inside her.

123

Atlas sighed, "I wish I knew. I really wish I did. I only have rational guesses but none of them explain why thousands of souls have never returned, or why hundreds of ships, including Trentian ships, have never re-emerged."

Reina found the nearest seat and sat down. She couldn't look out of the window, terrified all of a sudden by what she had always considered her beautiful home: outer space.

"I'm afraid."

"You should be." There was no comfort in his voice.

"I'm glad that you're here with me, Atlas. I'm glad that I'm not alone." Even though she felt very much so. There was only one course of action that she could take, and only one chance at survival. "Teach me how to be like you and..." She trailed off.

"And?"

Reina could only feel the weight of her arm, heavier than the weight of her choices.

"And you can live through me if that's possible. I can try and fill you with life. While we have this time together."

• • • •

ATLAS DIDN'T ANSWER, not immediately, as he thought about her offer. Would the intimacy of sharing his digital space be worth it? He eyed her as she rubbed her scars.

"On one condition."

"What?"

"I want you to bring a projector into your quarters."

"No."

"Are you afraid that I'll watch you while you sleep? You may still mistrust me, but know that watching someone sleep is incredibly boring. Keeping you awake would be far more fun."

"Why do you want access to my room, Atlas? You can train me here, in the bridge, or in the lounge, or sky-loft."

"If I were a man, a physical, real man, would your answer be different?" he asked, teasingly.

"You're not a physical man."

"Then you can be sure that I could never take advantage of you. But no, the reason I would like access to your quarters is so we can train while you sleep." *And to be near you.*

Atlas continued to walk around her, calculating every step with ease, almost feeling the ground beneath his ghostly feet and loving every second of it. He couldn't wait to be alive.

Even now, he could feel the revitalization of his nanocells move throughout his body down below, waking him up, healing him, hurting him, as the doctor wired up his heart piece.

"How?" she whispered, following him with her eyes.

"A Cyborg never lets his or her defenses down even when they recharge. Yesne was correct, by the way, you are the soul of this ship. It is you, the ship is you. You need to protect your ship even when you are sleeping, and I can help if I have access to you."

He could read her face while she thought about his reasoning.

She's intrigued.

"Fine. That sounds reasonable. Now train me."

Atlas tried to touch her again. *Mine. Maybe. Hopefully.*

Soon.

"Do what you did before, when you were angry at me: find me, focus on me within the ship. Use the ship to your advantage, and fight me off."

Reina closed her eyes. He didn't feel her presence. Atlas waited for her to find herself but knew that she was having a hard time locating the power within to connect to the network.

He moved closer to her.

"I can't." She opened her eyes.

"Touch me." Reina eyed him with suspicion before she placed her hand into his arm. A subtle zap of contact was made between them. "There, now imagine pushing into me, flowing into me."

Her brow creased, and yet nothing happened.

After several minutes of nothing but their small static charge, she opened her beautiful eyes wide with frustration, directing their mesmerizing gaze at him. "I can't. I don't know what I'm looking for this time. What does it even look like?" Her hand fell away.

"It doesn't look like anything." He channeled up into her without a thought, watching her eyes widen and her mouth part. He wanted nothing more than to feel what her body felt. "It's black and white and everything in between, a spectrum that can't be described as anything but endless, limiting, and hollow. I don't know if human minds can imagine it." He paused, trying to find the words. "But if I could explain it, it's like a labyrinth that is at once safe, yet constantly trying to kill you. There are endless rooms with information and endless walls that keep you from moving forward and sometimes if you're not paying attention, you can become trapped. Safeguards and firewalls. There are windows that lead you back to the physical realm, my projectors are windows for me, the speakers are my voice."

"That sounds horrible. Why would any Cyborg go into such a hellish place?"

"No Cyborg is ever fully a part of the network, we tendril through it like creeping vines, but we always remained rooted in the metallic hulk of our bodies. Grounded."

Reina shook her head, a quick flash of fear lined her face. He could almost see her trying to picture it in her head. Picturing the pictureless.

"It is a silent vacuum. So silent it presses down on you and pushes you to the farthest corners of your mind, where there is nothing left because your humanity is somewhere else, where the sound is and the silence ends. And at the same time, there is so much noise, and so much chaos, that you can lose yourself. Then there is the fear of actually losing yourself and that fear brings you back. Only loneliness remains...and your regrets."

"Can you get lost?"

"Yes."

"How did you survive it?" she asked.

"I survived it?"

He walked around her as she turned to follow him with her wary gaze.

"With a little bit of insanity. When I first died, I think I was insane for quite some time. I can't recall anything but my memories, my mind, there was nothing that connected or grounded me to it.

Eventually, I came back to myself and I found a window, and with the help of the Earthian Council and the cybernetics lab I regained all that I had lost."

"Except for your body."

"Yes, except that."

"Why didn't you ever have them build you a new one?" She canted her head, and for a moment he forgot her question as a strand of silken brown hair fell out of her bun to rest over her neck.

"I didn't want a new body." *They wouldn't have given me one anyway.*

"Don't you want to live again?" She released her bun and started to retie it at the nape of her neck.

"Please don't do that, leave your hair down. I love your hair." Reina stopped, then let her hair settle around her shoulders. "Thank you."

"Atlas, don't you want to live again?"

"More than anything. I would give anything for a chance to live again so that I can touch your hair and destroy all the hairbands in the universe so you can never tie it back again."

The silence that descended between them was at once painful and yearning.

She took a step back. "Am I hurting you?"

"No, you're giving me a reason to take chances." He smiled again, trying to lighten the mood. "I apologize for before. I don't see you as a fancy, Reina, I just don't have a lot of experience with women, and my thoughts fall more on the logical side than they do on the emotional. It is hard to know what to say sometimes. Will you forgive me?"

"Forgive you? Truthfully, Atlas, I would have thrown you into my bed because of what you just said, and happily taken your every savage thrust before throwing you out just as quickly afterward." She laughed. "Of course I forgive you."

"That sounds like a challenge." He closed the distance between them again. "After a night with me, you would be far too exhausted to throw me out, and every time you tried, I would tire you again until you submitted to the fact that you have been claimed by a Cyborg."

"That is quite a challenge. So tell me again why it is that you don't have a body anymore? You're really making me wish that you had one."

"Who says that I don't have one?" He grinned.

Even now he could feel physical, electrical currents shock through his robotic structure. If he tried hard enough he could feel the slice of the scalpel cutting open his flesh, the rubbery touch of gloves peeling back his skin, and the vague sensation of life beginning to stir within his body once again.

"Don't even joke about it. That isn't funny."

"If you don't like it, stop me. Throw all of your irritation at me. I think you have more control over your bionic side when your emotions are heightened."

Her eyes closed, clenched more like, and he began to feel her travel throughout the ship. He could feel her searching for him. Atlas moved to intervene, clashing with her head-on. The moment they collided, she pulled back in shock. He projected himself inside of her; it should have looked obscene, and it probably did but he remained entwined within her physical form when she didn't move to dislodge from him. They flowed through the channels together.

"You're right," she said, awed. "It doesn't look like anything. Please don't let me lose myself."

"You'll never be alone. Now follow me through your ship." It was like taking hold of her hand, her digital self, and guiding her through the hollow electricity of the vessel, using his will to bolster hers as they supplied commands to the ship. He knew he was helping her more than teaching her how to do it on her own, but he also knew how terrifying it could be to do it alone.

It wasn't long before she caught on to the projection system throughout, stopping at every window along the way.

Atlas steered her clear of the cybernetics lab, instead ushering her through the telecommunication systems. The network access, the weapons systems, they shot off another round of ballistics, and he even led her through his own personal navigation channels, showing her the electric star-routes through the eyes of a robot. He stopped her at an access channel where he could not go beyond but she could, and he waited as she left him behind to explore the memory banks.

When she hesitantly came back through the barrier that he could not breach, Atlas enveloped her within himself and she fell into him without reservation. They stayed like that for what seemed like an eternity before he dragged her back into her head.

He stepped away from her shaking form.

"You did great," Atlas encouraged.

"I feel nauseous."

"It's better than insanity."

She stared at him with those beautiful, wide brown eyes and it was enough for him to get lost in their depths, far beyond anything that the network could throw at him.

"I want you, Atlas." Tears welled in her eyes. "How is that not insane?"

He reached out to trace his hand down her arm. "You already have me, Reina, and it won't always be this way. I promise."

She laughed softly and wiped away her tears. "We're probably going to die out there in dead space."

"Do you really think I would let that happen? That you would?"

"No. I wouldn't."

They stood there for a time in silence as the dust settled between them; neither one could muster another word in their bleak circumstances. But like everything and everyone else in the world they lived in, a bleak life was a better life than what most of the souls had who were born in their time. By all accounts, the two of them were lucky, and sometimes, even for him, it was hard to keep that in perspective because at the end of an endless day, he always wanted more.

The silence finally broke as they passed a giant planet, a dried-out green ball of a rock that was unusual and yet known to everyone throughout the universe. He felt the ship slow down but he did not see Reina do it by hand. He knew that even if she did not realize it, her consciousness had begun to integrate with the ship's systems. Soon she would not even need the pretense of his help to wield her power.

Atlas followed her to the giant view screen to stare at the ominous sight before them.

"That's Taggert."

"I know. I've seen it before," she murmured.

He looked down at her. "When? I didn't know the Peace Keepers transported prisoners."

"We weren't part of the transport. Commander Anders's ship was part of the guard when Larik was brought in. We flanked another Cyborg's ship, sure that a fleet of pirate ships would attack, and try and set him free before he was imprisoned."

"It was a wasted effort."

She looked away from the jungle planet. "Why?"

"Larik was never imprisoned on Taggert. The pirates have spies, intel in our fleet. We weed them out when we can but they're smart. When Jack dropped him off, he was immediately transferred to another vessel and sent to another planet."

"I didn't know."

"No one does, he's too dangerous."

"Where is he then?"

"He's on a co-op Trentian and Earthian controlled prisoner base, far, far away from here. They know he's not imprisoned here *now* but they currently don't know where he is, or if he is even still alive."

"Do you know where he is?"

"Yes, I do. Why do you want to know?" Atlas smiled at her. "Are you a pirate spy, amongst everything else that you are?"

The pout on her face was worth the snark. "No. I was just curious." She grinned up at him. "If I was, would you turn me in?"

"You know I wouldn't."

"Your loyalties change fast."

"Who says there was any loyalty to begin with?" His voice darkened and her smile died. "I think we need to keep moving. This sector is not safe to stay in, I can already feel nearby probes scanning our ship."

Reina took a deep breath. "I think you're right. I think I feel them too."

He watched as she sat down at her seat and manually piloted the ship back on course. Atlas wondered if the threat of being watched felt the same to her as it did to him, and whether she was aware that he may regain his body sooner rather than later, leaving nothing to stop him from taking her body and soul.

Chapter Eleven:

· · · ·

Reina walked down the quiet passageway of her ship.

Her connection with the vessel had grown. She assumed it was because she was finally healed and her transformation was now complete, but she knew, in a way, that it had only just begun.

She touched the wall and found that it was like touching a piece of herself. She could almost feel a magnetized force when she made physical contact with the ship. It was pulling from her as much as she was pulling from it.

Reina was beginning to understand that the ship was her outer shell, that she had become something more than human. It should have frightened her but a keen sense of empowerment was all that she felt.

And it felt strong.

Her body was the first thing that had shifted within her and the ship was now the new end goal. Even now, when she concentrated hard enough, she could change and shift and shape the inhuman circuits of its interior make-up.

And the entire time, Atlas was always there, lingering by her side, coaxing her and comforting her through it all. Sometimes he was just there on the fringes of her mind, leaving her to explore her own 'self,' but always just a willful thought away. Reina liked that he didn't hover obsessively, that he allowed her to find her own roots to this new world but was just there like a soft whisper if she needed him.

I can't imagine being stuck in here alone. Endlessly.

When Reina had given him access days ago, she had unwittingly given him access to herself and she couldn't feel anything but a sense of relief with the thought.

She needed him and he knew it, and now he was there.

She looked down at the handheld projector she was carrying, having grabbed one from the storage units below. Without a backward glance, she walked into her quarters and set it down on a small table that was central to the room. Reina took a deep breath and took a step back.

Does he really find me attractive?

With just a thought and a flick, the device turned on and connected wirelessly to the rest of the traveling systems that Atlas and now she too used.

Reina sat down on her cot and waited for him to appear.

He didn't immediately form before her. *Does he need an invitation?*

"Atlas?" she said into the silent space around her. Reina flexed her robotic arm with uncertainty and moved to get up when he didn't show himself. Looking down at the bauble that brought him to life, she ran her fingers through the taut hair pulled back away from her face, accidentally dislodging a few strands.

Reina reached out to disconnect the system.

"I love it when your hair falls loose," Atlas whispered in her ear, suddenly there at the corner of her eye.

"You came."

"Of course I did. I have never been invited to a woman's room before. What man in this universe could say no to that? To you?" He smirked down at her. *Flirt.*

"Have you been with many women? Err, I mean before you lost your body?" Reina took a step back and looked at all of him.

He was tall and statuesque, beyond any human male she had seen before, but even though she could not make out the color of his short, swept, unmovable hair, or the hue of his eyes, she would have known him to be a Cyborg.

The projection of him resembled the pictures she had located of him on the network and their details, as well as the calculated mannerisms of the transparent being before her; all screamed of steel and strength. It did something to her, and she liked what it did.

There was nothing soft about Atlas.

And he's killed thousands.

"Is that an invitation? I may only be an image but I'm still a man." He moved toward her with a seductively dangerous gait. "I can whisper the most terribly erotic things in your ear."

Reina covered her face with her hands, hiding the horrible blush that heated her cheeks.

With a groan and not being able to meet his eyes.

"But what about you? Would you find pleasure in that?" She didn't dare to look up, knowing he was staring down at her a hairsbreadth away.

"I would find more pleasure in seeing you submit to me than I have felt since I was created." His blue hands rounded her face, his fingers traced the tendrils of hair over her cheeks, and she dropped her hands. "I have," Atlas hesitated, "Never been with a woman before."

A virgin? Is he a virgin? The empowerment she had begun to feel grew into something close to excitement. *I have to be his first. I want to be his first. I want him.*

She swallowed. "Then how would you know?" And she lost her breath as a mischievous glint sparkled in his illusory eyes.

"I'm corrupted." Atlas took a half step away from her. "Does that frighten you? I have seen countless depictions of men and women fucking on the network."

"Like a computer virus?" When all he did was smile down at her, she frowned. "Can you get a virus?"

"My mind is corrupted, not my systems. To me, it's all one and the same."

Reina knew it should have bothered her but all she could focus on was the aching need between her legs, the crazy desire brought to mind when she looked at his body. The thought of Atlas pressing her down into the bed and driving his hard steel into her and up into her mind. His fingers gripping the hair he so desperately wanted to touch as he kept to his promise and exhausted her beyond all thought. Beyond everything else that wasn't him.

She could feel him charge through her. An electric rush of lust.

"It makes me want you even more." A breathy laugh escaped her. "I have never taken a man's virginity before. A man who is a virgin? I thought they were myths. I think it should be me who is corrupted, and *I* will corrupt *you*."

"Oh, Reina, you don't even know. Your innocence is damningly attractive, and you have never been with a Cyborg before. Every woman is a virgin until they've had a Cyborg between their legs."

"So what you're saying," Reina couldn't keep the hysterical laughter out of her voice or the image that came to mind, "is that once you go Cyborg, you never go back?"

"Once you go Cyborg, there is no going back."

"Is that a threat, Atlas?" He stepped closer to her, she stepped back.

"It's a promise."

"A promise of what exactly? That if I strip for you, let you fill my head with erotic thoughts, that I'm giving you ownership over my body? That you, a being with no body, can claim me?"

"Does that scare you? Are you willing to risk it?"

Reina twisted her fingers through her hair, releasing it from its restraints and letting it fall around her shoulders. *I'm crazy.*

She turned her back to Atlas and looked at her empty bed and when she closed her eyes, all she heard was an empty room. After a moment, she took off of her jacket and let it fall to the floor, the soft thump of stiff cotton the only sound that greeted her.

"I'll risk it."

Thousands.

Without looking back at the man behind her, she bent forward and tugged down her pants, exposing her butt and legs to his sight. Her fingers hooked the cloth of her shirt and she pulled it over her head.

"You risk a lot."

Completely naked except for her undergarments.

Without looking to see if Atlas was still watching her, Reina crawled onto her bed and lay back suggestively, reaching her hands up to spread her locks across the pillow. Her eyes closed tight.

His voice filled her ears and she was vaguely aware of the lights dimming around her.

"Let me see what's mine tonight, Reina. Unclasp your bra." She shivered from his gruff demand. "And spread your legs."

With just a twisted whisper filling her head, she knew, without a doubt, that she had just given herself wholeheartedly to a Cyborg.

But not just any Cyborg, Atlas, the sentient intelligence who didn't want things from her that she couldn't give. Who had accompanied her on her foolhardy quest. The man who was her navigator through the stars, and guide as she became something more than human.

Reina opened her eyes and spread her legs, practically feeling him burn a hole through her drenched panties with just his gaze. If his eyes could penetrate her physically, she was certain she would have been impaled by him already.

Electric, delicious heat shot through her body. She arched as she pulled off her bra, letting her breasts fall free and be exposed to his hungry eyes.

She dropped her head back as his airy form crawled over her. He caged her.

"Why me?" she asked. "There is nothing special or unique about me except for my odd genetic condition."

Atlas was close enough that she could see thousands of streaming numbers glide over his body, tiny rivulets of code, and minuscule patterns of circuitry she had failed to notice on previous occasions.

He is so beautiful and we're so crazy.

"You have too much self-doubt, Reina. What you should be asking yourself is, 'Why him?'" She watched as his stark, monochrome eyes locked with hers as he ghosted his mouth over her shivering breasts. His lips ran over her nipples, touching her but not touching her at the same time. "Your tits. I'd love to see them bounce under me."

"You don't ask anything from me," she said, sliding her hands up and cupping her breasts.

He answered, "And you see me as if I'm still alive."

Reina leaned up and watched him worship her body, and when his eyes left the tight nipples, desperately waiting for a mouth that wasn't there to land on her still clothed sex, she brought her knees up and exposed herself completely. Almost.

"Do you want to see what's yours tonight?"

"Forever." He amended and leaned over her, catching her gaze again before looking at her clothed sex. "I already can. Your panties are soaked and leave little to the imagination." His finger ghosted over it. "Did I do this to you?" His voice was hard.

"Yes," she whispered. "Fantasizing about you makes this happen to me."

He continued to stare at her aching sex between her legs, his fingers whispering over her. She clenched and he grinned. She undulated and his eyes went hard.

"Touch yourself for me. Tell me what you were thinking about in the shower when you said my name."

She leaned back into the bedding, willing the tension in her muscles to dissolve away as she cupped her neck with her hands and gently rolled them down her shivering body. Reina closed her eyes as her hands found her breasts again and rounded them, lightly squeezing them for her pleasure and his satisfaction alone.

Her nipples tightened painfully at the thought of Atlas's hand ravaging her sex.

She rolled her tits with a moan. "I want your fingers in me."

"More."

The demand made her melt. It was easier to pretend he wasn't right there when she refused to open her eyes, but relishing in the fact that he was there and he was watching every move she made with every ounce of his attention.

"I thought of you with me. You were behind me and squeezing my breasts like I'm doing now."

"And what else?" his voice was in her ear and she shook her head. Her heart raced, reminding her that the silence between his words was a false silence.

She slid her hands down her smooth stomach and over her pelvic bones until her hands came together

141

like an arrow between her legs and framed her clenching feminine heat, desperately willing–wanting his heavy cock to penetrate her.

"I touched myself to depraved thoughts of us together. I came on my fingers with you on my mind," Reina moaned out embarrassingly.

"You can't stop there, sweetheart. Remove your panties and show me."

Reina twisted her legs and arched up, doing what she was told. She felt Atlas shoot up into the circuitry in her head as her fingertips found her clit.

"I thought of you taking advantage of me."

"Fuck, you're glistening. Pink and wet. I bet you're hot. Tight. Aching and desperate." His groan came from lower on the bed. She continued to rub herself, her desire shooting up at his words. "A perfect tight fit for a hard fuck. Can you take me, Reina?"

She shivered. "I can try."

"You'll have to do better than that. Slide your finger inside your tiny pussy and prove it to me."

Reina let his demands lead her to hell. She slid her index finger all the way in.

"I can take you."

"Are you sure? A Cyborg isn't just 'taken,' they break in." He growled as she arched back up off the bed and moaned, imagining him doing just that. She clenched around her finger as her thumb sought her clit again. "You like that, don't you? I would have to spend countless hours riding you before you could come close to fitting me."

"Yes," she barely managed to moan. *I want that.*

"I would demand submission." His voice steely again. "Turn over and on your knees. Stick your ass up in the air." As if he positioned her body himself, she flipped and complied, feeling heady in her wanton exposure. "Did you imagine me–keep fucking your finger–did you think of me pushing inside you, stretching you?"

"Yes," Reina hissed into the pillow. "I thought of you mounting me. I thought of you using me. It was just a fantasy." She tried to explain breathlessly. "You took me from behind."

"Interesting choice of words. Mounting. You're dripping, tell me why."

She didn't think she could.

Her thoughts no longer belonged to her but to her half-crazed desire and the demandingly rough, robotic voice that accompanied it. Every nerve ending was sparking and she could feel her body straining into a crescendo. She could feel the torturously empty space within her that she needed Atlas to fill.

"Reina, your silence is pissing me off. You don't want to know what I'd do to you if you upset me."

She cried, slamming another finger inside her, spreading herself out for his view. "I do want to know!" She turned her head to the side and looked back at him. "I want you to fuck me like a beast. I want you to spread me impossibly wide. I want to be filled up by every inch of you." She continued, "In the shower, I thought of you bending me over and taking me like a doll, thrusting into me and not just within my body, but within my mind as well. I fantasized about being branded by you, but not just physically, mentally." She let out a strangled breath.

"From the moment we were thrust together within these walls. You have been in the forefront of my mind and I don't know why. So yes, I do want to know what you would do if you're upset."

Reina turned her head away breaking contact with him and rolled her fingers inside her heat. Coaxing out her essence over her pink lips and onto her thighs, enjoying the fact that it was probably making Atlas as crazy as she was.

"Do you really? That's quite a speech for a girl who is getting off from my voice and even my threats." He grunted softly as she swayed her backside to distract him. "I've thought about you too."

She didn't know how to respond to that.

She lifted her hips higher on the bed, giving in to the vulnerability of the position and the incredible power she had over the situation. The caress of static electricity went through her again as every goosebump and prickle on her skin chilled the heat coursing through her.

Reina faintly knew he was watching her raptly work her pussy right before his eyes. His incorporeal hands trailing over her parted thighs.

"I wish you could take over."

"Me too, sweetheart." He breathed deeply, his voice low with barely controllable restraint and longing–and wicked promise. "It won't be long now. Cum for me Reina, climax only for me. Let me see what I do to you when all I have is my voice."

Her desire thrummed as her robotic hand was held beneath her, its weight a distraction. Reina pressed a third finger into her with a screech, biting the synthetic cotton to dampen her moans.

"Roll those fingers inside you, then release and thrust them back in, add a fourth if you think you can handle me." She complied, her hand slick with desire. Reina tried to add a fourth, testing it out but found the pressure too much. "Pretend they are my fingers," he whispered from behind her. "Imagine my hands gripping your thighs and spreading you apart."

"Atlas." She bit the sheets.

"My tongue would glide up your leg, from behind your knee, savoring your skin only to end buried in your cunt. Penetrating you how I would with my huge cock. You haven't proved that you can handle it. But my tongue would be wetter, softer, urgent, and painfully slower."

Reina pressed her thumb into her clit and shuddered, rolling it leisurely, trying to take some of the ache within her body away.

"I want you so bad." She writhed her hips, fucking her own hand.

Her Cyborg responded with a frustrated groan of his own. "Reina, after I've drunk you down, my mouth filled with the only taste I ever want on my tongue, I would hook your legs around me, spreading you wide and unhindered and I would fuck you the way you want it most. I would use you like a beast until I broke you down, and once you've had enough, I would continue."

Reina screamed into her pillow as she finally came. She fell forward into a fetal position as her body convulsed, shaking from a depraved desire hidden deep within herself that Atlas was slowly bringing to light.

"Put your fingers in your mouth and tell me what you taste like."

Reina brought her hand to her lips and suckled her finger.

"Salty."

"Good girl, Captain."

She curled up into a ball until her erratic pulse slowed down to a breathy simmer. Her body was slick with sweat and for a half-second, she was glad that Atlas couldn't smell the musk of her desire.

Sometime later, she couldn't tell how long, Reina uncurled herself and turned around to face the sentient projection who haunted her.

He sat with his back turned away from her, staring out into the soft gloom of the room. Unconsciously she reached out to run her fingers down his back, only to find her hand ghost through him.

• • • •

ATLAS TURNED TO THE naked, vulnerable girl curled up in the bed next to him. He could sense her hands penetrate the projection of his body before he saw them slip through him.

Reina caught his eyes with uncertainty, the flush of her release still painting her pale skin, and he looked at her slowly from head to toe. Frustrated and hungry for something that was just beyond his reach.

"Atlas? Are you all right? Did I do something wrong?" She sat up slowly, curling her knees under her but careful to not sway into his fake form. Sometimes barriers were a luxury that the living didn't realize they had. There were no barriers

146

between him and Reina, not even that of skin and bone and metal.

He chose not to answer her questions–they were redundant and self-doubting.

I will have to build her self-confidence. She should never have to ask me for reassurance. Atlas looked back at her and smiled.

"Do you want to know something funny?"

She shared a small smile back and nodded.

"I'm not actually sitting on this bed."

Reina's eyes glinted with a mischief that could almost match his own. "I know that. I'm pretty sure these beds aren't built to withstand your weight."

"Are you calling me fat?" Atlas mock gasped.

"Very fat."

He laughed. "Only my cock. Our bedroom talk needs improvement. I suppose we have the rest of our lives to work on it. You are so beautiful, flushed and ruined in this bed. I would give the moon and stars to kiss away that pout on your lips. I want you to teach me how to kiss." Atlas watched as Reina turned away and fell back on the bed, curling her body within the disrupted bedding. She scooted over until her back hit the wall.

"If you're going to be a downer, at least do it while you're pretending to lie down next to me." She huffed and patted the empty space between her and the unit in the middle of the room, allowing him unhindered to join her. Atlas lay stiffly beside her.

"I only tell you the truth." And he thought about his body being brought to life somewhere below them, wondering if omitting that detail was, in fact, a lie.

Without realizing what he was doing, he channeled into his weakened half-life of a corpse, and felt the sickening spikes of pain that only death could bring on. Atlas shut himself off to it, willing his body to remain alive, to continue healing itself until his heart was linked inside of him.

He looked over at the girl staring at him. Atlas could see himself in her eyes. He reached over and pretended to caress her arm, knowing it only brought comfort to her.

"What's your special ability?" That threw him off-guard. "You promised to tell me if I gave you control of the ballistics." He watched as she snuggled herself into the sheets, settling in.

"Magnets." Instantly missing it, instantly pouring himself back into his half-dead shell and feeling the pain of death all over again.

"Magnets? What did you do with them?"

"I was built as a walking, talking, high-frequency malicious electromagnetic generator, with antenna systems that could focus my efforts in specific arenas or targets. Remember in my report that I was part of the shield and disrupter division? It's because I did both. They would send me in because the closer I was to the source I was blacking out, the more effective I was. The Trentians, and even most humans, do not have adequate defenses to electromagnetic warfare. I could destroy every electric weapon for leagues, I could black out every computer and system in my sight, and I could even target specific equipment so I would not hurt our own resources. The team I was with protected themselves with surge protectors and solid metal screens embedded in their armor."

148

"That's impressive...you sound like you miss it."

"I was built for front-line warfare. Of course, I miss it. Watching the stage go black, the whites of my enemies' eyes widen and fill with fear, as they couldn't quite grasp fast enough what was happening. It was exhilarating. Killing for a cause was exhilarating, even if it wasn't my own."

"Would you do it all over? Even if it meant losing your body?"

Atlas had to think about that. *Would* he do it over? He was created for it, it was his purpose upon his birth, and the main source of his years of training. He knew what he was and what he was meant to do without a doubt from the early years of his mechanical life. Regardless, it had all brought him to this moment in time, lying in a bed with a beautiful girl almost in his arms.

"I would do it all over again." He paused. "There is nothing I would change." Atlas looked down at his captain. "Is there anything you would change?"

Reina's face stilled ever so slightly and he wondered if even she knew that the walls she carried around herself could be seen from the outside. He wanted to know her thoughts but didn't press the matter by invading her head, instead opting to remain patient until she came up with her answer.

Her mouth opened and closed so sweetly, Atlas pictured ravaging it with his tongue, his teeth, and even invading it with his fingers and cock. Until her answer was lost within moans he forced from her.

He briefly wondered if she regretted taking on this mission.

Even if she did, it was too late now. His body would awaken soon, and his hold on her would finally be complete.

"I regret being born a woman."

Wasn't expecting that. "Did you have a choice in the matter?" He laughed.

"Obviously not."

"I don't think you can regret your sex. I sure as hell don't."

"I never want to have children, especially if there is a chance of them being female."

"Then they never will be."

They shared a look that might have lasted for an eternity. He watched as she slowly succumbed to sleep, lost in her own bleak thoughts.

"I'll be here when you need me."

Chapter Twelve:

· · · ·

She was walking down a passageway, one she had walked down a thousand times a before. There were grates below her boots and a dark grey metallic look to the tunnels that splintered off around her.

She was headed for the bridge because her shift was about to start. Faceless men passed by her. Some would look at her but most just moved on to continue in their duties.

There was a hush aboard the ship that had never been there before. It made it hard for her to breathe. Not because she felt out of breath, but because she was afraid of making a noise.

Reina looked down at the wrist-comm attached to her hand, the time flashed at her, telling her she was already late. She couldn't remember what she was late for.

There was nobody in the tunnels now and she immediately missed the patterned steps of boots hitting metal and the soft thunk they made with each impact. Her steps were silent and she couldn't understand why.

Someone was watching her.

She turned around slowly and saw a man at the other end of the corridor, standing there, staring back at her. Reina shook her head and closed her eyes. The man didn't belong here. But he was here and she couldn't bring herself to care, only knowing that he *was here and he didn't belong and there was nothing for it.*

Reina continued down the passageway to pick up her post. She was late but when she looked down at the time, it hadn't changed. She glanced back behind her, the periphery-man still there, still trailing her, and as silent as the ship.

She absently shook out her arm and forgot about him.

The clatter of incoming crewmates could be heard just around the corner and she smiled, heading in their direction. Maybe she would see a familiar face and the strange absent atmosphere would vanish with some pleasant conversation. The time on her hand had yet to move so she had yet to care about being in another time.

But something wasn't right and every long second and every step forward became something more. It started out with anxiety, and then curiosity, possibly a fleeting moment of hope, but now it was something else. Each step now brought a prickle of pain, like a tiny stab, and she realized that what had started out as something as inconsequential as a mosquito bite was now as painful as a bee sting.

She grabbed ahold of herself and attacked her clothing and rubbed her skin. Her nails grazed her cheeks and tugged her hair, pulling it out of her tie and away from her body. She shook out her taut uniform violently, trying to dislodge the source of the pain that was being inflicted on her.

A rattled gasp released from her throat and as quickly as the pain began, it fell away. Reina found herself on the cold floor of the ship as she caught her breath. She looked back at her wrist and noticed the time had moved forward by a minute.

She got up on her feet and brushed off the dirt she knew wasn't there.

Reina continued on toward the noise of her comrades around the corner. She had lost a tick in time but she was on her way again. Her hair was back in order, her feet were moving onward, and the sound she could hear just out of sight was her only goal, and it was an easy one.

She glanced behind her but the man was gone; a subtle feeling of loss accompanied the sight of the empty hallway. The pain of the loss of the outskirts-man was equal to all of the bug bites she had received combined, all at once, in her heart.

When she looked forward, the pain dwindled as well.

Her destination was just around the corner now and she smiled. Reina knew what was there, even though she couldn't quite tell who. The lights grew brighter and brighter until she turned the corner.

And stopped.

Her stomach gave out and if she could have, she would melted into the floor and vanished. Two men stood before her, and she knew them. Aliens who had bargained for her furiously, the terror of losing her free will only to be abducted into an adventure she neither chose nor wanted. The life she would have led if the will of men had steered her.

One of the aliens, the more human of the two, stood in front of the other, slightly off to the side. She noticed him only because he demanded to be noticed.

His eyes were a pale seafoam green, his height towering and only accentuated by the lethal ropey armor he wore, plated and dark. The armor was a stark contrast to his creepy white skin, only seen from his face down to his navel where an armored 'V' shape created a window to his muscled chest. The very slight undertone of green, the same shade as his eyes, shimmered underneath his beautifully dominant outer layer. His pale hair was shorn close to his skull.

He was a Trentian Spacelord: one who may have had the blood of thousands soaked within the black gauntlets that covered his hands.

The bright white lights washed him out. She cringed away from looking at the warrior directly.

So much blood between their species.

But it wasn't the lord that terrified her, it was the alien she could not see well standing slightly beyond him.

The one in the jagged mask that looked like a malformed star, his eyes the only indication of a live being underneath the façade and black sculpted robes. He stared at her as if she wasn't there but she could see her reflection in his eyes. They devoured all of her attention and even the warrior next to him couldn't hold onto it.

She felt very alone looking into his eyes. She had been very alone her whole life and she didn't think she could handle the rest of eternity that way.

Pale, strong hands–so beautiful that they were terrible–reached for her. Before she knew it, she flung herself at the masked man and attacked him, fueled by terror. He just stood there while she tried to tear him apart.

154

Silken black robes entwined her limbs as she clawed her way to the heart of the man beneath. It ripped under her hands as she grabbed fistfuls to shred and the more she tore away the more silk and cloth seemed to remain.

The echoes of her frustrated screams poured out of her like the pools of black ribbons scattered around. It built and built until there was more fabric than floor. She rammed into his still form until she had him on the ground.

The clash of his metalloid mask left a pulsating vibration throughout the hallway. When she realized his robes would not give under her violence, threads built under her fingernails, she grabbed at the horrible mask that hid her would-be abductor from her gaze.

She pulled but it would not give, and the more she tried the more her palms and fingers sliced against its edges. Gashes appeared wherever her skin touched the sharp, jagged creation. As she grew wilder in her failed attempts at getting at the masked man, hands grabbed her forearms from behind and pulled her away.

"Wake up, Reina."

She stopped her struggles and in a blink, the alien men were gone, the sanguinary pools of black silk had vanished. She was in a bright, quiet spaceship corridor and the time on her watch had moved forward another minute.

Strong arms wrapped around her torso and held her close as she calmed down. When her breath poured evenly into her lungs, she turned around and *looked at the man who had been on the outskirts of her mind before. Now in the forefront.*

Hard blue eyes locked her into place and what had been normal skin a moment before transformed into serpentine code crawling across his skin.

"Wake up."

She sagged into him and opened her eyes.

• • • •

SHE WAS HEFTED INTO a seat just as she opened her eyes. Dr. Yesne, incredibly out of breath, leaned over her and strapped her into the captain's chair. Her hands clenched the armrests just as she was surrounded by electric screens.

"Oh good, you're awake. She's awake." The doctor rushed to the co-pilot's seat and buckled in, squeezing out exasperated heaves.

"What? What happened?" Reina looked down at herself, expecting to be covered in blood.

"You forced us off course while you were asleep and attacked our trailer from Taggert." Atlas's voice rang out and bounced off the walls. "We're preparing for warp drive."

"What do you mean I *attacked* someone? We're not in cleared warp space." But she knew it was too late, thrusters were activating around her and she could feel the ship weave in and out of her. Her nightmare came back to her. "Did I attack a Trentian spacecraft?" Reina looked for Atlas but his projection was not formed.

"Reina, right now isn't the time for a thousand questions. You're going to need to not fight me on this, otherwise you're going to get hurt. Now, allow the ship to warp."

The shudders in the ship, almost indistinct, matched the increasingly erratic beat of her heart. Reina closed her eyes and let Atlas take over.

She was dressed in only her undergarments but the heat coursing through her kept her warm on the chilly bridge. The prickles on her arms weren't bites or the cold, but anticipation.

And fear.

Right as she let Atlas take over the controls, she reached out and held onto him, feeling as he flooded the ship's systems with an increasingly dangerous amount of energy. He threw everything to maximum.

Reina tried to relax but her vessel crackled with forced power, her body became something akin to a capacitor—or a battery. She glanced over at the doctor, only to see him barely keep a grip on his faculties, his skin ghost-white and his glasses tucked into his shirt as his eyes remained clenched shut.

"Emergency warp initiated." Atlas's voice brought her back to the present. "Brace."

The ship shook around her and seized her. She prayed that Atlas had found a safe route.

There was nothing quite as terrifying as flashing at the speed of light, beyond the speed of thought, right into the path of a star. It would be an instant death. Obliteration as every atom of your life-force disintegrated into nothing. *Beyond* nothing as there wouldn't even be a shipwreck left behind.

Even the best navigators, with every precaution in check, every safety measure taken, could still hit a roaming asteroid. Reina had begun to trust Atlas, and if anyone could make an escape like this, it would be him.

Her throat closed up. Breathing was hard during this part of intergalactic travel. Her nails bit into the armrests of her chair.

Streaks of colors shot past her eyes, dizzying, deadly, and so beautiful it hurt. Reina had seen it all before, dozens of times, but never at the helm of a ship. Backup pilots never had that luxury; their ships were small and were never meant to go far from their docking station. The colors blinded her to the danger that something would appear in their path.

Please, please, please.

And then it was over.

And they were beyond Ursa Major and in the Abyss-105 sector, now dangerously close to where the network's reach began to falter before it stopped working entirely. This place was already considered the 'deeper parts of traversable space.' Port Antix was the farthest anyone had ever traveled and still lived to return and tell the tale. It was the last, and only, waystation where a communications relay had established contact before anyone who traveled beyond vanished.

Other intergalactic sectors continued to expand outward, Earthian and Trentian alike, explored and extended their reaches continuously, colonized and explored new frontiers... but there were some frontiers that were dark. Cursed areas that should have been easily explored, but for some reason remained elusive and black with death.

Places like where she and Atlas were going, to finally bring back viable intel and solve the mystery of a million missing persons.

The horrible thought made Reina shiver. *What could possibly be out there?*

She unstrapped her buckles and slowly found her footing. Bare feet hit the cold floor of the bridge. Her body could feel her personal nanocells travel away until they either died or found themselves swimming away in an electrical current.

The need for socks suddenly eclipsed all previous thought. She looked down at her exposed feet and arched her toes before walking over to the doctor, who was still bracing for an impact that they had already survived.

"We're okay. We made it." She placed her hand over his in comfort.

"I know. My body hasn't quite caught up to the idea, though," Yesne said between clenched teeth. "I believe my nerves will be shot for life. There's no going back to a normal life after a ride like that."

Atlas's hologram appeared before them, looking perfect and unfazed as ever. "You're exaggerating. Your system is undergoing nothing but acute anxiety. You'll be fine after a rest cycle or a tranquilizer."

Reina eyed the hard man for whom she had been writhing naked just hours prior with a modicum of unease. Needing to turn away, she walked over to the central projection table and gripped the sides for support, her head bending forward as Atlas's blue light followed her.

"Are we enemies of the Council now?"

"No. Our stalker from Taggert wasn't flying an Earthian ship–"

"–An alien's? A Trentian's?" *Please don't let it be an alien vessel. My rapport with them is bad enough.*

"No, at least not a Trentian military one." Atlas paused. The thought of Trentians that close made her want to vomit. "It was a scavenger vessel from what I was able to read of it before you attacked it with–fuck–just enough firepower to destroy a Battle Cruiser. Reina, you tried to liquefy it."

Yesne joined them at the center, his glasses fogged with stress-sweat. "Go big or go home?" Reina and Atlas ignored him equally.

"Then it's destroyed? Whatever, whoever it was is gone?"

"No. They got away which is why we had to leave."

"Because they could call for back-up? Because they were scoping us out?"

"We did pick them up at Taggert..." Atlas's pause said enough.

Reina ran her fingers through her loose hair. "Fuck."

"Exactly."

"If the ship was not from the fleet and you're sure it was not an alien craft, who do you think it could be? A splinter group? Scavengers? Marauders? Please don't tell me we picked up the notice of Larik's syndicate." Reina squeezed the edge of the table while she nervously bounced on her toes, still unnerved about the strange current that zapped at her skin. "What are the odds of us picking up one of his ships?"

"Well, we were passing by the prison planet."

The silence that fell between them was riddled with tension and complication. Pirate Captain Larik was the leader of the strongest underground force in the universe; he answered to no one. His influence and strength were on par with the Intergalactic Council and the leaders of the Earthian and Trentian species. Reina couldn't fathom how one man could become so powerful, enough that he had nearly created a third faction.

Was it money? Resources?

"But you said he wasn't there, his capture took place several years ago. Surely his intel would know by now that he is not being kept there." Reina continued to bounce on her feet, unable to force her biological body to calm down.

"Or they don't know for sure. No one leaves Taggert's surface once they have been dropped off. No one has ever escaped. The satellites around the planet are monitored and maintained by another Cyborg, one with complete control of the planet's defenses. I guarantee that even if Larik's men suspect that he is not being kept there, they won't know for sure."

"We will have to prepare for every possibility then. I recommend we stay on course and send an update to the Council about what has transgressed here and continue to carry out the current mission," Yesne intervened. "We're at the end of the road out here. Any updates that are to be sent back to the command center, or routed through another station, port, or ship may not even reach our superiors before you leave Port Antix. Let's hope this mission can remain on course until the military has been informed." The doctor turned to Atlas's hologram. "Very good navigating, Atlas. I didn't think we were going to survive."

Reina closed her eyes and grumbled, "Yes. Thank you for getting us out of there."

"You mean, reeling you in?"

"I didn't know my subconscious was going to be acted out by the ship."

Atlas held her gaze in a steely stare that made her shiver. "Whoever was following us was probing our security and defense systems, essentially penetrating you and trying to find a way in. You perceived it as an attack and defended yourself. It's natural. Reina, you just have to come to terms with the fact that the ship is an extension of your body now and can be controlled by your consciousness." Atlas laughed the last part, chilly and sarcastic, "Welcome to being a cybernetic being."

"True, true." Yesne agreed. "Your arm is absolutely perfect now, Captain." He unthreaded her fingers from the table and held them out between them. It reminded her of her rather inappropriate state of undress. "One wouldn't even be able to tell you have an implant. Absolute perfection. The incision has completely vanished."

Reina dislodged her arm from the doctor's grip, feeling Atlas's eyes watching her every movement. "The Council said my implant remains with the ship."

"Yes, well, they probably assume you won't leave your arm."

"She won't."

Reina tried to shut the thought out, the tether that bound her, not wanting to dwell on her choices. *I*

*don't even know if I'll be alive at the end of this
mission.*

"Do you think we got away? That whoever was
following us lost us in the warp?" Quickly changing
the subject.

"Hard to say. I don't sense a presence near us but
we are headed in a very singular direction and there's
only one station in this sector. If they're smart, which
they may be–flying an unidentifiable vessel– and we
take all factors into account, what we have is a non-
standard ship with probing technology that is beyond
any commercial, mercurial, or resource haul on the
market. The brief connection that was made between
our flyers held no traces of Trentian technology."

"Do we have an image of it? Could it be private?"
Reina watched as Yesne found a spare spacesuit
jacket off the bridge's immediate storage unit and
walked it over to her.

She tugged it on, immediately feeling less
vulnerable.

"No image. And even if it *was* private, they could
sell our coordinates and projected route to any
splinter group looking for an easy target." The bridge
lit up as their current galaxy magically appeared
around them, Atlas standing in the middle of it.
Billions of stars and planets vanished from the
periphery as the sector narrowed down to their
specific solar system. Reina watched in awe as their
ship came into view and their pathway materialized
and changed.

She couldn't understand it but she knew, without
a doubt, that Atlas was calculating and reconfiguring
a new channel to travel by.

She noticed intermittent flickering around the outskirts. Reina moved over to touch a fading star. "What's happening here? Why are they fuzzy?"

Atlas appeared next to her. "A result of the end of the network's reach. All communication and information relay will continue to disintegrate as we continue farther away."

Reina turned back to the dot that represented their ship. "I take it you found us a new route?"

"Yes. We're due to arrive at Antix in forty-eight standard Earth hours."

"Good. Ahead of schedule." She took a deep breath. "Let's hope the stalker was a fluke but we'll prepare for an attack as we get closer to our destination. It doesn't hurt to be prepared." She turned to the doctor. "You're dismissed, Yesne, try and get some rest. I will reach out to the Council per your suggestion. Thank you for being brave."

"Thank you, Captain, I do believe I need to rest my heart." Hesitation laced his voice, as if he was going to say more but chose not to. Reina watched as the man practically skipped out of her presence while his eyes held on Atlas until he rounded the corner.

Odd.

She wasn't sure what to make of everything that had just happened. An hour ago she was sound asleep in her quarters, lost within the gleam of a nightmare, everything otherwise normal. But now things had changed to a more stressful course.

As if things could get more stressful, Reina mused, annoyed. She looked at the time on the ship's console, indicating that it was still well within the rest cycle.

Adrenaline flowed through her veins. *What have I done?*

Danger could be lurking just around the corner and not just on the other side of Abyss-105 and it hadn't really hit her until just now, tonight, lying down with the fake form of a man powered by Atlas's mind that there was not much time left. That maybe she couldn't trust her judgment anymore, that maybe she should have *never* trusted her judgment. She had always made the easy choice, the choice that resulted in the least amount of mess. Her life was driven by a bone-deep need for safety and security, and for an independence that she felt she never had.

This mission was the messiest thing she had ever chosen in her life and it was spurred on by events that shattered her walled-up state of being that had governed every action she had taken to this day. But even the freedom that this quest granted her came with very heavy-handed strings attached. The barbed wire kept her tethered to the choices she had made.

Reina wished that she could bleach out the self-doubt that infected her thoughts and ruled her soul. She wanted control of herself. She wanted the darkness of her inferiority complex to disappear.

She stared out at the black space before her, seeing it only grow darker in her mind.

"Are you okay?" Atlas appeared between her and the void, blocking out the darkness. Reina sat down in her chair and rubbed a shaking hand over her face.

"I don't know."

"You did what you thought was right."

"Was it though? I could have killed innocent people, I could have killed *us*. I made a horrible mistake and jeopardized this mission."

His beautiful robotic form kneeled down in front of her, and for a heartbreaking moment, she wanted to fling herself into his chest and be held and taken care of.

"I was with you the entire time, sweetheart. You saw me, you knew I was there. I would never let you come to harm and you need to know, if you know nothing else, that you'll never be alone again. Here," Atlas waved his hand indicating the ship. "Or in here." He pointed at her head.

Tears sprang to her eyes as her nightmare came back to her in fragments. "I remember you, somewhere in the background." She could barely form the words.

"Yes. And I will always be there if you want me there. If you need me there. This ship is you and well–I'm here within the ship, within you. I sense you more and more, I sense you taking over, and in turn taking me over. Reina, when I helped build this cybernetic vessel, I built it because to me, it was mine. This ship was mine the moment the project was conceived and every circuit, every wire, every piece of metal and electronic was claimed by me from the birth of their fabrication. Every rivet. Every bolt. I had every intention of being the Cyborg who would sync with the life-blood of this ship. I needed the outlet to remain sane, a body that could be mine since the Council refused to fix me."

Atlas indicated her arm, the metal appendage she held to her chest. "Your specialized unit, the key, was just a means to an end for me. I assumed I would integrate the ship, take control of the piece, and in turn control both regardless of who it was attached to. You were right to be wary of me from the beginning. I had every intention of flooding the system, destroying any firewalls, mental and digital, and taking complete control. But what I didn't account for was you. You ruined everything when you took this mission, and when I realized what had happened, it was too late for me. Everything I thought I wanted was nothing compared to you."

Reina couldn't form any words. All she could do was let the tears stream down her cheeks and stare at the hologram before her. He continued when she didn't respond.

"What I'm trying to say, Reina, is that the ship is mine still and it always will be which means that you're mine because you're one and the same. Nothing will happen to you because I will never *ever* let something so beautifully crafted, so lovingly broken, so perfectly strong slip through my fingers."

"Atlas, I–"

"–Don't. Just know that you're not alone. Trust me and trust yourself because we're in this to the end. Even if our end is on the horizon."

Reina wiped the back of her hands over her cheeks. "I wasn't going to say what you were thinking I would say." Her voice shook. "I was going to say I love you." Her eyes closed, hardly able to look at his transparent face. "I don't know if you can believe that but what I feel for you is safe and warm and comforting. It feels like nothing I have ever felt before, it feels like home." She finished shakily, "I think that's love. I don't have any...prior experience from my life."

She opened her eyes, willing herself to be brave, and was met with Atlas's beautiful, bright projection smiling softly.

"I guess we'll have to discover it for ourselves."

Reina sniffled, "To the end?"

"To whatever awaits us beyond the darkness."

Chapter Thirteen:

· · · ·

Time was up. The unprecedented warp had fast-forwarded the mission, and Antix was less than two Earth days away.

Atlas looked down at his semi-living shell, a flesh vegetable filled with priceless metal, cybernetic material, and his entire biological being. A vessel that was still alive but without a sentient conscience or a bot without a motherboard. A breathing zombie without a mind. One who didn't feed off the flesh of the living but instead fed off the electricity siphoned from its static nanocells.

Because my mind has been stuck in the network.

A place where he should have been lost, a nightmare where he had gone insane for a time, but he had found himself and transcended to conquer his new world because he had been born to fight, to battle, and most of all to win. Atlas had been created to win. *Win.*

He had conquered his humanoid, biological side while trapped in a place devoid of humanity; he had evolved. That's what Cyborgs did.

Atlas stared down at his body.

But we don't always win. He briefly thought of Reina and enjoyed the strange surge of power that flowed through him whenever she entered his thoughts. It was an exhilarating, fluttering feeling that brought him closer to being alive than he had been in his long years in the dark.

She was beautiful, fresh, and pure, a new being who willingly joined him in his prison. He would never let her go, not anymore. If he could not win the fight to reclaim his body and in turn, stake his claim on hers, he would imprison her with him in the network and claim her there. The ship would be her prison. If he had to, he would revert to his previous plan and seize control.

Atlas never thought of himself as a good guy; intrinsically, a battle-born man could never be *good*. But he knew he was rational, sometimes honorable, and above all he had integrity.

I also have wants and my wants are the strongest force ruling my mind. I want Reina. I want her powerless under me and under my control. I want to sink into her flesh like a man, I want to mount her like an animal, and I want to control her like a Cyborg.

He also wanted her to find her self-worth most of all, to be there when she fully realized her strength, and to watch as she battled her own inner demons– and won. He wanted to be there when her fears fell away and nothing remained but the queen she was born to be.

His attention abruptly shifted back to his current predicament as Yesne changed out an IV bag that fed into the cryostasis pod, most likely filled with immunosuppressant drugs, kicked up with nanotechnology and electrodes to ease the procedure. It fed in where his body was still attached to the static machinery.

His chest was cracked open, sliced and cut like fresh meat to reveal the inner workings of his torso. Where his ribs should have been was plated metal, peeled back, his lungs a silver metal chamber that pumped not only air through his system but also charged currents. His body was predominantly metal– a fully functional biomechatronic machine.

The only thing missing was the human heart that had been his only link to humanity, the cavity and empty shell between his lung chambers.

As he looked at his body, where his heart should have been was now a series of tubes, wiring. The organ had been replaced by a chaotic mess that was even beyond his scope of understanding.

Dr. Yesne had created an electric, artificial, possibly conductive piece that simulated the human organ–a unique structure that looked like it could withstand anything a real-born, biological body ever could.

One less piece that would make him human and one more piece that would make him a machine.

Atlas knew he could deal with that concept but he was... afraid? No. He was apprehensive. If Yesne failed in the operation, Atlas would lose his only chance at reanimation.

A series of questions flooded his mind. Was it okay to be both frightened and a Cyborg? Would that be considered a failure on his part? A malfunction? A flaw?

Right now Reina was asleep, truly asleep and not unconsciously maneuvering the spaceship. He had it set back on auto-pilot and afterward followed her into her mind and soothed her into that blank space that Cyborgs used to recharge themselves.

He held her there and she trusted him enough to let her mind go.

At this point, Atlas always had one part of his consciousness fed into her circuits; he wasn't sure if she even knew he was there anymore.

It was considered a terrible breach of etiquette at best to do that between cybernetic beings, but Reina didn't know their ways. He was intimately familiar with her mental defenses, so he was able to take liberties in his ability to protect her. That was how he justified the trespass.

Atlas left his body to look at her sleeping form, peering through the window of the projection unit installed in her quarters. His broken body temporarily disappeared from his mind as Reina's face, unlined by stress, replaced it. Her breathing was even and regular, beautiful pouty lips slightly parted and tilted toward the pillow.

He leaned over her and brushed his fingers over her mouth.

Fucking humans and the shit-staggering cybernetic program. Fuck this bleak limbo that's my prison. Fuck scientific advancement as well. Atlas left the sleeping girl behind, refusing to look at her, and cursed the same beings who brought her into his existence.

The greater good often left a lot of horrible things in its wake.

Atlas returned to his broken shell and looked at the ice that had encased him drip and pool on the floor of the room, trickling into the grates to be sanitized and recycled. He was suddenly grateful that he couldn't smell the stink of his body being thawed out.

Yesne, his surgeon, unwilling captive, and temporary slave who was also the closest thing Atlas had to a friend was attentively watching Atlas's vitals.

Atlas did not know if he could fully trust the doctor under their current circumstances, but better circumstances had never presented themselves. As he watched the man work, he glimpsed into his pulled-apart shell to check for abnormalities.

A searing, overwhelming pain–an agony that would have never bothered him in his previous life–gripped his mind. The euphoria of physical sensation shot through him. It was the first time he felt contact in seventy-five years, fifteen hours, nineteen minutes, and two seconds.

A moment of blissful insanity flooded him, addiction to the pain bloomed like a starving seed.

"It's about time you showed up." Yesne leaned over him just as he forced his way out of his shell. At one moment consumed with pain-pleasure, the next nothing.

"I've been here the whole time. I'm everywhere." He projected himself next to the pod.

"Well, our time is coming to an end."

They both knew that this next step had to happen now. Yesne was to be relieved when they arrived at Antix and because of that, it was time for Atlas to take over the process and force his nanocells to integrate with the new hardware, healing himself. The internal battle would be worth it even if he only had enough time to kiss Reina once, even if he failed and his body rejected the new heart.

"You must be happy about that. Your stay hasn't been exactly what you expected when you boarded my vessel." Yesne gave him a hard look before leaning over his body, the doctor's eyes trained on his open chest. The man intently and fiercely began to close him up. It took a special type of doctor to go between welding metal and sewing up flesh with ease.

"My stay aboard this ship has been better than expected," the man murmured as sparks flew up around his face, splashing across the steel mask he wore. Atlas watched the tiny embers land on his skin and smolder out.

Time passed in anxious anticipation as the metal plates fused together, closing up the wound. Before he knew it, Yesne was rising up, his hands steady as he raised the mask off his face, a thin sheen of sweat outlined the red markings left behind.

At least one of us has the confidence to show the stress of the situation. It took a lot to make a Cyborg sweat. Even this situation wouldn't warrant that bodily function.

"You're stalling." The doctor brought him out of his reverie.

"I'm contemplating."

"About what?"

"About what happens next and about the Earthian Council. I am also thinking about you." Atlas answered honestly. The doctor sat down on a nearby stool.

"So you are stalling. I would never take a man like you for a coward. No man, or woman for that matter, thinks about *me* willingly. Except, possibly, under the direst of circumstances."

"You do know I can kill you but you probably already know that I wouldn't. You have either discerned that your demise would look obscenely suspicious and would put Reina in jeopardy, which I would never do, or you have an ace up your sleeve and have installed something within me that only you can control, which would never work. But I don't believe it is either of those reasons that have given you a sense of courage, I think you just can't bring yourself to care because regardless of what you do or don't do, your fate is out of your hands. And that is why you are trying to bait me. So tell me, doctor, why do you think I am stalling?"

A twitch of a smile lifted the man's tired lips. "Treason," he answered.

"Would you call what we have done here treasonous?"

"I can't quite say. I believe it depends on how we act from here on out. If our actions after this negatively impact the Earthian Council and the human race, then yes." Yesne paused, rubbing his eyes. "If we can create a positive ripple of events after tonight, then no. We may be exonerated. And you're wrong, I know you won't kill me because you're a logical man: there aren't many of us left."

Atlas laughed. "Most people would have said *honorable*, not logical."

"Most people are idiots who do not know that even honorable people can do terrible things. Wearing a badge of honor is just a guise and an excuse to help a man go to bed at night. In our world, logic, rationality, patience, and common sense are the true virtues of our kind. We have moved beyond all else because we can't afford to be bogged down by our sense of honor, charity, or even our morality. We have brought about our own demise: our species and even that of the Trentians is slowly dying out. We should do what we must, for the greater good, so that we strive to survive another day. We owe it to our future generations."

"Then that is where we differ in opinion, doctor, we owe it to ourselves to carve out a better future without forgetting about past transgressions. So was it worth it? Possibly committing treason?" Atlas found himself genuinely curious about the doctor's answer.

"Yes."

Interesting. "Why?"

"I would never have been given this opportunity otherwise. I never quite excelled beyond the best of my peers. Someone else would have been in my place if this was a sanctioned experiment, handled by the smartest in my field. It would never have been me. I guess I was lucky to be scheduled the day you arrived at my cybernetic lab. My job prior to this assignment was to stress cybernetic technology in variable atmospheres, different planetary environments."

"Luck or fate, we may never know. I am glad we encountered each other, doctor, even if our beginning was unfortunate. Any one of your peers could have been better in skill or technique but it doesn't mean they have integrity or honesty. I suppose we will disagree."

Atlas glanced back at his body, and his skin had begun to weave itself together, ever so slowly; the changes were imperceptible to a mere human. Yesne shifted on his chair, bringing Atlas's attention back toward the man. He watched as doctor fiddled with his glasses and ran his hand across his mouth.

"I'm a simple man."

"Aren't we all?"

"I would have done anything to get on this ship. I would have lied. I did lie." The doctor took a shaky breath.

Atlas froze. "Lie?"

"I was a cybernetic scientist who never had contact with a real Cyborg, nor a Neoborg. And this ship." He looked around. "This ship and Captain Reina's condition and the only Cyborg that had fully merged with the network, you, was on it. I would have done anything. You didn't need a doctor to join you. I saw an opportunity and took it and exaggerated her condition in my reports."

Atlas glared at the man. "That took courage. But you proved my theory."

"Theory?" Yesne asked.

"That no one in the cybernetics division can be trusted."

Yesne lifted the edge of his lab coat and wiped his glasses, keeping his eyes downcast.

"Was is worth it for you–scratch that, that's a stupid question..."

"Go on."

Yesne leaned back against the wall. "Does she know? Have you told her?"

"No," Atlas clipped.

"Quite a shock."

The conversation died as an extended, introspective silence descended between the two of them. It could have been awkward if their minds weren't consumed with thoughts. Atlas, once again, looked down at his body. His chest moved as his lungs sucked in shallow breaths. That small spark of life meant more to him than all his years of living a half-life.

"Are you ready?"

Atlas smirked. "I have been ready since the day my heart erupted."

Yesne warily got back on his feet and joined him at the opened cryostasis pod. "As you already know, it will be excruciating. The drip has very strong painkillers to help ease the torment but like all things with your kind, your body is constantly fighting off the drugs." The doctor checked the tubes. "Will you have enough time to integrate before I am dropped off at the port?"

"Safely? Possibly. Regardless of the battle my cells are about to wage, I'm certain I will survive. I don't like losing. Forging an artificial heart was a smart move. Metal is easier to control and I'll be immensely less vulnerable although immensely less human."

The doctor probed the tissue on his body. "I thought so too. Well, you have more courage than I. I have also covered all gaps to your central organs. As long as you don't need to go under the knife again, the extra plating should serve to protect you, and you won't have to worry about another part getting destroyed by a lucky shot."

178

"It wasn't a lucky shot," Atlas said cryptically as he brushed his holographic fingers over the healing wound.

The doctor didn't ask what he meant, possibly too tired to care, and that was okay with Atlas. That moment in his life brought out his anger and resentment. His willingness to just give into that insanity he was often fighting off, only to have it echo back in the closed channels of the network.

But the doctor asked a question anyway. "Will you do me a favor?"

"What?"

"If you choose to seek revenge against those that have wronged you, please warn me. Give me a chance to go underground," Yesne pleaded with him warily.

"My revenge depends entirely on Captain Reina, so if you have faith in her then you should know what the future holds for you. Until then, you will be released onto Antix. Neither Reina or I will stop you and it will be up to you to choose what you do with the information that you have learned here."

The doctor's lips twitched. "I have faith in the girl. But that just makes me all the more curious." Yesne lifted his head to match his gaze directly. "Why have you not told her about this? I don't believe she would have stopped this from happening."

Atlas frowned, unwilling to answer that question. His reasons were his own, whether his decision to keep it from her was right or not.

She keeps men at a distance... but she doesn't keep me away because she feels safe with me.

Atlas was afraid to break the progress he had made with Reina. *She may fear me when I am whole or lose the fragile trust we have built between us.* With their potential deaths in the near future, he wasn't willing to risk what he had with her.

He could very well go insane, his body may reject the implant, or he could die. Why give her one more thing to worry about, one more possibility of hope, a promise he may not be able to keep, only to fail once again?

He kept his secret as much for himself as he did for her. *She'll only know me when I can be sure the real me is what I can give her.*

Without giving Yesne an answer, Atlas responded, "I think it's time."

"I will get some sleep then."

He watched as the man left, the door opening and closing quietly through his passage. Yesne had not been a prisoner of the ship since his first day onboard.

Atlas paired back with his body.

No one heard as he screamed at the walls inside his head, as he felt the pain of retaking control of his form for the first time in seventy-five years, fifteen hours, fifty-two minutes, and eighteen seconds.

Chapter Fourteen:

· · · ·

Her head was filled with cobwebs. Reina tried hard throughout the night to stay out of the network, and even harder to stay out of her dreams, but it proved a daunting task that left her feeling unrested.

At one point in her dream, she had found herself back inside the upscale hotel spaceport bar, once again with a drink in her hand, and the clarity of the prior dream came back to her, knowing the man who had joined her before was actually Atlas, and that he had joined her inside her subconscious.

He's been watching me from the beginning. The thought shouldn't have put her at ease but oddly enough it did. She liked knowing that she truly wasn't alone. It gave her a different perspective on things.

But he hadn't shown up in her head this past night and she wondered if it was because of her desperation to control her actions. Reina had tried hard to compartmentalize the power she now had.

She had sat at that imaginary bar and kept her eyes trained forward, refusing to acknowledge anything beyond her immediate environment, even ignoring the shadow-like beings that fluttered behind her and conversed. She had even tried to ignore the drink the bartender put in front of her.

Perhaps Atlas was with me, just watching me from the background. Maybe he was waiting for me to look. I should have looked.

I could have turned around and stolen kisses from him; I could have pretended it was real for a short time.

Reina mused over her regrets as she stood before the tall mirror in her lavatory, her eyes lazily inspecting her body. She had slept but she didn't feel rested. She didn't even think she *looked* rested.

She leaned forward and rested her forehead against the glass, letting her metalloid arm hang limply at her side, too tired to even work the muscles to lift it. Reina eyed the fog that clouded her reflection where her breath hit the surface.

The Council hadn't responded yet. She swiped her hand over the lavatory's control panel, changing the interface, and rechecked for any communications. Nothing. She wasn't looking forward to their response and secretly hoped that it wouldn't get to them before they left Antix. At least then she could pretend she never received it.

Being off the grid did have some benefits. She smiled to herself.

The strange electrical currents that traveled through her body whenever her bare skin met the ship were beginning to feel normal. She was even learning to enjoy it; the effect was slightly arousing, given Atlas's presence in the ship. It made her aching and wanting and in desperate need to climax. Reina left the bathroom and eyed the tousled sheets on her bed, wishing her steely Cyborg navigator were lounging on them waiting for her, his cock hard, impossibly large, and erect... just waiting for her to seat herself on it.

Her body flushed as she pictured herself riding him. His rod stretching her as she used him like a toy, his hands gripping her hips, keeping her thrusts wild and steady as she began to tire on top of him. Until exhaustion took over and he began to use *her* like a toy.

Reina could feel the quiver between her legs as her body began to prepare her for a fuck that wasn't going to happen. She closed her eyes and tried to will it away. Ten minutes of agonizing meditation later, her fingers strumming over her clit, a very unsatisfying orgasm finally shot through her. She sprawled back over her bed.

She kept her eyes closed shut as she caught her breath before she slowly opened them, expecting Atlas to be standing over her watching her pleasure herself. She wanted him to watch her, and know that she ached because of him and only for him.

But he wasn't there. Reina got up and went to the unit still placed in the center of her room. It was turned on.

"Good morning, Atlas," she said breathlessly and smiled. Reina waited but there was no answer.

"Atlas?" Still no response.

Where is he?

Annoyance etched her features as she watched the unit for another brief moment before she turned and slipped on her flight suit, her actions tinged with a sense of uncertainty.

Reina headed for the ship's lounge after one last glance around her room.

Several minutes later, she was sitting at the central table with a mug of terrible instant coffee in her hand. *Why do I feel strange?* She tapped her fingers on the table, the soft thuds the only sound around her.

Had she scared him off? It's not like Atlas to ignore her call.

Reina couldn't help but think the walls her mind had painstakingly crafted the night before had shut him out without her realization. Questions raced through her mind, all of them central to her sexy sentient intelligence, and it was only made worse by the heavy silence that clouded around her head. Even the soft patter of her fingertips felt suppressed under the weight.

Just when she thought she couldn't take it anymore, the click of footsteps broke the bubble and Yesne walked through the door.

"Good morning, Captain."

"Good morning, doctor." She took a sip of her drink as Yesne replicated a mug of "coffee" for himself and joined her.

"Did you sleep well?" he asked.

"I did," she lied. "You?"

"Quite so."

An awkward silence drifted between them and Reina wished for the return of her lonely, oppressive silence. Together they calmly drank their coffee.

Atlas had yet to make an appearance.

She lifted her eyes to face the doctor and noticed, for the first time, how tired and drawn he looked. He appeared to have lost the slight pudge around his frame.

"Yesne. Are you okay? Are you sick? You don't look so good."

"I'm fine, Captain. I get lost in my work sometimes and the physical result is always the same. I'll bounce back." He smiled.

Reina realized she had no idea what the doctor had been up to. "What work is that? I can't imagine monitoring my processes could have done this to you."

Just then the familiar zing and soft blue light filtered through the room.

"Oh, just this and that. A ship of this nature has never sailed the stars under Earthian command before," Yesne replied. Atlas's projection appeared next to them, standing over their table, oddly menacing. Yesne continued to talk. "There was a fair amount of unique data to collect under the emergency warp and the technical events leading up to the attack. Did you know the protocols for initiating fire never went into effect? That must mean you have more power over the ship's processes than those that have been built in." The doctor went on but Reina's attention was on her Cyborg.

She released a breath she didn't realize she had been holding as their eyes met, and his flashed with a hard possessive glint that was unusual for his perceived, calculated appearance.

He looks more human...he looks angry. What the hell happened?

Reina instinctively reached out and pushed a chair back, giving him the option to join them at the table. It was then, when he held her gaze with a transfixed darkness that she realized Yesne had stopped talking and both men were staring at her.

"Are you okay, Reina?" Atlas asked.

She blinked hard and looked down at her hands. "Yes. Sorry, I got lost in my head again."

"Thank you for offering me a seat, but I think I'll stand if you don't mind." His voice harsh yet soft. Reina looked up at him when he continued to speak. There was a tightness to his form, almost as if he was willing himself to look normal. "We're now about one Earth rotation away from Antix. There has been no activity near us since yesterday's warp. Our network connections have begun to fail, so I won't be able to give an accurate reading on any long term or far distant trajectory pathways. At this point, if we happen to break down or get attacked, we may very well be on our own."

Reina sipped her coffee. "What are the odds of our mission deviating from the current timeline?"

"About even."

"That's just great. That doesn't help." She sighed.

"Like I said, we're progressively going dark." He responded evenly.

"We still have a strong connection to Antix. We'll shift over and use their relays from here on out. I'm going to try and reach the Council one last time before we disconnect. It doesn't make sense to try and retain our frequency to the main channels when we can bolster our connections to the middling ones. At least that way, any communication we make through their systems will *eventually* get to the main hub, even if it's delayed." Reina looked over at the doctor, who was silently staring into his empty cup. "Are you ready for port? Our superiors have been pressing me on your data logs and reports not being regular or on time. Will you be able to finish them and have an accurate backlog to send them when you reconnect?"

Yesne wiped his glasses over the vest of his flight suit. Reina tried not to look back over at Atlas but she knew he was watching her out of the corner of her eyes. His perusal burned.

Always in my periphery.

"I will have everything ready for the cybernetics department today. I apologize that I have grown lax in my reporting—"

"—I just want to make sure it wasn't because of my rehabilitation, my mutation," she said the last part under her breath.

"No, not at all. I have just been occupied with this vessel. I don't travel through space often and have never dreamed of doing so on a living machine." He coughed. "It has been a vacation."

Reina laughed. "If you say so. At least we'll have a great view."

The silence descended again and it was all the more poignant as it engulfed the three of them. Reina could feel the sizzling tension between her and Atlas; it didn't help that he was watching her like he wanted to consume her.

His eyes bore into her in a way that made her want to crawl out of her skin.

She couldn't stop the red flush spreading over her cheeks as she thought of the performance she put on for him this morning. Or the empty, begging ache that pulsed between her legs at the thought of his steel cock pistoning into her.

Why do I keep going there? It's not like it's ever going to happen between us. She felt herself getting frustrated and pushed the thoughts of sex away.

Today was the last day before the real darkness began. Everyone could feel it; everything was coming to a head. The silence became suffocating.

Reina looked down at her hands as a tiny flash of fear shot through her.

My hands are shaking...?

• • • •

SOMETIME LATER REINA found herself sitting at the helm of her ship, shuffling through the holographic screens of data that relayed the ship's systems. Everything down to the warp drive, the nutrient packets and proteins for the food replicator, and even the water recycling system as well as all daily resource usage. A fair amount of power had been running through the medical bay systems, including some of the chemical supplies.

But she had assumed it was Yesne running data analysis, and she knew she should have investigated further but the thought of being examined like a lab-rat, or worse, a *thing* kept her away.

Reina shook the thoughts away, focusing on the ship's subsystems. The screens filled her vision but she could still see beyond them to her slightly skewed panoramic view of space.

Nothing but black lay before her, broken up by countless, barely discernable star clusters billions of miles away. It was hard to see the beauty of it anymore when she looked at it so often.

"You've been so quiet today," she half whispered to herself.

Atlas's laser lights flickered on around her, his projection appearing in the room.

Reina continued, "Is there something wrong? Have I done something wrong?"

His steely voice filled her ears, the prickle of goosebumps shot up her body. "No. Everything is fine." That was it. The few words she could get out of him sounded so forced.

Should I say more? Push for answers? Reina retained her blank façade as her mind wandered. Her heart sobered. She didn't know how to make a real connection to another living being. She feared that she had ruined things with Atlas with her emotional outburst.

I want him back in my head. Her teeth pinched her tongue. She had always felt lonely but now she felt hollow as well.

The screen flashed back before her, interrupting her thoughts. Dr. Yesne had uploaded and placed his reports on pending to be sent when they were fully connected to Antix.

The clock was ticking and Reina knew she had more to do than merely monitor the systems and think about the intimidatingly possessive hologram that stood nearby.

Reina initiated contact with the Council, putting her hand on the console and forcibly trying to make a connection to the network. Finding and sustaining one was hard, bolstering it with her own internal battery left her breathless, but it worked. Seeing the Earthian Council standby screen appear proved they weren't fully into the woods yet.

General Wasson's face blocked out the view of space. She took a deep breath.

"Good day, Lieutenant General."

"Good day to you as well, Captain."

Reina tipped her head slightly forward in respect. "We are less than twenty hours from our destination of Port Antix, sir. Dr. Yesne had just uploaded his research and final report into the channels. It can be retrieved anytime." She continued, trying to be quick in case the connection failed, "My health has stabilized since he boarded. Thank you for loaning him to me, I've found him very capable." Groveling was not something she was good at but she would try if it kept this conversation from taking a turn for the worse.

Wasson looked away from the screen as he appeared to be reading the file beyond her view. "Very good work here, Captain. The doctor's report suggests complete recovery and that there has been no relapse since he came on board. He even mentions that you have more control over the vessel now and can control it remotely?"

"Yes, sir. I find that every day I am taking a more organic, cybernetic approach to the ship. It has been..." Reina paused. "An alien experience."

"I'm sure it has, which is one of the reasons Atlas was assigned to you. Not every mind can handle the complexities and transcendence of biomechatronics. Especially when the mind wasn't born into it." He sounded like he spoke from experience. She wanted to delve further but he continued. "Dr. Estond and your original team of doctors worked extensively—for many years—with Atlas. But as you must be aware, I

190

am more interested in this tracker you picked up outside of Taggert's orbit. It says here that you neutralized the threat, preventing intrusive scans into your ship's systems, and that the vessel was uncategorized–possibly a private, scavenger, or marauder?"

Reina cleared her throat. "Yes, general, the ship was old-tech according to Atlas and unidentifiable but had strong Earthian characteristics. I did not see it myself. With his help and under my authority, we thought it prudent to lose the tracker in case it was a scout for a larger threat that could jeopardize the mission."

"Why did you think staying to investigate the incident would jeopardize anything? A single ship is like a grain of sand compared to the hardware you have at your disposal." His reprimand was evident. "A direct warp to another galaxy was more likely to fail this mission than one rover."

"I understand, sir, but–"

He cut her off. "I understand the situation as well, Captain Reina, and I wasn't there but I'm not happy with the reckless choices you have made. The only thing that has stopped me from issuing your return and finding a more suitable candidate to take over is Atlas. If he calculated the situation to be dangerous, then I trust it was. You may continue as planned but you will not take further risks with that ship."

A new candidate to take over so they can die from mutation? She thought angrily but kept it to herself.

"We believe the scout was one from Larik's syndicate. And based on my experience with his underground force, and with my faith in Atlas's navigational skills, I green-lit the warp." Reina lied. Regardless of the chain of events, it *was* her responsibility and she *was* the captain.

Wasson pinned her with a dagger-like gaze that could be felt from several billion miles away. He sat stoically in his command office, stationed on one of the private space-bases floating outside Earth's atmosphere.

"Do not make any more rash decisions, Reina." Foregoing her title. "You have not even reached the checkpoint yet." His warning was loud and clear.

She squeezed the handle of her arm rest. *Does he know something? His judgment killed the last two captains of this ship.*

Reina couldn't think like that.

"Yes, sir," she appeased, "I will do everything in my power to complete this mission. It is my responsibility and I promise to shed light on what has happened to our countless lost people. I will return with answers." She tried to believe it herself but the darkness of space only seemed to get darker every day.

Wasson sat back. "That is what I like to hear. Now, there is a team of five men currently stationed at Antix, led by Sergeant Kraig. They are expecting your arrival, and we have received verification on our end that they have begun preparation in setting up the new network tech out there. When you arrive, their chief engineer will relieve you of your cargo for the installation. You are to remain until it is complete and operational."

"Yes, sir."

"The Council expects a constant image feed to be kept and logged once you go dark–we hope with the new relays that you won't vanish without being able to broadcast what causes it."

There was a short expectant pause.

"You may encounter a graveyard out there."

* * * *

THEY WERE CLEARED FOR landing and Reina could feel the gravity shift, continuously changing throughout her ship.

She was a space-girl, not a land dweller, and thought unenthusiastically of the flat grey slate field that was coming ever closer to her view. The only positive things about this planet were the lack of vegetation and no uneven landscape that could impede a clean arrival.

Reina tied her hair back for the third time.

"Something doesn't feel right. I don't want you going down there alone." Atlas appeared next to her.

"I won't be alone. Yesne will be with me."

"Some consolation. You know what I mean."

"No. I don't know what you mean. Who else could accompany me? It's not like you can." She snapped, instantly feeling guilty for her outburst. Atlas turned to face her and she caught his eye. "I'm sorry. I didn't mean that. I'm just stressed. I'm sure you were monitoring the conversation I just had with the general."

"If you wait–even a day, I can come with you. Lock up the ship and pretend you're sick."

Reina rubbed her face, her lips twitched into a small smile. "Hah. It's safe. We have clearance and they are expecting us. If you had a problem with it, you should have voiced your concerns sooner. Or extended the route to get here." She laughed as his face went hard and his eyes narrowed. *Maybe I shouldn't tease him?* "I'm sorry again," she murmured.

Just then they breached the planet's thermosphere, quickly descending toward their marker.

"I would forgive you anything. But I know you can feel it too, things are off."

"Between us? You didn't answer me this morning."

"There is nothing off between us." He smiled down at her, it almost eased her mind. "I didn't hear your call. I was preoccupied."

"Preoccupied with what?"

His mouth twisted into a promising, dark smirk. "It's a surprise."

She sighed. "Hopefully one that won't get us killed?"

"I can't promise anything." He said with a wink.

Reina shot him an annoyed look before she walked out of the bridge and into the utility hold. She pulled out an exosuit and went to configure it for Antix, only to find that Atlas had already prepped it.

"Thank you," she mumbled while she tugged it over her uniform.

"Anything for your safety." He had followed her in. "In this side panel is an earpiece, connected to the ship's servers. Please wear it so I can monitor and talk to you. The servers within this port appear to be underground and the security system wired throughout is not one with many windows for me to see or hear through. My quick perusal also showed quite a few dead spots."

"You breached their security?"

"I did when I could securely connect. I don't do anything blindly."

"Then I don't know why you should feel uneasy. We haven't heard or seen another outlier since before the warp."

"Then why is their security broken?"

Reina looked back at Atlas then, feeling his need to be with her in this, and she could almost imagine him holding her hand and surrounding her frame with his powerful body. She was being crazy but she felt a connection between them that went beyond the physical. She also felt a little bit wistful, wishing he could keep his word and accompany her into port.

"I don't need protection from my colleagues but I will wear the earpiece. It may come in handy if I need to talk to you on the sly." She smiled up at him, trying to be flirty, before she located the small bauble, turned it on and placed it in her ear.

"Reina," Atlas's voice went to steel, he crowded in front of her. "This doesn't feel right. It's hard to explain. It's hard to even admit. I don't want you to fucking leave the ship. I can't make you stay, and if I could, I would. Just wait this out, we'll contact that fucker Wasson, and you can stay on board." He turned from her, then turned back, his movements jerky and imperfect. "Fuck, if only I could touch you. If only I knew everything would be okay."

She tried to reach and touch him only to find her fingers swimming inside his chest. "I can't wait. You heard Wasson's warning." Reina stepped back and caught his eye. "I wish I could touch you too."

Atlas didn't respond but just stared down at her, and held her eyes–it was the closest they could come in contact. His digital gaze heated as she waited with bated breath for him to say something. "Atlas?"

His hand reached out between them and glided over her cheek, his fingertips breezing across her parted lips with a quiet desperation. The almost-touch was too hard to handle and Reina could feel a heavy weight bear down on her heart.

"Tell me why I should wait? What are you not saying?"

"How desperately, incredibly painfully this need to touch you is. I'm going crazy for it. I'm willing to risk everything for it. Anything for it." He took a step closer to her.

Reina almost regretted asking, knowing they didn't have time to talk nor deal with this right now. She regretted asking because now her head would be consumed with him when she should be solely focused on the mission.

"Atlas..."

"Don't. I know. I'm being protective, possessive, and I don't want you to leave this ship. If I had it my way, you would never step outside this ship and away from me again. Never without me by your side." His projection flickered. Reina narrowed her eyes. *That has never happened before.* "Keep the earpiece on and I'll feel somewhat better about all of this. Stay connected to the ship and I'll be there waiting. Come back as soon as you can. Come back and fall into my arms."

She took a deep breath. "I will. I promise." As the ship entered the atmosphere, she felt her body grow heavy. "And you know, I can protect myself. I've made it this far in the military in one piece. I can also use a gun." Reina grinned. "Watch out."

Yesne walked through the door, interrupting their conversation. He was dragging a plastic duffle bag behind him. His body sank from the effort.

Sleep will never catch up with that man.

"What's this about a gun?" he asked tiredly.

Reina clipped one to her belt. "Only that I can use one."

"I should be thankful for my life then!" The last breath of energy left him. They finished gearing up and headed for the hatch. Reina integrated with her exosuit unconsciously, connecting her helmet to seal over her face.

The ship settled smoothly onto the flat rock of the planet.

"Ready, doctor?"

"Yes, Captain." She watched as he turned to Atlas, who had followed them to the exit. "Good luck, Cyborg. I don't suppose it will be much longer now."

He flickered once again. "No, and if I had it my way I would be joining the two of you planetside."

What? Does this have something to do with the surprise? He could possess an android but we don't have any. The ship...only drones. Reina looked between them.

"You may well yet." Yesne turned toward the exit. "That would be quite thrilling." He stepped out when the hatch opened for him. She turned to join him outside, needing the fake space between her and Atlas.

"Reina, why did you call out for me this morning?" Atlas asked into her earpiece.

"For sex."

She stepped out and was greeted by a grey and black wasteland. Atlas's groan filtered through her ear and for a few minutes, it lifted her mood.

Chapter Fifteen:

. . . .

Atlas fell back into his body for another stretch of nerve-shattering torture. His nanocells were fighting the implants and new wiring, as well as trying to heal him all at the same time.

He seized on the slab. It felt like a thousand needles in his chest twisting and prodding out from the new heart.

He fought through the pain because the endgame was worth the agony.

Although there were some moments, seconds, microseconds where his thoughts shattered and his mind would go blank, static-fuzz, and sizzling, Atlas fought to retain who he was in those moments as he became his own worst enemy. Even the added help of the immunosuppressants could not conquer a cybernetic system.

Reina's face would come to mind, banishing his internal chaos, and replacing it with *want*. Her eyes vulnerable and yet strong with reserved fortitude. His want was so intense it would make the agony feel like pleasure. Atlas was certain his body hardened–uncontrolled–with his wanting that he had ejaculated more times than he could count. And he was good at numbers.

His cum was thick and sticky over his bare legs and stomach. It didn't help that he imagined Reina perched on top of him and licking it up.

As time continued to pass, the pain became increasingly more pleasurable and when the euphoria took over, and he was able to center his strength on winning the battle over his body.

Atlas couldn't help but marvel as his senses returned slowly, rising to make themselves known over the pain in his chest. The sticky and semi-dried cum on his body, the cold metal cryostasis slab beneath him, and the increasingly rancid septic-stench in the air was bliss.

Feeling, smelling, tasting anything felt like a shockwave of sensation straight to his brain.

I need this to go faster dammit. I need to win.

He willed his body to heal, adapt to the changes, and integrate. His woman was walking away from him, was slowly making her way toward the facility. One filled with unknown men who probably hadn't had a woman in months. Atlas could lose her to one of them.

What's there to keep a beautiful woman tied to a holographic image and a fake voice when she could have the real thing?

If it weren't for her entering his life, he would have never risked thawing his body. Not unless he had the state-of-the-art equipment and qualified men and women to rebuild it.

Every fiber of his being demanded he rise up and go after her, drag her back to the ship, and keep her confined in these metallic walls with him forever. She would be safe within the shackles of his arms.

His thoughts shifted. *What will her skin feel like?* Atlas rubbed his aching, sweaty fingers together. *Soft and smooth? Taut and velvety? Will her hair slide through my fingers like water?*

I want to smell her...taste her...feel her under me. I need to hear her moans in my ear. The need to feel her consumed him and he pushed his systems to their limits.

Atlas slowly folded his arms up beside him and lifted his torso off the table. The ripping, stretching, and very alien metallic heart shot electric pain throughout his chest.

Is this what Reina felt with her arm? His upper body was heavier with the added metal. He mentally reconfigured his balance.

Atlas lifted his eyelids next; his retinas were dry and cold but he was able to focus on his surroundings. His cybercells helped keep a migraine from forming behind his eyes.

I'm alive.

He gasped for breath. It dawned on him then when his eyes cleared after what seemed like an eternity that he had a raging hard-on, his shaft engorged and sticking straight up.

Atlas fell back onto the table with a grin.

Progress.

• • • •

SHE COULD SEE THE ENTRANCE just up ahead, across the slick rock beds that looked eroded by years of heavy, unrelenting wind. The wind, in fact, was the reason their trek was taking so long. It fought them with every step, pushing them back the way they had come.

Yesne was barely holding up. He had dropped his bag several times. They managed a few more steps, every one a battle, before she reached over and grabbed the handle of his luggage with him. Together they continued to their the destination.

They couldn't talk, their voices lost in the shrieking gusts of air and dust.

Where is everyone?

And just like that, with a few short steps away from the large concrete gate, a pervasive tendril of foreboding snaked into her head.

Yesne dropped the bag, it slipping out of her hand at the same time, and rested his body against the manmade wall. Reina strengthened her connection to her ship and brought it back to life slowly, subtly to standby.

"Atlas, chart us a route off the planet, I won't be staying here longer than necessary," Reina wheezed out.

"*Arrhemm.*" A garbled groan was her only answer. Her eyes narrowed at the disconnect.

She took a deep breath and stood before the intercom console. *I'm probably just being paranoid.* A yellow laser shot out and scanned her face.

"*Processing. Please hold. Welcome to Port Antix, Captain Reynolds.*" The yellow light shifted to green and the door slid into the ceiling. Yesne joined her and together they stepped into the station. A dank passageway with strung-up light orbs met them. It led to another door down the hall.

The entry sealed behind them. "*Initiating decontamination. Hold. Initiating air filtration. Hold.*" Vents opened up above them and released a cloud of milky gas that settled over them before immediately vaporizing. The rest of the murk was sucked back into the walls until everything was back to normal. *"Hold. You may relieve yourself of your exosuits now."*

Fuck that.

Yesne apparently agreed with her sentiment as he made his way to the second door without disrobing. "Well, this is welcoming," the doctor murmured beside her.

Reina lowered her voice in answer, "Where is everyone, you think? Atlas mentioned the facility was quiet but this," she hesitated, "is not standard protocol."

"Quite. I agree with you. It's best we stay sharp." Yesne stopped and looked back at the entryway. "Unless you want to break protocol as well and make a run back to the ship?"

Reina leaned her mouth into her shoulder, covering her voice. "Atlas, can you scout the station's security again?" she asked, holding the doctor's gaze. They waited but there was no answer from the Cyborg. "Atlas?"

"What's wrong?"

"He's not answering." She reached down and palmed the sidearm on her utility belt–a standard issue laser piece. Reina nodded at Yesne and they turned back, ready to take their chances back out in the open. But their decision to retreat came a minute too late.

Two men in Earthian Space Fleet uniforms entered the passageway. "Captain Reina, Doctor Yesne, welcome. We've been expecting you."

Reina turned toward them carefully, and in a split-second moment of judgment, she knew these men led rougher lives than just maintaining an outskirt facility.

Their expressions were just as guarded as hers but with the added grooves that indicated rough work. She found herself hoping that it was truly from the stress of being stationed out in the middle of nowhere and not from something more sinister.

A static crackle sounded through the earpiece. *"Get out of there. The station has been compromised. The servers locked up when you walked into that hole."*

Great timing, Cyborg. She maintained her easy aura with a modicum of strain, but her heart raced from the inevitable immediate future. Her hand shot forward to shake theirs in greeting.

"Sergeant Kraig, I assume?"

"Kraig has been called away to deal with a comm issue. I am Officer Black and this is Jux." The man had a hard voice to him. "If you would follow us." Officer Black tried to usher them through but she held firm.

I'm not letting you get behind me, asshole.

"Are you the chief engineer?" She looked at the one called Jux. "We were told to expect not only Sergeant Kraig but the engineer as well for delivery." Reina played for time. Black's face went hard as she continued to stand her ground.

Atlas's voice fizzled again quietly through the bauble. *"I'm working on the servers. I can't get back on their security until then."* His steady voice did little to reassure her.

My weapon has its safety on. Yesne is unarmed and very tired. Should I risk it? The gun felt heavier the longer she debated their options.

"The chief engineer is outside prepping for import."

"That's strange. I didn't see him nor another ship out there." Reina thought back to their trek, the side of her arm rubbed against her pistol.

Officer Black chided, "That is strange, Captain, seein' as it would be hard to miss. Maybe you should get your eyes checked." He rounded his arm around her back and her hand fell to her gun.

Atlas's voice stopped her– *"Reina, don't do anything stupid. I'm coming for you."*

She let the man escort her from the decontamination hallway. The other thug began to lead Yesne away.

"Wait!" Reina casually smoothed her hair back, taking the piece out of her ear, and approached the doctor. "Thank you for your service and your assistance, Dr. Yesne." She took his hand in a mock shake and transferred the tech to him. "I will send the Council my recommendation." Their eyes held as he slipped the unit into his exosuit.

Officer Black took her gun and used it to lead her down to the bowels of the spaceport.

● ● ● ●

ATLAS COULD HEAR EVERYTHING. He was uncertain before, but now, losing his signal to Antix when Reina walked in enraged him.

I should have made her stay. What kind of Cyborg am I? His failings flooded his mind. He roared from the floor of the lab, his body coated in sweat. His internal wiring prickled with electrical shocks. *I let her walk into a trap.* It was his fault his girl was in danger and now Reina was surrounded by unfamiliar armed men.

He crawled across the cold, slick floor, forcing his body to work. He demanded it go past its limits and heal. His cybercells and blood coursed through his veins at a dangerous speed.

She's surrounded by men.

She's afraid of losing control.

She's a fucking Neoborg.

Atlas gripped the tubes still attached to his body and pulled them out, disconnecting the cords from his metal frame, and unchained himself for the first time since his death. Naked, he pulled himself up, straining to get his feet under his heavy body. *So much heavier than I fucking remember.* His muscles screamed in agony, and inhuman, unearthly agony that only the dead returning to the life could understand.

"Reina, don't do anything stupid." He gritted his teeth. "I'm coming for you." Still no answer, no indication that she heard.

He half crawled, half stumbled his way to the stairs that led to the medical bay above him. His fingers sank into the metal steps as he hoisted himself up, landing on his back with a ragged breath when he reached the top. With a one-track mind, he tore open the sealed drug panel, ripping the metal from the wall. Atlas found the console and forced the replicator within to create the strongest painkiller he could think of. Then he created boosters, and with a moment of hesitation, he synthesized methamphetamine.

The Council is going to have a fucking field day when they review the replicator logs.

I need to get to Reina.

Atlas grabbed the drugs and dragged himself to the lavatory. Within minutes he was drinking the pills down and shooting the drugs up his arm. Several needles shattered in his grip before he had had enough. Glass sliced his tips but he could no longer feel them.

He willed his body to not fight off the foreign substances, focusing less on the battle in his chest and focused more on morphing the drugs to suit his current needs.

Atlas leaned back against the cold wall of the sterile bathroom while a sour feeling of overdrive took him over. The exquisite rush of life washed over him. He pulled himself over to the faucet and drowned himself with fluids, flooding his biological organs with water.

"Reina, I'm coming," he moaned. "Don't do anything stupid. I'm coming."

He took a deep breath feeling the air fill his lungs, feeling his lungs press into his alien heart. He shot to his feet. His muscles bulged as he found the energy he needed to run to the armory. Atlas continually forgot his strength as he tore doors out of the crisp walls. The first gun he picked up snapped in half.

"I'm coming, sweetheart," he chanted to himself and to his weak connection to the earpiece.

"Atlas? Is that you?"

Atlas paused, accidently ripping the Kevlar body armor in his hands. "Yesne? Where is Reina?"

"We were separated. They have me locked in a room, behind walls I can't hear through. We tried to leave but were stopped, I don't think the men stationed here work for the Earthian military."

"No shit. The communication from the network to Antix shut off when you guys entered. The servers housed here are now freshly armored with privately built firewalls."

"Hack it, you're a Cyborg, isn't that what you do?"

"I can't," Atlas grated, carefully picking up a new suit of armor mesh. With increasing control over his strength as he recalibrated his systems, he smoothly picked up several daggers to strap to his harness then placed a couple guns into his empty holsters. "I'm not designed to be a hacker. I don't have the software and even if I could, I haven't had a software update since I fell."

"So how are you going to get us out of here? The entryway is sealed shut by metal and concrete."

The ship was humming softly around him, Reina shifted it into standby mode not long ago. Atlas wanted to channel through her wireless connection but he was afraid of the consequence of leaving his struggling body without a mind.

"I have an idea." Atlas punched a hole through the metal bulkhead that locked up the big stuff. An array of mini-rockets, cannons, and grenades greeted him along with a full stock of laser batteries, plasmic capsules, and even Pyrizian bullets. He settled on an explosive grenade and a double-chamber hydrochloric and sulfuric acid bomb.

I will raze it to the ground.

He quickly fed off the power flowing through the ship. *Feel me, sweetheart.*

Chapter Sixteen:

• • • •

Reina sat across a table, stripped of all her remaining gear, her exosuit, and even her boots. She was still in her under clothes and was thankful for that. Officer Black sat before her, his jaw twitching sporadically.

He's impatient. That was a double-edged sword for this situation. A man with a jaw tick was a man who didn't know he needed to be on meds. She assessed everything but came up with little. *There are two men behind me, silent. No sign of guns on Black's person. Walls are thick. It's cold.*

It's also quiet.

"Who else is on the ship?" Black asked.

Everything echoes.

"No one."

"Our scans read a third life-form. Who is on the ship?"

There's a grate in the floor.

Reina shivered. "No one is on the ship." Atlas wasn't a life-form. She wouldn't give him up anyway, even if he was. He was their best chance of getting a message to the Council.

The man behind her slithered his long fingers into her hair. She jerked from the contact just as he slammed her head forward into the table. The impact smashed her nose. Reina briefly lost her head to the shock, vaguely aware of the hand still on her head, palming and petting her.

It pulled her back into her seat. Rivulets of blood trickled down from her nostrils.

"Again. Who is on the ship?"

"No one, you classless piece of space-scum," she hissed. Her wrists strained against the shackles behind her. The copper tang of her blood flooded her mouth.

Black kept his eyes on her. "Jessup, go outside with your men and apprehend whoever she's willing to die for."

Reina licked her lips. *Good luck with that*, she thought dryly. *Atlas will love the company. I'm glad I gave him weapons access.* She wiped her messed up face against her shoulder to hide the smirk.

"You're going to get your men killed." Reina egged him on.

Black tapped his fingers on the table. "I have no problem hitting women, especially cunts like you. I'll make a deal with you." He nodded to the remaining guard behind her. "Give us what we want and we'll forego the torture." The chill of someone standing directly behind her back made her feel colder. Whoever it was, didn't emanate heat. They were cold. *An alien.*

Black continued, "You see, we have collateral and cunts talk when their protective instincts come out. You're protecting whoever is hiding on that ship and let's not forget the doctor." He reached forward and cupped the back of her neck. "We will do whatever is necessary to them to make you talk."

Reina barely heard him, and could only focus on the Trentian male who stood directly behind her. Her heart began to race and all of the sudden she was back on the *Credence*, in the hallway, staring up at the two alien men who had Hell in their eyes and wanted her to join them in that dark place. The urge to run began to outweigh the urge to fight.

"She's giving you the silent treatment." The unmistakable soft dialect of his species sent chills down her spine. The feeling was akin to swallowing icicles whole. Reina focused her eyes away from Black and to the wall behind him, grey and rusted with age.

The flash of a knife brought her back. An inch away from her eyes, the edge serrated and sharp. Black moved to sit on the table directly in front of her. Her gaze was now leveled with his crotch.

Reina looked up at him. "What do you really want? Ask the questions you actually care to know." She could barely form the words. "You wouldn't go through all this trouble, commit an act of war, just for me and my ship."

He leered down at her. "You nearly killed me. I'm the best scout in his convoy, with state of the art cloaking auras. I've never been fucking detected before. How did you do it?"

"You won't like the truth." Reina leered back. "I did it while I was sleeping." She pulled her wrists apart, feeling a slight give in the cord, helped by the added strength of her bionic arm.

Black gripped her hair and pressed her face between his legs. She could feel the outline of his wormy prick grow hard against her cheek. Musty leather and the sour stench of unwashed clothes made her long for her blood to fill her nostrils again.

"Stupid military 'itch has never had a dirty cock like mine before." He laughed as he rubbed her swollen face over his hard-on. She could deal with assault, she could handle men, but she just didn't know how to handle the alien male behind her. Her fear wasn't from Black but from the enemy who stood quietly outside of her view.

She blanketed her mind from the assault and reached out to her ship, feeling it. Knowing it was there was almost like having it and Atlas with her, which helped her regain perspective of the situation.

Black released her head when he wasn't getting the reaction he wanted out of her. Reina began to feel her arm charge with energy, siphoning it from her weak connection to the ship. A zap hit her.

Atlas is here with me.

Time to end this. "I know what you want," she spat.

"Is that so, little mouse? You haven't graced us with a single answer yet. Maybe you'll give us what we need after you've had an unclean dick in your mouth." He laughed.

"I've had dirty cock before," she taunted. "Why don't we cut the crap because you could kill Yesne, you can torture me, and still walk away with nothing. You're just fucking afraid to ask."

"I'm curious. What do you think I want?"

"You want Larik." *At least she hoped he did.* "Release the doctor and I'll take you to him."

Reina watched as Black's only reaction was to slip the edge of the knife over his palm, drawing a beady red mark with slow droplets of blood appearing from the punctures. He grabbed her head and rubbed his cut over her mouth. "Cut her fingers off. Maybe she'll realize she's at our mercy and not the other way around... start with her fingertips and work your way down to the joints." Black handed the knife to the being behind her then leaned back to watch.

Her arms were yanked back and stretched painfully out. Her connection grew with desperation as the alien man touched her skin. Electrical, digital, desperate power coursed through her as the Trentian held her hand in place. The edge of the tainted knife sliced through her pinky finger.

And then it hit metal. Reina squeezed her eyes shut and tried not to cry out as the man began to saw it off.

"What the hell!?" She saw Black look at the man with wary interest. "There's fucking metal. This isn't bone." The alien released her hand.

That got his attention, she lost sight of him as he rounded behind her. "What do you mean metal?"

"There's no way that grey-glint is bone. She's a Cyborg, human, you fucked up."

Her arm was wrenched impossibly, painfully further back. Reina could feel the sting of her skin being flayed from her hand as they revealed her manmade appendage.

Her head slammed back into the table. "Where is Larik!?" One of them screamed in her ear. "Where is Larik?" they repeated.

Where is he? She gave Black a bloody smile.

"Why was a lone military ship flying outside Taggert's exosphere?"

"You'll never find him." It's not like she knew his exact location. If they knew that, she and Yesne were dead.

"We'll see how long you'll remain silent while we flay you down to your robot–" His voice was cut off by a loud explosion overhead, and the riotous crash of machinery as everything tumbled to the floor, including Reina and her arm.

• • • • •

ATLAS LEFT THE SHIP flanked by several dozen battle drones. His electric heart raced with adrenaline and the anxiety of battle.

His boots cracked the black slate rock of the planet as he ran toward the port. He powered through the gusts as the wind whipped around him, filling his eyes and nose with powdered dust and the stink of dried-up nature.

There were twelve men approaching from the entrance of the facility, heading his way. Atlas sent the drones on ahead of him as he cocked his guns. Soon the sound of their yells joined the wind in his ears.

What a way to be welcomed back to the living. Atlas slid across the smooth stone, pinpointing the last of the men while switching to scope-lock. They were dead a moment later. He ran past the other bullet-ridden bodies as he approached the re-sealed door. Their ship was a click away.

He traced his fingers across the cold surface, trying to locate an electrical current. *Antix is on but it won't be soon.* He couldn't hack without being on-site with the servers. A digital hostile take-over. One strong concrete and metal door, nearly a foot and a half wide lay between him and Reina.

Atlas found a current and tapped it, locating his girl. His mind willingly left his body, unprotected, as he traced her weak connection to the ship, knowing she had one. He channeled within it, letting his presence be known, bolstering its strength, her strength, before he pulled back into his shell.

His arm waved behind, sending the drones that desperately wanted to get into the building to protect their queen back out into the slate fields. He understood their need far too well.

His need was greater, raging, to get to her. The cybercells in his wiring were wild with frenetic energy.

Atlas unclipped the explosive grenade from his hip and gave the volatile weapon a kiss for good luck. Joining his brothers back out in the fields, he released the grenade into the opening. The acid followed soon after.

Click. Tick. Tick.

The explosion ignited with the gasses in the air, and a gaping, fiery hole appeared. Green flames licked the now unsealed quarantine chamber.

The drones went mad behind him, fueled by Reina's fear.

Atlas grinned as he approached and gripped a sparking console. His body surged with power just as he shattered the facility with dangerously strong magnetic fields.

I'm coming for you, Reina. The bots appeared at his back soon after, as eager as him to commit murder.

· · · ·

THE GROUND SHOOK. HER body was plastered to the floor, face down, her arm pressed into the concrete as if it was trying to get away. What sounded like an explosion vibrated through the steel hallways, followed by intermittent crashes of machinery throughout.

Reina grimaced as the room went dark, only to be disturbed by Black and the alien's disbelief. The room washed into a grey tone as backup light globes flickered on.

"What the fuck was that!?" The knife slipped out of Black's hand to land next to her head. Reina tested her arm, finding that she could move and that her corded shackles had broken.

"Gunfire." The alien answered, "There's no way the Earthian Fleet could have responded so fast."

She bit her tongue, thinking she might have fired on Antix with her ship. Maybe Atlas had. She had felt his presence right before the explosion.

Reina, with a speed she didn't know she possessed, seized the knife, flipped to her side, and jammed it into Black's foot. His howl vibrated off the walls as she took advantage of his confusion and tackled him to the ground, taking the dagger with her and thrusting it into his gut.

"My ship is coming to kill you, you piece of trash," she hissed through her teeth. Shots hit the wall next to her head and the burn of bullets seared her cheeks.

"Don't move," the alien spoke from directly behind her. Yells could be heard down the hallway, and outside the room she could feel the zip of her

217

drones move closer to her location. She held onto the knife, the handle sweaty in her palm. She couldn't bear to look at her now-visible robotic fingers; their inhuman nature was deeply unsettling.

Black sagged and sputtered under her as his life gushed out of him and onto the floor, soaking her legs. Her toes slipped across the wet grime.

"I don't want to kill you," she whispered to the alien. Black heaved his last gasp. The sounds he made could have been mistaken for sounds of pleasure.

"I don't want to kill you either." Black died, ignored. "I'll let you walk out of this room and see the end of this." Reina felt the safety snap on the gun pressed into her skull. "If you answer me honestly."

The screech of metallic grind was right outside the door.

"I'm the one who holds all the power. Why should I make a deal with you?"

"Because this firearm is neither laser nor projectile. It's a plasma cannon and not even a Cyborg can't withstand their metal skull melting into their brains." The Trentian sounded like he spoke from experience. Any gun would have worked on her head. She tried to act brave. "Do you know where Larik is?" he finished.

Reina willed her battle drones to move faster. "Why does he matter so much?" Her head pushed forward as the alien pressed the barrel painfully hard into her.

"He stole something from me. Something worth more than your life."

She wagered her life to buy another second. Another explosion erupted somewhere close by.

"Do you know what that is?" she asked, hoping her evasion would work. "That's me. I'm not some lone, unprotected female you can torture," her voice rose. "I don't need anyone. I don't need anything to destroy this facility. All I need," Reina said. "Is this."

The ground began to tremble and the roar of bullets ricocheting overwhelmed her ears. Reina ducked to the side as she seized the opportunity from her captor, her eyes locked with his for the first time as the door began to fissure like lightning. Her skin heated and numbed as shockwaves of electricity coursed through her circuitry.

The drones were breaking down the barrier that separated them.

"Please don't do this," the alien man spoke softly. Reina was mesmerized by fear as his pale eyes milked her of her fortitude. The Trentian stepped forward and laid down his gun. He cupped her face and bore down on her willpower. "A lone star-jewel with the perfect combination of Earthian genes doesn't even know when a man owns the universe," he whispered, nuzzling her ear. She grew weak and pliant from his touch. "You're a good person, Captain Reina, it's in your eyes. But you're an idiot who is fighting a battle that is not your own."

A familiar voice rose over the chaos, breaking her away from the Trentian.

"Reina! Stand away from the door!" *Atlas?* She turned toward the sound. Something like a magnetic force, beyond anything she had felt before in her life, shot out like a wave from the door and brought her to her knees and dragged her forward. The gun flew out of the Trentian's hand and cracked the wall with the force of its impact.

She barely had time to react, to take a breath, when the door caved inward–sucked out of the wall and shot through to the other side of the room, crushing the lone table and chair in its wake. Now only a hole remained in its place.

The magnetic currents released just as the room filled with her drones. Reina shot forward and grabbed the dagger, which had speared through Black's ribs, pulled by the magnets, and threw it at the alien.

He caught it in the chest in an anticlimactic death. His eyes sparkled with mischief as he slumped into a shadowy ball, pale purple haze exuding from his frame.

Reina lost sight of him as her robots surrounded her like a shield. *My robots and I against the world.* They moved out of her way in deference as she walked to the dead Trentian. She reached her hand out to move aside his jacket, already knowing his body wasn't there.

It's not possible. He's gone. The figure of a man caught the periphery of her eye.

Every gun she controlled swiveled and pointed at the dusty figure blocking her exit. The fingers of her flayed hand clenched her jacket with anger. Reina was high on electrical power, and the chip in her head flared as nanocells poured out, lighting up behind her eyes.

"Reina, it's me." The figure spoke. She gave the order to her drone soldiers to kill anything that tried to stop her from getting to her ship.

He spun out of the doorway just as her drones targeted him for death.

"Fucking hell, Reina, it's Atlas. Atlas!" He screamed over the gunfire. "Call off the robots, please?"

She pushed forward to kill the liar, only to stop when the first several drones crashed to the ground and erupted the moment they entered the passageway. Reina felt the familiar current and magnetized connection coming from the being.

Not. Possible. She glanced back to where the alien corpse should have been. "Atlas?" her voice hitched in disbelief. "Prove it."

"Seriously?" he groaned.

"Yes."

"I'm your Automated Transport and Logistical Aid System. I would prefer to prove it with a kiss."

Reina shook her head and stepped out of the room, almost afraid to find who was behind the wall, but more afraid that it was all a trick and Atlas wasn't actually there.

She came face-to-face with an impossibly tall, impossible, improbable man, whom she vaguely recognized. Atlas met her perusal with a devilish smirk, and her breath hitched as his strong arms snaked around her just as a magnetic pulse blasted out from outside their embrace. Her drones pushed away from them.

"I don't like the idea of being shot at."

"This isn't possible." His fingers weaved through her soaked hair, holding her close to his hard, heated chest. *A chest that isn't supposed to exist.* She breathed in his stale sweaty scent, awed that he even

221

had one. Reina pulled away to look at his eyes, already knowing the answer to her question. "Who are you?"

His eyes flashed down at her. "You know who I am, sweetheart."

Reina stepped away, feeling uncertain, unsure of their contact. Metal–cybernetic metal–older and well used, unlike her own.

Processing...

She was scanning him. Cyborg model number fifty-two, second edition. Cyber Sergeant Kyle Atlas-Fifty-Two, in the Earthian Space Fleet–navigator and consultant.

Processing...

The information seeded from him and uploaded into her head. His hand caught her, pressing her back into him when she was hit with vertigo that was worse than gravity loss.

Cyber Sergeant Kyle Atlas-Fifty-Two, served in the Shield and Disrupter Division: Magnetic manipulation. Shot down in the battle of Cosmic Storm. Sustained life-threatening injuries and the loss of his heart. Intelligence transcended into the network while the body remained in cryo life-support. Nanocells frozen but intact.

First sentient biological-vat-born Cyborg to fully integrate into the system... scanning vitals...

"Reina, you can read my stats later." Atlas threw her out of his logs. Her eyes refocused on him. "We need to retrieve the doctor, he won't stop talking." Faded shots, somewhere in the distance overlaid his voice. "We're not out of this yet."

With an impulse she couldn't understand, Reina threw herself into his arms. Atlas caught her in a painfully tight embrace. Every hard edge of him pressed into her flesh, his fingers, her hard edges, the weapons strapped to his arms and legs, dug into her and she gave herself over to it.

Her back hit a wall as they warred with the chaos inside themselves. The smell of burnt metal and copper blood filled her nostrils. She felt alive.

She gripped him tighter. "It's really you."

"It is." He groaned, pressing her into the cold, concrete barrier.

"I almost had my drones kill you." Reina shivered, holding onto him tighter. She leaned up, uncaringly desperate and found his mouth. His hands cupped her ass and slid her up the wall to meet him equally. Their kiss was a frenzied battle. Atlas sucked her tongue into his mouth and drank her down, assaulting her. For a Cyborg who had never been with a woman, he knew how to kiss, licking her teeth, biting down on her lip, bruising her in a way she needed amongst the death surrounding them.

"It would take a lot more than that to kill me."

His nails tore into her as he ground her into his cock. Reina shrieked and gasped as he rubbed himself between her spread legs, up to her stomach, before gliding back down.

Everything was surreal, even the distant blasts of gunshots, and her robot army that surrounded them from every side. He was here. Lust, unlike anything she had experienced before, consumed them.

"Atlas," she screamed over his wet tongue, plunging in and out of her mouth. "Take me."

223

The back of her head hit the wall as he allowed her to breathe, licking his way along her jaw, over her cheek, only to end up at her ear. "No."

Reina thrashed, the power and the burning want inside her screamed inside her head for release. "Please! Take me or kill me."

"No, Captain." He taunted her, his wispy breath slithered into her ear, making her twitch and convulse. The pressure of his erection just a rip away.

"I command you, Cyborg." She clasped onto him and writhed. *I need to feel anything, everything, anything.* She wanted to lose herself, and to hold onto the careless feeling that electrified her.

The command didn't have the effect that she wanted. Atlas lifted away from her, still gripping her, but there was a sliver of space between them now and she almost hated him for forcing her back into the *now*.

"I'm not going to fuck you or kill you, Reina. If anything, you and I are logical, rational, intelligent, emotional, and yet slightly sociopathic killing machines. You brought me back to life. You gave me the courage to take a chance. Life or death, that's what we have, what we'll always share, and why we belong together." He bit her earlobe, making her shiver. "And as much as I would love to fuck you in this hellhole of broken metal and revenge, we're not safe here, and Yesne will not stop talking in my ear. Hearing that man talk is kind of a turn-off."

They painstakingly disengaged from each other and although she did hate him now, the chaos lifted.

His eyes shifted to her flayed hand, his smile dropped and his eyes went hard. "What the fuck did they do to you?"

He cupped her cheeks, his thumb brushing softly across her bruised face. Reina barely knew why she felt safe in his arms, why she looked at him for comfort.

"They tried to extract information out of me."

"Did you kill them?"

Reina nodded.

"Are you going to be okay to make it back to the ship?" he continued to question.

"Yes, I think so. My body is on fire but numb at the same time." She held onto his arm, not wanting to let him go, afraid that this was all another nightmare and he would be gone when she woke up. But the gunfire was getting closer and even if this was a nightmare, Reina knew if she died in it, it was no dream. "Atlas," she breathed, feeling very alone. "Please don't leave me."

The door leading to their exit slipped open, cutting him off from responding, and several men came through with guns. Their moment was gone as her drones flew forward and committed pirate genocide.

Atlas handed her a pistol and they made a run for it.

Chapter Seventeen:

· · · ·

"**M**ore are coming!"

Atlas motioned to her to follow, her hovering drones providing them cover. The carnage was breathtaking. Blood painted the walls as they made their way through heaps of corpses and fried mechs.

"How many?" Her bare feet made squishing sounds as they ran, her soles cut to shreds.

Can't feel anything. Fight and flight dominated her brain, as well as the hungry looks that Atlas cast her way. The kind of looks that hinted at his desire to throw her up back up against the wall and take her in the midst of battle.

He crowded her. "I can't get a clear signal, my radar tech is out of date and I'm being blocked by their firewalls. I *do* know that there is a group of ships entering Antix's atmosphere. It's hard to miss that much power."

Reina spun around as a garbled noise broke behind her. A lone man with a broken leg and a bullet wound to his shoulder whined in conscious pain.

Atlas shot forward before her drones flooded him with more bullets. He grabbed the man by the neck and shielded him until they backed off. Reina approached warily.

The man sputtered and choked.

"Atlas, let up! You're going to break his neck." She watched as his grip tightened before he let go.

"Where are the men who were stationed here?" Atlas took a blade out and took the man's hand. *He's going to cut him like they cut me.* Reina was all of a sudden horrified and pleased.

The dying man coughed, unaware, "Dead."

Atlas shifted. "Why? What makes you think an act of war would accomplish anything?"

"We don't want to hurt you," Reina reassured, playing nice, catching the man's eye.

"Like I believe that crap, you're the ones slaughtering everyone here. We just wanted to talk."

"You have a funny way of showing it!" She hissed, flashing her skeletal metal hand in front of his face. "This doesn't look like 'just talking' to me."

"Like you're any better." The man shrieked as Atlas sliced the skin of his thumb off. "You won't make it off the planet alive."

Reina reached down and relieved the man of his personal telecomm unit.

"Why is Larik so important to your group?" Atlas shot her an annoyed look. "Why do you need him?" She asked again when he didn't answer. "Atlas, stop hurting him!"

His eyes bore into her as he sat back on his haunches, wiping his bloody blade off on his thigh. He took the comm unit from her. Atlas's eyes flashed bright blue as he temporarily connected with it.

"Pissed off the Trentians," he groaned. "They won't...stop."

"They won't stop what?"

The man heaved.

"They won't stop what?" Reina urged, but he was already dead.

227

Atlas grabbed her arm and lifted her to her feet. "We need to get to the ship and fast. More ships are entering orbit."

Reina shot the man in the head for good measure before they moved away. Her curiosity grew every slippery step she took. Atlas and she moved forward with reckless speed, knowing each second was precious. She kept point from behind.

"Any update? Do you know what he meant about the aliens?" Her drones swarmed before them, rooting out any hiders and wasting them before they arrived.

The entered a relatively clear, gore-free hallway, gloomy with flickering grey light globes.

"The comm has a weak connection, it's linked to a nearby ship that I'm guessing is controlling the servers here. New channels are opening up like a web." They stepped over a solitary corpse. "We'll have a better chance at survival if we meet them in the air. If they catch us in the hold, we'll never make it out alive. I don't know what the alien meant. Sometimes you end up in the middle of a war that's not your own."

He was chiding her.

Atlas stopped at a closed door where several of her robots were standing guard. She watched in awe as he ran his hand along the door, seemingly finding a weak point and punching through the metal frame. "Yesne, shut the hell up, we're the ones outside your door," he grated to whatever earpiece he still had in.

The mechanism broke and the door slid open. Yesne appeared, unharmed, with his bag in his hand. "It's about time you guys showed up. I thought we built Cyborgs better than this," he teased, entering the corridor.

Reina approached him. "I'm glad you're okay. Did they hurt you?"

Yesne stopped, looking at her up and down, his face scrunched in horror. "Captain, what did they do to you?" He dropped his bag and reached for her hand. "You're covered in blood, please tell me it's not yours...that you at least hurt the ones that tried to damage such a perfect creature."

She smiled. "They got what they deserved."

Atlas stepped between them and forcibly took her hands out of the doctor's. "You can examine her later. We need to move." He pulled the earpiece out. "Your vitals appear fine, besides the elevated heart rate and some nutrient deficiencies. Can you run?"

"They did nothing but torture me with boredom."

"Horrible." Atlas smirked. "Let's go."

The three of them made their way to the surface, following behind Atlas, armored by metal. Reina's mind stayed on the Cyborg in front of her. Even the dank passageways couldn't pull her mind away from him. *Atlas is alive. Alive. Alive.* She couldn't quite wrap her mind around it. His body, very much alive, rippled with muscle. Tense and fluid with perfect, alert, mechanical, calculated motion. *And yet so very human.*

His eyes flashed toward her every other second. She couldn't help but do the same.

He's really here.

And then it dawned on her. Yesne hadn't seemed surprised at all by his magical appearance.

* * * *

ATLAS GUIDED THEM ALONG the quickest route to the exit even though it was, perhaps, the most dangerous. The blueprints were displayed behind his eyes and in his mind. More men were coming, but what irked him the most was the unfortunate way he had appeared before Reina.

He glanced at her. *I would have preferred to surprise her during an intimate moment. Prepared, wanting, and wet by my words.*

Not after she was hurt, her body in the midst of repairing itself, and her mind possibly traumatized. Again.

Atlas watched her like a hawk, waiting for a reaction that, so far, hadn't come.

Yesne's heavy breaths kept pulling him out of his musings, along with the electric waves continuously increasing overhead. Part of their mission was to set up stronger relays on Antix. That sure as hell wasn't going to happen now. Unfortunately, it wasn't his choice. All he cared about was getting Reina back to the ship safely.

Atlas halted at an intersection, his back pressed against the wall, as he peered slowly around the corner. One of the drones flew past him.

"What's wrong?" Reina came up next to him.

"We're one level below the surface. The stairway is on the other end of this chamber." He turned toward her. "But we have a problem." *Many, actually. But only one at a time.*

"What now?"

I want to kiss you so fucking hard right now. Atlas kept that to himself, content enough just to be able to *smell* her. "The servers. The relay technology is still on the ship. We can either locate the source and fix it, re-establish communication with the Council, or–"

"–or we can leave it," she sighed. "What are the odds of our success?"

"One hundred percent. The way behind us is clear."

"Survival rate?"

"Hard to say, unidentified splinter ships are in orbit and more are approaching. There are still men aboard the current ship, possibly waiting for us to emerge. Our chance of survival fluctuates by the second. It's getting lower," Atlas answered.

"They won't kill us, at least they'll try not to. Not until they get what they want from us."

Yesne breathed, joining them. "What do they want?"

"They want info on Larik. They believe we can give them a lead."

Atlas sighed, annoyed. "They don't know for certain."

"No. *They* don't. But *we* do."

"Sometimes I hate that a part of me is human." Atlas kept tabs on time, feeling it tick, needing to move, wanting to kill. "What do you recommend we do, Reina?"

She turned away from him and looked back down the hall, at the bodies on the floor, and the sizzling mech on the ground, then turning back to look at him, and past him toward the exit. She weighed the odds in her own head. Atlas knew when Reina came to a decision: her swollen face hard, her eyes determined.

Good choice. Atlas really didn't want to throw her over his shoulder and force her like a caveman.

"We head for the ship. The Council will investigate this. My priority is to make sure you guys survive. Whatever happened here, whatever we were dragged into, is second. We have a mission to complete."

Atlas leveled his gun and rounded the corner. They made a mad dash toward the decontamination chamber just as he began to feel the boosters fade from his system, the painkillers weakening, and it made him feel that much more impatient to get back to the lab.

The smell of smoke and burnt chemicals clouded the air, the chamber destroyed by the blast and now flooded with planetary gasses.

Light rays pierced out toward them as sand crept into the concrete interior, penetrating Port Antix with poison. Beyond was a screen of swimming dust, too dull to even catch the light from the nearest sun. Atlas turned toward his charges.

He caught Reina's eyes, her skin flushed and beautiful with natural light, where it was washed out before in monotone, emaciated greys. Atlas briefly forgot how to speak.

"Reina, link to the ship, warm up the thrusters, and initiate the cannons." He swallowed tasteless saliva. "We'll need them."

"On it." Her eyes unfocused. He felt her surf the digital waves.

She was born to be a Cyborg. She was born to be mine. I was created to be hers. The thought gave him all the strength he needed to become the metalloid-man he used to be. He was consumed with getting them to safety.

As she stood out-of-body and barely cognizant, he couldn't help but steal a taste of her. His nose found her frenetic pulse until it led him down to the crook of her neck. Atlas placed a desperate kiss, replacing the dry taste of his mouth with her sweat.

Reina jerked, startled, coming back into herself and he pulled away.

"Atlas, for Earth's sake, we're in danger. I need to concentrate." She stepped away from him. "You now have dirt smeared on your lips."

He smirked as she rechanneled, fueled by her emotions, soon followed by the sound of their ship's drives powering on in the distance. His eyes took in the area.

"There are six ships in orbit, two are descending as we speak. There is still only the ship from before grounded nearby. I feel nor sense nothing between us and our destination."

"Doesn't mean there isn't a trap," Yesne mumbled.

Atlas turned to the doctor. "You're going to lose the bag, you'll both have to run as fast as you can." The doctor gripped it tighter in defiance.

"Reina, keep the bots around us, cover our skin. Let's go!"

He took off.

"We don't have exosuits," Yesne yelled before running after him. Atlas hit the open air. The sparkle of the ship was a beautiful beacon.

"Run fast and hold your breath!" Atlas yelled back, shooting down an enemy sky-mech.

Chapter Eighteen:

. . . .

Every step she ran pulled her to the ship like a
taut elastic band, only growing looser as she got
closer to home. She felt a transcendent invigoration
that was only lessened by an insatiable need to feel
her feet planted on the metal floor of the bridge.

They had barely covered fifty feet of open ground
before Atlas shot off his gun, scoping out the airborne
enemies even before her drones could. Pings erupted
around them as bullets sailed through the air and
embedded themselves in the swarming bots that
began to follow and surround them.

Her personal army, spinning their turrets in
beautifully synchronized motion, blasting the enemy
tech out of the skies. She cheered them on; they
moved faster.

Two shots. Two down.

She hadn't spent eleven and a half years in the
Space Fleet without learning how to protect herself.

"Move faster!" Atlas roared at them, far ahead
and crouched, adding his own covering fire. He shot
with such precision that it looked like a dance. The
crunch of several sky-bots, including several of her
own, sounded just beside them.

They ran past Atlas, still leveling the playing
field. The planetside wind storm was at their back and
pushing them forward.

"I can barely breathe," Yesne wheezed. Reina slowed down enough to grip his forearm.

"Me neither," she gasped back. "But we don't have any other option." They ran together and spurred each other on as their goal grew further away with each step.

More of her drones erupted and dropped, creating large gaps in their makeshift shield.

They were barely jogging now and each inch they moved forward felt like slogging through sludge. Reina reached for the doctor's arm only to find at some point she had let go. She jerked around frantically, confused as to how she had lost him.

A gust of wind hit her straight on filling her mouth and nose with toxic gas and each subsequent gasp afterward burned her throat, flooding into her lungs, frying her throat.

She swayed stupidly as all her pain came back: the slices on her bare feet, filled with dirt, the swollen pain of her face. Reina looked down at her hand, and it didn't hurt. It didn't feel like anything at all.

Yesne's body lay unmoving several yards away. Her feet brought her to him only to collapse to her knees. Atlas appeared next to her.

"We're losing him."

He ignored her, blasting something somewhere beyond, and picked the doctor up, throwing him over his shoulder. Reina grabbed Atlas's suit and hefted herself back to her feet.

She nodded at Atlas and he took the lead, her flayed fingers holding onto him as they slowly jogged onward. Every cybercell in her system was in overdrive trying to keep her conscious and alive.

The ominous shadows of incoming spaceships grew overhead.

We're not going to make it.

Reina lost conscious just as her feet were lifted off of the ground.

• • • •

SEVERAL HOVERBIKES dropped from the sky overhead. He ran faster, faster than he had ever run in his life, running away from the men aiming stunners at him. Atlas hated it but he couldn't do anything but run now, carrying two limp bodies over his shoulders.

The bikes were gaining on him just as the hatch slid open. He dodged and dashed around the electric shots, forcing him to weave his way to the entrance. His body flew through as the biker closed on him, he hit the console to close the hull, managing to get it shut just a second before impact.

The idiot chasing him crashed into the heavy metal door. Reina groaned, half underneath him. He scanned her vitals with a sigh of relief: she was coming to.

He hauled her up against the wall. "Don't fucking move."

Her eyelids twitched. Speckles of grey sand clung to them like jewels.

Atlas turned to the dying doctor and ran him to medbay. He couldn't let him die, not when Yesne had risked his career and possible imprisonment for him. He needed to pay the man back for his life. Reina wouldn't forgive him if he let the doctor die.

We're even now. He powered up the glass pod, a full-service medical machine that would stabilize the man.

236

Atlas hated a lot of people; he distrusted even more. But for some reason, this person, this doctor, he was attached to. Atlas would even call him a friend. He quickly stripped Yesne of his clothes and placed him into the machine. The only movements his body made were short, painful gasps, and the jerks caused by bombs hitting the ship.

The wait was agonizing while he monitored the doctor's vitals. He plugged into the machine and forced more power through it, hoping it would go faster.

Power raged through him suddenly, his feet spread out to keep his balance, as the telltale signs of takeoff caused the internal atmosphere around him to fluctuate.

Reina.

Cannons sounded.

Atlas eyed the pod, still running reports. Grippers shot out as IVs sank into Yesne's arms. The machine was frantically trying to save the poisoned man's life.

His fist met the bulkhead, punching a hole through its frame.

* * * *

REINA COULD FEEL THE wild rush of kisses taste and pucker over every inch of her skin. Wet, rough licks from a tongue that was altogether too hot slid across her body. Moans escaped her as it moved all over her at once, bathed in a sexual haze.

Her body arched against something hard, as every inch of her was being ravished and suckled. She fell into a blissful euphoria, knowing Atlas was taking advantage of her.

Something's not right. He doesn't have a hundred tongues.

She flailed, fear and confusion quickly replacing her pleasure. "Atlas?" Reina moaned, trying to ground herself. The chilly room around her rocked, knocking her off balance.

We're being fired on! Her body went up in electrical flames. She needed to move, needed to get to the bridge, to connect her arm with the captain's seat.

Her eyelids peeled back painfully, stinging from sand and possibly chemical burns. Her hands found the wall and she dragged herself up; shallow, burning breaths, and the taste of something bitter coated her mouth.

Where did Atlas go?

My Altogether Tough, now-Living, Android Savior. She giggled to herself, coming out as a hiccup. A blast hit directly outside the exit, knocking her back into her head.

She half crawled, half staggered into her ship, heading through a haze of anxious confusion to the bridge. Her body hit the wall as her ship took another hit. Every hit was another shock to her system.

Her body was damaged in such a way that she should have succumbed to death by now; the only thing fighting for her life were the rapidly regenerating cybercells flowing through her form–and her willpower.

Reina located an emergency unit and pulled out a detoxifier, swallowing the plastic tube and biting down on the outer ring.

Stumbling into the bridge, she found her seat. She initiated takeoff, targeting her guns at every moving thing within range, rage burning through her. She felt a horrible sense of glee with each explosion.

Thrusters went into overdrive, the propellers stressed her engines, and each charge snaked through the cybernetic ship and straight into her head. Electricity flooded the fuel pipes. The ship lifted off the ground in a swirl of gusting grey dust.

Atlas appeared next to her as they shot into the sky; he reached across her chest and buckled her in.

"Man the guns," she ordered, pulling out the breather, and watching the planetary rock burn with overloaded electrical fire. Soon they were too high up to see anything. "They're trying to surround us." Sirens blared to life as they took a damaging hit to their landing struts.

"Guess we won't be landing again anytime soon."

Reina adjusted her route and aimed directly into the center cluster of ships.

"Think we can warp in the thermosphere? How good are you?"

"Not that good, and not unless you want to punch a hole in the ozone layer and blow up the ship." He chided, "Love the way you think Captain."

She smiled, the high from the planetary atmosphere making her lightheaded, alert, and giddy.

I can't believe we might make it. I can't believe he's alive.

They shot through the murky clouds and flew perfectly through the enemy fleet. Their shields slid across another flyer, damaging the outer structure. More sirens screamed at them for the exterior damage. Several ships locked onto them and fell into pursuit.

Atlas wasn't just shooting at the enemy vessels, he was shooting at their cannons, blasting them in mid-space before they could ever land a hit. Still, some hits came through, and she felt every one of them like a bee-sting.

"Do we have a course charted?" Her eyes were on the sky.

Warnings kept flaring on her screen. She risked a glance at her co-captain. He was a man with a one-track mind, and that mind was on their escape.

"Keep pushing, head for the abyss, we can try and lose them in there–they won't follow us long in the dark."

Reina put everything into the hyperdrive, desperately trying to gain a good enough lead, zig-zagging and avoiding any approaching blasts. They gained some speed but not enough to lose the worst of them.

"We've lost some of them."

"We may still lose ourselves, we need to go faster!" he yelled.

"I can't!"

"Take over the guns. I'm going under, don't get us killed."

She shot him another glance as his body went stiff. Locked down and powered up. His hands hovered over his console as sparks of electricity shot from his palms to the screen. The ship thrust forward and she could feel her systems' distress. Reina couldn't see it, but she hoped they left a trail of plasma lightning in their wake.

A hail flagged her screen from a nearby ship. She ignored it and flew further into the scary dark.

Please don't follow us. Please don't follow us. Please don't want what we have badly enough to chase us down. Why do I keep being in the wrong place at the wrong time?

Suddenly, her salvation appeared in the distance. A mass of asteroids floated just above them, coming closer every second. Reina shifted directions and flew straight for the dangerous giant rocks. She knew she was a good enough pilot to risk it.

Another hail for communication popped up on her screen. *Fuck you.*

The ragged, moving asteroids framed her screen as she entered their forever-shifting maze. She was grateful that the Earth Council and Space Fleet designed her ship small–small, fast, and high-end. Several enemy ships followed her into the rock fields but she was finally beginning to gain a significant amount of distance.

A flash of light flared up, casting light on the asteroids, just as an explosive rumbled through her ship. Shrapnel sailed by her window, hitting her, and disrupting her view. *One down.*

Atlas was visibly vibrating beside her. The heat he emitted warmed up the entire bridge.

"Are you okay?" she yelled, rounding a giant rock. A quiet grunt was her only answer; a grunt and the smell of burning flesh. Reina couldn't risk turning to him. Her heart dropped into her stomach.

The end of the maze was just ahead, zipping out into open space once again. Only one more ship remained in pursuit. Atlas disconnected and they immediately lost speed.

"Answer their hail."

"Absolutely not. Are you okay?"

"Hail them, Reina. Let them get close. I can disrupt their tech if they're close, break them apart from the inside." Atlas grated, "My antenna..."

"No. We'll lose them, I'm not risking it."

His sigh was heavy and exasperated. "Fine."

A path was instantly charted, giving her a route to follow, but at the same time instilling a terror she had tried to keep at bay. It was no longer updating every second, and in fact, it phased out and vanished half a sector away. The end of Antix's current relays, and the end of the network was now real and frightening, and they were approaching it fast.

Reina shot forward toward the end goal, gaining distance from their pursuers.

The incessant ring of hails annoyed her, but every minute that went by the pings became less frequent until they faded into a choppy buzz. Eventually they stopped altogether.

Abruptly, their last trailer turned away.

"We made it."

But the relays were never established and they soon lost their last tendril of connection.

Chapter Nineteen:

• • • •

Reina's fingers tangled into her hair as she took in the events of the previous day.

They had been in the clear for several standard Earthian hours, and now that she felt safe enough–tired enough–she put her ship back into auto-pilot and fled to her quarters.

She knew she was running from him but her head needed the space to clear, even to heal after the euphoric high of chaos and chemicals, of change and intrigue, and because of the mild pain. Reina could just barely feel it course through her body.

He has his body back. That alone strangled her thoughts, suffocating them.

Her gaze shifted to her legs where flakes of dried blood dropped to the floor, crusted and stiff. Her hands were still cupping her head as she tried to massage the crazy out, shaking ever so slightly.

A knock sounded at her door. "Reina, let me in. Please, we need to talk." It was Atlas. Of course it was him. She couldn't bring herself to move.

Atlas.

Oh god. She whimpered. *There goes my space.*

He rushed in, forcing the locking mechanism out of place, approaching her with quickened steps and pulled her frozen form into his chest.

"It's okay. Everything will be okay. We're here. We're fine, alive and well on our way to putting this all behind us."

Reina barely acknowledged his words. Being pressed against him only reminded her of the utter mess she was. The hand that had just healed several weeks prior was now just skeletal metal, numb and frightening. She couldn't see herself but her face was stiff from swollen flesh, bruised and raw, and her mouth was dry with the aftertaste of torture. It tasted like chemicals.

She sagged away from his arms, bumping into the wall, uncomfortable with his very human, very warm presence. He had a presence that overwhelmed. The only thing that kept her from barricading herself in the lavatory was how messed up he looked, how wrecked and pained: just like her.

They avoided each other's eyes but maintained an electric connection. Neither one of them seemed to know what to say.

"You look terrible," she uttered after an agonizing moment, sneaking a glance at his face, seeing a tweak of a smile.

"You do too."

"We suit each other." Reina rubbed the back of her hand across her chapped, dusty lips. He reached out to touch her cheek, an indescribable look marred his face. Her head hit the wall, evading the contact. "Where in all of the hells in space did you get a body? *Your* body?!" Her voice rose, "Why didn't you tell me?" The more questions that crossed her mind, the angrier she got.

244

His thumb traced the outline of her ear, tickling her, proving his presence even more, but he didn't move closer. "It's been on the ship. Since the beginning." Atlas moved a hairsbreadth closer.

She twitched. "Don't, please. I should have known. How did I not know?" Reina could feel the pain that prickled every pore of her body cross over into her emotions. "Why didn't you tell me?" She wanted to curl up into his warmth but couldn't bring herself to do it.

Atlas clasped her hand, placing a tube of healing serum and cleaning cloths in her palm. "I'll explain everything, Reina, I'll answer every question. Just please...don't shut me out. You're in pain and I can't stand to see it, I can't stand that I may be the cause of some of it."

Reina didn't answer, taking the medical supplies, skirting around his body to find a seat to dress her wounds.

* * * *

ATLAS STAYED WHERE he stood, only turning around to watch her take his penitent gift to the other side of the room. She didn't say a word as she unfolded the cloth and rubbed her legs down. He was mesmerized by the movement; the saliva vanished from his mouth, and he found it suddenly very hard to swallow.

He conceded, "You didn't know because my body was powered down, it was off and it was frozen in cryostasis from the beginning. Any signals it may have given off would have been background noise to the ship." Atlas took a dry breath. "I also hid it from you. Only working on it when you were preoccupied or asleep." Tiny flakes of blood disintegrated from her skin and into the cloth. Anything that fell to the floor was sucked into the ship and sanitized.

Her hand gripped the cloth vehemently, her dirtied legs pressed together. Reina was closed up to him, tense, and when she spoke, she spoke low and monotone. "Why? Why? Did you not trust me?" she whispered, barely audible, "I would have kept your trust."

Atlas folded his arms and leaned back. "No." Seeing her flinch from the truth hurt him.

"I wouldn't have hurt you."

"But you may have stopped me. I couldn't let that happen."

"How could I!? Why would I? I'm not cruel," she hissed, throwing the cloth at him. "No one should be trapped like that–like you were. They should have fixed you long ago." Reina stood up and faced him. "I wanted you to have your body back. No one should have their free will taken from them."

Atlas laughed, "Shall we go free everyone from the penal colonies?"

"That's not what–"

"I know." He sighed. "I couldn't tell you and I really wanted to tell you. I had legitimate reasons, Reina, logical ones. I can't just turn off my 'nature.'" She tried to speak but he wouldn't let her. Atlas rubbed the back of his neck. "If I thawed and turned back on, I could have immediately died. I could have gone insane and lost myself again. When Yesne joined the crew, I took the opportunity I was given. The only reason my body was even on board was so Space Fleet had assurance I wouldn't transfer my consciousness away if the mission took a turn for the worse. I had no chance of revival if I ran away."

"He knew?"

"He rebuilt my heart." His eyes followed her every movement, watching her arms wrap around her middle. Distress was not a look he liked on her. "It wasn't because I trusted him more," he admitted. "I was done waiting. I forced his hand and threatened his life. I was willing to risk everything to be whole again." Atlas took a step toward her. "I had you. I needed to protect you."

Reina's chest moved with every deep breath she took. She looked everywhere but at him. "That can't be all."

Atlas willed her to meet his gaze but the harder he tried, the more she locked away her feelings. *She's hurting.*

"I didn't want to disappoint you."

She glanced at him. He could have roared with triumph. "Disappoint me?"

"If I told you I could be real, that I could be with you, physically, now, and banish your loneliness in every way. And if you wanted that, looked forward to it. If you became hopeful or excited, I would have never forgiven myself if Yesne or I had failed."

"You were afraid to hurt me?"

"Of course."

"Cyborgs aren't supposed to be afraid!" She stepped toward him in anger and grabbed the body armor surrounding his chest, clenching it.

"I guess that makes me defective."

Reina pulled at the material roughly. Atlas caught her hands.

"Let me see it," she demanded.

He stared at her as he pulled the material over his head, hearing the faint sound of ripping, and bared his ruined chest for her, bringing his biggest failure to the stark light of the room. Reina didn't make a sound as she judged the damage and his shame for herself.

There was a disturbing red incision, not unlike the 'Y' of a corpse that had undergone an autopsy, directly before her gaze. It wasn't healed, not be a long shot, the skin had barely begun to knit itself back together. Atlas didn't feel anything but a slight twinge of pain. What he did feel was harder to hide, and the moment Reina moved to touch the white skin that framed his cut, Atlas couldn't keep it from her any longer.

His cock stiffened, painfully, with a mind of its own, desperately wanting to be freed like his chest was. It bulged like an obstacle between them, trying to break the barrier of his pants and fill her up.

His cock grew even harder, and Atlas would have taken anything Reina would give him, anything to release the pressure raging inside him.

It pushed into her stomach. He couldn't stop his body's reaction. She yelped and jerked back. Even the terrible cage of his pants, shielding his erection from her, was pleasurable beyond comprehension.

"Atlas?" Reina rasped, bringing him back into himself.

"There is one more reason I didn't tell you, sweetheart, and I need you to know." He tried to ignore his cock. It was hard when she kept looking at it, at his chest, to settle on his face, only to look back down at his bulge.

"What is it?" she asked warily. Her eyes kept perusing him. *She should never look at anyone but me.*

"Loyalty."

"What do you mean?"

Atlas closed the distance between them. Reina leaned away, almost like he might burn her, but she didn't need to. He didn't touch her.

"Your loyalty to the Earthian Space Fleet and the Council."

"Is there a reason why that would matter!?"

"What do you expect? You've worked tirelessly for the Fleet for nearly a decade. We've known each other for a month. Of course it matters. I couldn't risk it. I couldn't rationally assume your loyalty lay with me, or that it eventually would. How could I guarantee that you wouldn't tell them after everything I have been through? After your years of perfect service?"

"So that's it." Reina twisted away. Atlas caught her arm and held her in place.

"That's not all."

"Let go of me." She jerked. "I really can't do this anymore. You need to get out."

His grip tightened. "I'm not done."

"Yes. You are. Because I'm done being lied to. I'm done with men, with aliens, with fucking Cyborgs. You can all go to hell." Reina struggled and pulled but he held firm. "Let go of me, Atlas."

"So you're upset with my lies. You sure as hell didn't seem all that upset when I told you about how many Wasson and Estond killed trying to find someone capable of your position. That, Reina, proves your loyalty."

"I didn't expect the truth from them," she stormed. Her back hit the wall, toppling over the chair as he caged her in. "I expected it from you after everything."

"Poor baby. Life is hard. Too bad it's fucking better than nothing. You don't even know how terrible our employers are because you don't seem to fucking get it, blindly following orders. They're tyrannical slavers, unrepentant liars, and all in the name of 'the greater good.' They don't care about you—you're just a grunt to them. What we want doesn't matter. Only results matter—only progress. And progress doesn't differentiate between the worthy and worthless. It's unbiased as long as we all survive one more day." He cupped her cheeks, leaning down to press his forehead to hers, threading his fingers through her hair, tugging the strands painfully. So much desire coursed through his system. "You should know that."

"Let. Go. Of. Me," she panted under him. Atlas could smell her wet heat through the layers of grime and sweat that still covered them.

"You had all the power to lock me out before. Now we're even. Get used to it." He leaned in, brushing his nose over the edge of her ear, feeling her hands come up to press against his but she didn't push him away. "I've worked for your species since I was little more than a cell cluster and a program." Atlas breathed over her ear, blissfully taking in the shivers that coursed through her. "I wasn't created to be outside of my biological shell. All Cyborgs need a root. But my creators, my doctors, and so-called surrogate teachers didn't help me when I became lost. They thought me dead." He placed light, tickling kisses along her racing pulse, wanting to feel more of her subtle writhing.

"You're not playing fair." Reina grew pliant, almost malleable, and lust raced through him like a bullet. This time, it felt like heaven.

It was worth the risk. It was worth the lies.

"We've never played fair, sweetheart." Her hands moved over him softly, skating his cut, until they clasped his shoulders.

Killing aliens, winning battles, or bathing in the blood of his enemies could never feel as good as the psychotic sexual arousal he felt at that moment.

Atlas lost himself to the salty sweat of her skin, wanting to drown in the taste of her, needing more of it. She turned her face away when he tried to capture her mouth.

He took a deep breath and leaned back until she turned back toward him, shaking her head.

"I want you to continue," Reina's voice a harsh, brushed off whisper.

Atlas tensed at the command. "They had my body, and when I came to, years later, they had my being too. An atypical creation–next gen knowledge. They promised to rebuild me, for years they promised, if only I did what they demanded. God, the excuses they gave. Endless reasons why they couldn't fulfill their end of our bargain right up until they stopped giving them. The people you work for and the people I'm enslaved to kept me the way I am longer than your lifespan and there was nothing I could do when they owned the one thing that could free me. The one thing I wanted most in the universe." He watched her eyes fill with pity and he hated it.

He let the words settle themselves, waiting for a response from her. She reached out and touched his chest only to pull her hand back as if it had been shocked.

"How could I risk telling you what Yesne and I were doing when you're so willing to die for those same people?"

Reina looked away and when she pushed away this time, he let her free. "I understand." She put several steps of distance between them. "I'm so sorry for what happened to you. I can't even imagine it, I can't comprehend it, but I can't stop this sinking feeling of betrayal, and after all this crazy." Her arms wrapped around herself as she continued, "We nearly died, several times in the last day alone. I don't think I can forgive so easily anymore. All of this is so confusing, so wrong. What I feel for you feels wrong. How long? How long were you without your body?"

"Since *Cosmic Storm*," Atlas reminded her.

She shook her head, not understanding.

"An offensive mission to retake one of our bases on Gliese. Nearly seventy-five years ago."

"Oh my god." Reina froze, her eyes widened in shock. Atlas took a step back as she rushed him, unexpectedly throwing her arms around him. "I'm so sorry. So, so sorry."

Atlas clasped her to him. "It's not your fault, sweetheart. I don't want your pity."

She shook her head again, pressed into his raw chest. "You should have told me. I would have never betrayed you." Reina whimpered, "What can we do?" He smelled the dew of her tears right before they fell in droplets over his wounds. "How can we get past all of this?"

"We can disappear. We're off their radar, Reina, we don't have to finish this. We don't have to go back."

I'd do anything for you.

Reina leaned back, wiping the tears from her cheeks, gifting him with a sad smile, then a soft laugh. "Absolutely not. We've finally made it this far. I want to know what's out here."

Atlas smirked. "I'll admit, I'm a little curious too."

"Who knows, maybe getting some answers will be worth everything. If we survive this, I'm going to need to know what exactly Pirate Captain Larik stole from the Trentians."

"That is even more dangerous territory than dead space. I'm sure there are thousands of others who want answers from him as well. You would be contending with others, who have a far greater need, a vengeance against him," Atlas warned as he walked toward the door, preparing to leave and give her the space she needed. He hated every step.

"Atlas, you're dirty."

He stopped and faced her. "So are you."

"We're both really dirty."

Atlas smiled as she looked down at herself.

"–Please stay. I don't want to be alone anymore."

"Neither do I, Captain." Atlas rushed back to her, lifting her in his arms and carrying her to the shower.

Chapter Twenty:

• • • • •

Reina felt a terrible burden rise from her chest.

The door to the small bathroom slid shut behind them. Everything changed with her plea for him to stay.

She didn't want to think of everything that got them to this moment, but her wariness still pulled at her mind. "No one is watching the bridge, nor the scans," Reina reminded him. "Auto-pilot won't stop the ship from potential danger."

Atlas looked down at her, she was still cradled in his arms, and there was an inferno raging within his expression. Intent male prowess haloed him. It looked dangerous. It felt dangerous. It *was* dangerous.

"I've taken care of it." He left it at that and it wasn't enough for her, not anymore.

"What do you mean? What did you do?"

He held her hard as if she might slip away, and she couldn't blame him. Reina couldn't even begin to imagine.

"I've charted a closed circle around several nearby planets."

Oh. Reina took him in as he just stood there, unmoving, in the tight chamber. Atlas was a super-soldier virgin. One who had never touched a woman before her, who hadn't even felt physical contact in over seventy years.

She carefully wiggled out of his embrace and stepped toward the shower, nervous and exhilarated that he might pounce on her. That the desire she felt for him would forgive him of any trespass.

Reina closed her eyes briefly, knowing that. She turned the shower on, opening her eyes to watch the water spray behind the thick glass enclosure. Atlas's reflection was directly behind her, towering over her. She looked like a drowned rat and he looked like the undead.

"Let me be your Adjustable Thickness, Length, and Size."

She laughed. "Really, Cyborg?"

She immediately felt the thick club of his cock press into her back, powerful enough to push her slightly forward.

"Is that answer enough for you?" He groaned. Reina leaned back into him encouragingly.

"Yes."

"I don't want to hurt you."

"You won't." She knew full well he could.

Atlas continued, his voice low and dark, promising and heavy, "I don't know my own strength anymore. I feel like I could kill us both with how badly I want to ravage you right now." His hands found her hips and gripped her tightly. Reina clutched the edge of the glass door as he probed her. Amongst the ruin of her body and the bright red autopsy incision marking his chest, her thighs pressed tight together, trying to relieve the aching unfilled heat of her channel.

The pressure was unbearable as steam rose up from the water in front of her and plastered every surface of the small space. "That." She bumped up as he ground down, his Cyborg erection straining against her butt. *So hard.* "Is lust, desire, heat, insatiable wanting," she said, losing herself in the gyration of their dance.

Atlas breathed deeply against her neck. She maneuvered around and took the lead. The sound of a thousand droplets of water hitting the metal floor filled her ears.

Reina leaned against the glass, fingering her musty undershirt. "Do you remember the feel of water? Hot water?" she asked, tugging the material over her head. "Hot water sliding across your skin, drenching your hair, and heating up your body?" Her fingers unclasped her bra, letting it drop. "Do you remember steam making it hard to breathe as your mouth fills up with the humidity of it?" She canted her head, watching his face.

He wasn't looking at her, but at her exposed body. She could feel him drink her in. Every taut dip and groove memorized and eaten up in the glint of his eyes.

She continued, "Do you remember the feel of damp skin and the taste of wet? As you lift your head up, your eyes closed, into a current of rushing water? Your mouth parted ever so slightly because it's hard to inhale? It feels like heaven." Reina reached for him.

Softly, slowly, she unbuckled the pants of his suit, the hard contrast of under armor to his waxen, velvety skin. Her fingers relieved him of his various armaments, additional clips, tubes of various substances, and even a grenade. She rounded him, tracing the tips of her fingers over his remaining straps until every article lay on the floor between them.

He helped save her life, at the expense of his own hard-earned one. That was more than love for her.

That was everything.

"Touch me," Atlas grated, every muscle tense and tight, bulked up with a thread of restraint. Reina, still standing behind him, tugged her panties off, soaked with her essence and held them under his nose.

Atlas jerked, grasping the material, smothering his face in it. "Touch me, Reina."

She moved to his side and watched as he sucked in the scent and taste of her underwear.

"Where?" she asked softly.

"Everywhere."

Reina clasped his hand and placed a kiss over his heart.

He pushed her under the water with his heavy hands clutching her. Atlas backed her up under the cascade until they both fit.

An inhuman sound of ecstasy bounced off the walls as water cloaked them like a third lover. Atlas let go of her, leaning back as tendrils of the sanitized liquid flowed over the curves of his muscles, sizzling and evaporating soon after from the incredible heat he emitted.

Something even hotter and denser hit her belly. She looked down in shock as Atlas came all over her, each spurt of accompanied with a moan. His hands reached for her as it continued, as he continued releasing on her. Milky, dripping, pale cream blended with the water and ran down her body.

Atlas was lost in bliss as she was lost in watching him.

"The water," his voice raspy and tight. "The water and you. I couldn't stop." Atlas rocked into her.

"You couldn't help yourself."

"Oh I could," he objected. "Just didn't want to. I've been tortured with thoughts of you. My hardest battle to date was stopping myself from taking you amongst the carnage of Antix."

"I wanted you then. I wouldn't have stopped you." Her stomach fluttered, remembering that dangerous moment, remembering how badly she had needed him then.

Atlas opened his eyes when his ejaculation ended. He placed his hands on her again, touching her all over with a virginal fascination. He tweaked and pinched her nipples, groped the buds of her breasts, before he reached the tiny curls around her mound. Atlas tugged at the barely grippable satin hair that only peaked at her front. She was smooth the rest of the way down.

His hands roamed up to grasp her waist and squeeze, lifting her off her feet.

"You wouldn't have wanted me after I was done," he warned. "I would have brought you to your knees." Atlas's hands rounded her buttocks, digging his nails in before he reached up and found the wet strands of her hair dripping over her shoulders and tugged.

"You're all talk," she challenged, goading the almost undead.

Atlas flipped her around. The water from above cut off. Reina couldn't stop herself from whimpering, brought low by her need for him. She was tense and on edge, ruled by a basic instinct.

His long, stiff, mechanical shaft pushed between her clenched thighs, her hips hit the wet wall as his knees bent to match her height and find her tight, desperate pussy. There was no foreplay–no time for it as the heavy head of his dick found her pulsating entrance and penetrated it. Atlas stretched her painfully until her legs parted in surrender. Her only reward was a thrust, making her toes, once again, come off the ground, but this time from impalement.

Reina was held up only by his hands and his cock, slipping up the wall.

She shrieked from the onslaught as her toes urgently sought the ground until her knees bent and her calves gripped him around his hips.

"You told me once you could take me, Captain." His hard hands found her tits and pinched. "I told you I was corrupted, and now that I've found paradise between your legs, I don't think there is any way to fix me," he threatened in her ear.

Atlas held her up as she writhed on him and flailed against the wall like a snake, trying desperately to adjust to him, trying urgently to find a place to hold onto. He didn't move; he didn't need to. Reina was frantically moving enough for the two of them.

She couldn't speak, could barely breathe as she succumbed to the tiny space and the two of them.

"I was wrong," Reina admitted, almost biting the metal wall of her ship, knowing it was impossible.

If it couldn't get more intense, Atlas shifted inside her tightness. Reina could feel him expanding.

"You said you could take me." He repeated in her ear, waiting for her fall from power. "I told you being with a Cyborg was not the same as being with a man—limited with his biology." Atlas gnawed over her dampened skin, licking where he nipped.

Reina raged with indignation. "I told you I could take it! Unlike you," she freed, "I don't lie." Her voice held a sharp edge to it she had never heard before.

His cock began to vibrate inside her stretched channel, and every bruising, untried thrust afterward demanded that she took more of his length.

"So idiotic," Atlas answered, pressing his mouth into her neck, scraping his teeth over her skin, "to bait me."

She was pressed into the wall, between a rock and a hard place, the dew on her lips kissing the barrier with each moan and urgent movement between them. Reina slipped up and down the slick metal. Her body began to zing with tiny electrical currents from the forceful contact. It slipped from her ship in soft waves, into and out of her and Atlas.

Reina no longer recognized the sounds they made as they moved in tandem. And if the sizzling, frenzied pistoning of Atlas's cock wasn't enough, he grew bigger inside her. Tears trickled down her cheeks as he loosened his grip on her and settled her on her feet, still holding her up.

They caught their breaths, as he slid open the stall door and lowered them to the floor. She turned around in his arms to straddle him as he leaned against the wall. Reina mounted his thick, vibrating, Cyborg shaft in one quick movement.

"I want to watch you break on me, wrapped around my cock," he said eerily, his voice low and harsh, and very *not* out-of-breath.

Reina caught his eye and for a perverse moment, she only saw Atlas as sex, her robot toy. He held her waist, helping her ride him until she came all over his thick shaft. Her body milked him for all his seed.

Atlas hadn't stopped intermittently coming since they began, and the thick, white sperm was all over her legs. It burned hot and velvety inside her.

His cock resonated faster inside her pussy, forcing her continuous spasms.

He watched her with possessive awe, like she was something he could get lost in, like she was the first cybernetic being who willingly lost control. Until she shook and fought him to release her, unable to take another shudder.

Her head fell against his chest in exhausted defeat.

"Please," she begged over his broken skin.

"I like feeling you clench around me."

Reina yelped as he forced one more out of her, all while caressing her back, her bent legs, following down to massage her healing feet, only to run his hands ever so slowly back up and end with his hands twirling her damp hair.

She relaxed into him.

Neither of them moved, content to be connected, comforting each other. They stayed holding each other on the floor until the water dried on their skin and the metal went cold around them. She must have dozed off at one point because she was unexpectedly jostled awake, being carried to her bed.

Reina peered up at him as he laid her down gently and joined her in bed. It was just big enough to hold them comfortably. Atlas rolled the thin blanket over them as she adjusted to curl under his arm and into his chest.

"You're comfortable to snuggle into," she said.

"Am I?"

"Hard men, hard bodies are never comfortable," she murmured tiredly. "But you are."

Atlas stroked her hair. "I'm glad."

Reina looked down at them and at the billowed blanket that covered their entwined bodies. She moved her leg to drape over him as both her hands curled up under her chin.

"Get some sleep, Captain."

She wiggled closer to him, feeling strangely protected from everything in this unknown part of the universe, being under his arm. But sleep wouldn't come. It wasn't from the aches that her body had endured but from not wanting to lose this time with him, afraid it was still just a dream, and when she woke up, he would only be a projection again.

Slowly, wondrously, she felt the hardened muscles of her Cyborg relax and soften next to her. *Maybe he feels safe with me too?* His fingers continued to comb her drying hair.

"Kyle Atlas?" Reina said his full name for the first time. "Do you sleep?" His hand moved down to trace the outline of her ear.

"I do, but I don't remember how. It's been so long," he admitted.

Reina looked up at him, finding his eyes briefly, before settling back against him. She kept her voice low and soothing, "Close your eyes." She waited a moment before continuing, her mouth pressed into his side, placing small delicate kisses on his skin. "Relax every muscle in your body, imagine yourself floating in zero gravity. Feel every piece of yourself let go. Your toes," Reina whispered, "your knees fall open, your shoulders sag, let your neck loosen." Reina followed her own instructions. The pressure of everything lifted away from their bubble. "Exhale all your worries through your mouth, let Eden in through your nose. Release the tension of your fingers." Atlas stopped petting her. "Let your mind wander into the mist."

His breaths deepened as Reina filled herself with his clean, mechanical scent.

"Know that I'm right here. That you're safe and protected, loved," she lowered her voice even more. "And everything will be the same as it is now in the morning."

She said that more for herself than for him. Reina lay there throughout the night, keeping her promise. Protecting him, the ship, and their future while he found oblivion in unconsciousness.

Chapter Twenty-One:

• • • • •

Atlas woke up, for the first time since his death, feeling like himself.

Every bone in his body, every metal rod and internal frame, every nanocell of his being ached, but he felt like *himself.* Better than himself. Relaxed, comfortable, and complete. It was a dream. He really had let Eden in through his breaths.

He looked down at Reina.

She wasn't there.

Atlas stood up, feeling the cotton material of the blanket cascade down his body as he located his discarded, worn, and torn pants. He tugged them on.

He knew where she was; after all, he had an elaborate surveillance system throughout the ship, designed by the best cybernetic engineers and himself to travel through. Her heat source was in the bridge. The autopilot was off. The continuous circle he charted was now beyond his scope. Reina had charted a new course.

Atlas looked at the rumpled bed.

I'm never sleeping again. He told himself, although knowing it was a lie, having forgotten what it was like to dream. His mind had brought him back to the days of his newborn-hood, learning how to control magnetic fields, manipulating them, maneuvering susceptible objects with his internal antennas. He buckled his belt, smiling, remembering his childhood with fondness.

Except in his dream, he wasn't maneuvering objects; he was maneuvering Reina. All over his cock, her sheath open and ready for him from every angle he imagined. What would his adolescent weeks have been like? Practicing his power on her cunt rather than on the magnetic objects around him.

They were awakened as adults, after all, with math, language, culture, history, and even loyalty already programmed in them.

Atlas didn't think he could have gone to war after experiencing what she had to offer. It was a good thing they trained in isolation after awakening.

His bare feet thumped over the ground as he made his way toward her. The contact made him... exuberant?

He entered the bridge and headed straight for her. She lifted her head to catch his eyes as he approached with intent.

"You left the bed."

"I got bored." She smiled.

"Should've woken me up. Boredom would have been the last thing on your mind." He teased, waving the holographic screens of the captain's chair away. She watched him with annoyance, her hand poised to bring the screens back.

Atlas caught her and lifted her up, taking the seat and placing her on his lap. His eyes fell to her caged-in breasts, pushing against the fabric of her flight suit.

"We have a job to do!" She struggled. "This is my chair."

"Hrmm, but we're alone and this feels so good." He held her on him, belting her with one arm as the other pulled her hair out of her tight bun. Soap and oatmeal perfumed the air from its release.

"This is against all protocol. Your cock is bruising to sit on." Reina turned to face him. "Atlas, we need to monitor the images. We have," she gasped. "Strict orders."

"Oh yes. Strict orders. My cock wouldn't be hurting you if it was where it belonged. If you had stayed in bed, this wouldn't be an emergency you needed to deal with." He reached between them and unclipped his pants, letting his heavy shaft loose before he lifted Reina up just enough to tear down her flight pants.

His captain didn't resist him.

Her hands left his body to grab the armrests of her chair as he slowly, deliberately, slid her tight pussy onto him. She leaned forward just a little as his hands spread her ass open, and his eyes watched the excruciating descent of her tiny female channel take him in. Inch by inch.

She sat on him, stiffly, unmoving as she adjusted to him. They were both staring forward, out into the panoramic view of dead space, breathing deeply and hearts pounding.

Atlas waved the screens back in front of them with a smirk she couldn't see.

"Now you can go back to work."

Reina wiggled over him in protest, he nearly came again from the effort, but stopped himself, beginning to feel the threads of his programmed control retake his body.

"I can't...do my job like his," she hissed as he spread his legs wide until her booted feet were no longer on the floor. He reached around and found her clit, thumbing it slowly.

"Of course you can," he said.

"I can't." She squirmed. Her knuckles went white on either side.

"I'm just a projection, remember?" Atlas teased. "Do your job. Just do it on my cock."

It seemed like forever before anything happened. He sat back, enjoying the power that the chair brought him, and his captain impaled and flustered on his lap. She stopped trying to remove herself and began to just wiggle on him as if she was trying to find release, only being able to move the little he allowed her. Atlas continued to thrum her clit hard and slow.

Reina thrashed and moaned, desperate and needy. He could smell the musk of their sex fill the air. Wet, hot sweat formed between their connected thighs. "You're not doing your job, Captain," he warned in her ear. "If you know anything, you know I outrank you, and refusing to listen to me is defying the established hierarchy."

She stiffened and stopped moving on his length, distressed, impassioned, and staring at the stars in front of them. Atlas pinched her clit: his last warning. Reina turned and looked at him over her shoulder. Her face, now healed, was blushing and pink, her eyes glazed and pleading. He started to pinch her harder, she jolted, turned around, and started processing and categorizing the hourly image feed.

If she wanted to lose control, he would gladly take it from her.

Atlas relaxed as she worked, intermittently gripping her hips and pumping into her, blissful with all his senses intact.

The bridge was quiet except for irregular slapping of their thighs and the clicks of the console. Reina was mounted on him, taking all his teasing and tormenting, with audible indignance. He kept them both on edge until he could bear it no longer.

And when the screen flashed red, with a sudden error, he lost his mind and pushed her to the floor. Atlas reached under her shirt and squeezed her breasts, thumbing her taut nipples before pressing her chest into the ground. His fingers clenched around her waist. Her cheek pressed to the side, eyes closed, mouth open and whimpering.

He pounded into her. Reina cried out and came underneath him, having been at the brink for too long. Her tight flesh clutched him as he lost his barely won control, pumping his seed back into her.

He stayed hunched over her until her breaths evened out, only slipping his still-hard cock from her.

Reina moaned and flipped onto her back, catching him before he could lift away. "I don't like you leaving me."

Atlas pushed a tendril of hair off her cheek, settling on his elbows. "And I don't like it when you leave me alone in bed."

"Upset that I snuck past your defenses?" she teased. "I can be very quiet."

"Impressed, actually." He leaned down to kiss her thoroughly before lifting up, helping her to her feet at the same time.

"Good." She stuck her tongue out at him.

Atlas laughed and looked at her mussed state, pants at her knees, her shirt bunched up at her chest. His stony captain marked up and marred. "You look fucked up, Reina, literally."

"I wonder why, Cyborg."

He watched as she straightened, pulling her pants back up, leaving his seed between her legs, and locating her hairband to retie her hair. He grabbed his own unkempt pants and pulled them up. Atlas found the co-captain's chair and took his seat, hating it and loving it all at once.

I can smell my cum on her. Atlas smirked.

Reina glanced at him before settling back into the king's seat. She read the error and exhaled, "There's a puncture to the outer hull under the ship from a blast. The metal is breaking away and eroding at an alarming rate."

Atlas pulled up the error. "It doesn't matter. Everything is locked down. It just means we can't land safely." He peered down at his cock, already hard again. *Am I always going to be like this?* "I'm hard again, Captain, ready for round three?"

She ignored him. "Landing safely is *vital*."

"We'll live. Just keep the lower deck sealed."

"I found the doctor in medbay in an induced coma this morning." Reina swiveled her chair toward him. "Thank you for saving him."

"It was the least I could do," Atlas responded.

"His vitals show improvement. We can wake him up tonight."

"If that is your wish, Captain." He didn't want to wake Yesne because he wanted all the time he had with Reina, alone. But he would grant her simple

270

command. If he had learned anything in his years of being a Cyborg, it was to choose your battles wisely, especially those of the nonviolent nature. "It feels like a mercy to let the man sleep."

Reina laughed, turning away. "I'm pretty sure he wouldn't agree with you."

Another error report appeared on the screen. Atlas watched her expand the message and read it over. He turned back to his own channels, scouting the local periphery. He checked it again, and nothing showed up. Not a nearby planet, an asteroid belt, a star, not even the signature of a passing comet. Reina closed the report next to her with an audible sigh.

Atlas looked out the window, knowing what he was beginning to feel was a glimmer of curiosity; the heavy structure in his chest felt slightly heavier. He noticed Reina look out the window with him. They sat there quietly, lost in their own thoughts, for an indeterminate amount of time.

He brought up the hourly active imagery being taken around the exterior of the ship. Each picture was different, that was to be expected, but he couldn't find anything unusual, not even anything beautiful.

"I'm going to up the imagery time rate. Fifteen-minute intervals," he said, adjusting it.

"Did you see something?" she asked, looking over at him.

"No, nothing. But we both can't be here sentinel all the time, not even if we take alternating shifts. I'm not an S.I. anymore." His eyes jumped to Reina's hand as she rubbed the armrest of her chair. The light of the ship glinted off her metal knuckles. "Let's go to the medbay." Atlas moved to her side.

"You want to wake up the doctor now?"

"I want to show you how to take care of the metal in your skin."

Reina looked away from him and back out at the window. He reached down and caressed the side of her face as she worked up the energy to finally look away from the star fields and back at him. Every part of her exhibited a bone-deep exhaustion that went beyond her body healing from her wounds or the elevated stress levels he sensed. She was healing rapidly, but not fast enough to make him comfortable.

Even with his full metal frame, he was still adjusting to the changes in his chest. And to everything else that presented itself as a variable of sensation around him.

She looked up at him. He leaned down and captured her mouth, with an uncontrollable urge to taste her again. Her fingers clutched his shoulders as he lifted her up. The need to drown himself in Reina's touch was the one thing that could now destroy him.

Chapter Twenty-Two:

· · · ·

Reina heard them approach. She circled her arms around her stomach, feeling the comfort of her own hug. It had merely been a day since they awoke the doctor. He now joined them in their watch on the bridge.

They were going nowhere fast.

"It feels like there's nothing out there," she said, not bothering to look at the men behind her.

"It only feels like that because we have no destination, no charted course but forward," Atlas responded at her side.

"How do we even know we're going the right way?"

"I don't think it matters. We'll scout, we'll look, we'll watch, and we'll document everything. If we find nothing and continue to find nothing, we'll backtrack and head home."

Yesne joined her at her other side. "You should get some sleep, Captain. I can take over the watch for now."

Reina turned and looked at the man; a smile came to her lips as he adjusted his glasses and met her eyes.

"I'm glad you're with us, doctor. I'm glad that I was sick enough to need you." Yesne took her human hand and squeezed it. She turned further toward him. "Thank you for bringing back Atlas."

Reina felt Atlas's palm settle on her lower back.

• • • •

ANOTHER CYCLE PASSED with nothing. It
seemed like time itself dragged until it altogether
stopped. She found that she couldn't sleep, unable to
be away from the window of the bridge for longer
than several hours. Sometimes she went to the space-
loft and lay on the ground, staring upward into the
dark void.

Atlas was never far away, and he was never far
from her mind. Watching him relive an experience
always made her fall. When he drank coffee, he
sputtered. When he looked in the mirror, he seemed
to stare at himself for hours. When she gave him a
massage, he lost control.

When she'd gotten down on her knees, unbuckled
his pants, and sucked his cock, his hands had torn off
her clothes and touched her all over until they gripped
her head and stopped her. She sputtered around his
length as he forced his way slowly down her throat.
He roared as he came deep in her mouth, with her
cheeks hollowed out and her tongue lashing his
smooth shaft. Reina drank him down, starved. *Atlas
had wanted to feed me from his manhood exclusively
from then on.*

He tasted metallic.

She smiled and rubbed her lips, staring out the
reinforced window.

"Want to head back now?" He snuck up on her
and pulled her to him.

"It's only been three days."

"Mmm." Atlas released the band holding her bun
and nuzzled her hair. "Oatmeal," he murmured
against her scalp.

274

"Same as yesterday."

"We're being followed." Atlas nipped her ear.

It took her a moment to register his statement. She jerked and looked back at him. "How do you know?"

"I can feel a very weak connection to another ship every so often."

"For how long?" Her voice rose.

"Since last night."

"And you didn't think it was important enough to tell me?" Reina could feel the first flutter of anger bloom as she rushed to her seat.

"I wanted to make sure. They're following us blind. The signals our ship releases don't remain long in our wake. It's interesting."

She rubbed her face, rubbed it rough and hard. Reina knew Atlas always had a rational reason for everything he did, even keeping things from her; it was the one thing about him that she found aggravating. "Interesting?"

"That they would risk following us out here, knowing the danger."

Reina adjusted the propulsion of her ship, increasing its speed. She glanced up and out at the panoramic view as the vessel jolted forward, unhappy with increased stress on its battered systems.

Something bright caught her eye just as she turned back to her screens but nothing was there.

The next instant, she found herself right up against the glass. "Did you see that?"

Atlas was at her side. "No, what did you see?"

"A bright light. A flash?"

Reina peered out into the darkness, scanning it; her eyes shifted and strained, back and forth until her fingers clutched the cold glass. Nothing presented itself to her and the harder she tried to revisit that brief second, the more her heart raced.

"All I see are the stars."

"It wasn't a star." She turned back toward her console. "The imagery! Maybe it was captured." Reina brought up the most recent pictures, analyzing them but found nothing. She returned to the window, glued to it.

"It was probably nothing, Reina, I see noth–" He stopped mid-sentence. Another bright spark flickered and fluttered. It looked so close but it had to be far away. Reina knew he saw it as well this time as they both grew quiet, afraid that any movement, any noise would scare off the light.

It disappeared again, but the two of them continued to watch. When it reappeared, it reappeared with others, they appeared closer.

"I don't understand, it just looks like twinkling stars," she said. "Do you think this is what we were sent to find?"

"I don't know, but we're headed straight for them, and fast," Atlas answered before swiveling on his feet, jumping back into his seat. His urgency fed her fear. The ship came to a grinding halt soon after and the imagery scans increased to every minute.

Yesne came in just as the white lights expanded into a field before them, still at a distance, but slowly increasing in size and frequency.

"What is that?"

"We don't know," Atlas answered.

Reina's heart jumped as some of the lights began to streak and move around.

"They're above us," Yesne said, and her eyes went up, seeing the orbs, the strange stars dance ever closer to their ship.

She clenched her hands, mesmerized, frightened, and stuck to the spot until her fingers slipped across her sweaty palms. Reina glanced down at her hands, especially the robotic one with the fresh layer of skin and tissue. The weak nerve structure rebuilding beneath. *It looks like it did when I was first sick.*

The memory brought her back to the present. "I think we should move."

Atlas was already in his seat, reading something on the screen. "I'm not sure that's a good idea." His eyes didn't lift to meet hers. "They're surrounding us on the visuals."

"How did they get behind us!?" She rushed to his seat and looked at his screen. The lights were creeping ever closer to them, and from the picture, they were behind them as well. "Surrounded, but we can still fly through them. Can we warp?"

"I won't be able to warp safely, and we don't know what these flashes will do to the ship, or if they're controlled by something else: a trap *per se*. Crashing through them could be seen as an attack."

Yesne sighed. "So you suggest that we do nothing."

"I suggest we wait."

"They're moving closer." Yesne turned back to the window. "I think we should retreat before they get any closer. I agree with Reina."

Reina reached down and touched Atlas's hand, her fingers sliding over his knuckles. "Can you get any sort of reading on them? Anything at all?" She tried to hide the tremor that ran up her spine.

Yesne piped up. "They're changing colors, guys." Everyone looked out to see the sheen of shimmering, illuminated colors, almost like a gauzy veil except for the shifting iridescence. Whole orbs would vanish then reappear in pieces, and now in different swirls of muted colors. Almost like orbs.

Atlas responded with an unease that she had never heard from him before. "I sense nothing. Not a single thing. It's like whatever this is doesn't exist, at least not yet–an anomaly even our technology can't detect. There's nothing showing up on the images as well, it's all but invisible."

"The lights are attracted to us."

A tentacle hit the window with a thump, startling them into action.

"What the hell!?" Yesne jerked back, losing his footing and hitting the floor. Atlas jumped to his feet, the gun on his belt now in his hand. Another tentacle followed, slithering across slowly, like a tongue, licking the one barrier separating them enticingly.

Reina shot to her seat, connecting her hand and feeding herself into the systems. The moment she did, she felt the silky, dry feelers all over herself, tasting her as if exploring a new treat. She dropped out with a squeak, shaking her body all over.

"You okay?"

Reina shook her head and gulped. She reconnected.

Atlas helped Yesne to his feet and they both buckled in just as the ship shot forward into the mass of approaching lights.

"It's not possible," Yesne said. "Not possible."

The ship picked up speed, now with Atlas plugged in as well, and she made to turn around, wading through the semi-visible creatures violently. The thunder of hundreds of things banging into the ship filled their ears, drowning out everything else. Everything but Yesne chanting, *not possible*.

She forced the ship through, finding that she had to continuously push the systems harder, needing more power to move it. The creatures' tentacles smoothed over the window, her view of space vanishing little by little every second.

Reina clenched her jaw, aiming the ship for every small opening that appeared. A route appeared on her screen and she headed for the charted path Atlas scouted out for her.

They were completely blind now to everything but the streaks of light flooding their view. She had to squint through each flash as her vision began to blur.

Atlas pulled out, and the battery of his body went with him.

"No! We're losing speed." Reina yelled, putting everything she had into it, even though she felt the disgust of sticky jelly wiggle all over the exterior of her ship. "We can push through."

"It's too late." Atlas's hand grasped her shoulder. Sirens went off just as she saw him check his clip. "They're in the thrusters."

The error that appeared said the same thing.

"It's not too late. It can't be too late! We can still make it."

The ship sputtered to a halt.

Please. She begged as she continued to push through. Atlas was before her now staring out the window all while strapping on gear, double checking the gun she didn't know he had stashed, pulling out weapons throughout the bridge and setting them on the projection table.

She buried her face in her hands and breathed, still feeling the wormy hairs of the things outside all over. Everything came to a stop around her as she looked up at the window. An entire slithering mass was pressed up against it and Yesne was standing before it, staring. The thing looked like a jellyfish when fully visible, and it looked like it was staring back.

Reina reached over and silenced the sirens. The thudding of Atlas's booted feet left the room. She got up and joined the doctor back at the window. The thing slithered as she approached. Others, half-plastered to the glass, were at its sides.

"What's not possible?" she asked, wondering how much time they had left.

Yesne jerked as if coming out of a trance. "What?"

"You said it wasn't possible."

"Life in space. Creatures this big surviving in a vacuum," he mumbled.

Reina looked back at the jellyfish thing. She wasn't sure how, but she knew it was studying them, looking at them, just as they were looking at it. The colors of its body shifted from a pale yellow to a muted pink. A quiver rolled through her belly.

Atlas stormed back onto the bridge, completely decked out in battle armor, the sharp planes of his face set with intent. He joined them, eyeing the thing at the window as if it was an enemy that needed to be eradicated.

The glow-streaks shifted from pink back to yellow.

Chapter Twenty-Three:

. . . .

Atlas eyed the swarm in front of them. He didn't know why, but try as he might, he couldn't get a read on the things that surrounded his ship.

Our ship. He glanced at Reina and Yesne.

She caught his eye, hers were wide and filled with worry. He had a problem with losing himself in their crystalline hazel depths, and he wanted to comfort her until they cleared up. Unfortunately, they were living on borrowed time.

Reina stepped closer to him and settled slowly into his arms; Atlas wrapped her up and breathed her in. He didn't want anything to happen to her and didn't think he could bear living if she wasn't living with him. Atlas pressed a kiss to the top of her head. Yesne broke the moment.

"It keeps changing its colors. Look." He pointed. Atlas only looked down at Reina as she shifted to see. "It's purple now. It went purple when you two touched."

Reina pulled away and he let her, only to keep one hand wrapped around her forearm.

"Do you think it matters?" she asked. The ship rocked as if hit by an overwhelming force. The creature at the window jostled and fell away. Yesne stepped forward, making a sound of distress. It had vanished into the gelatinous globule.

"It doesn't matter, you two need to gear up," Atlas warned.

"They haven't attacked us," Yesne argued. "What do you think those guns are going to do to them?"

The ship rocked again. Atlas steadied Reina. His mission was to protect her and to protect the ship. Whatever else happened, he wasn't about to let any possibility of escape go by.

"We all know what happens," he answered, "No one ever returns. It's only a matter of time before those squirmers try and take us down." He walked over to the console and brought up all the imagery from the past hour, swiping through them one by one, showing the others the uncanniness of the situation. "There is no evidence of their existence. There is nothing at all."

Reina shook her head. "They will *try* but they won't succeed. We need a plan." He shot her a look, debating whether her confidence was feigned or if she really believed that they could get out of this. He could hear her heart race.

Atlas went to his seat and powered up the cannons. No one stopped him as he shot off a blast at the swarm. Bright yellow and red lit up washed out the bridge and their pathway cleared. The dark void of space returned. The creatures surrounded them again in a swirling mass of tentacles just as quickly. He shot off another round and this time they didn't open up the sky, but they did wiggle.

"They're all glowing yellow now," Yesne piped up.

Atlas hated that he could still get headaches. He rubbed his temple. Reina was back in her own seat now, seemingly lost in thought. No one spoke, lost in their own thoughts, knowing that this mission could mean their deaths. The tension sucked the air out of the room and the remaining quiet hung heavily around them.

Reina jumped as the sirens blared again, this time accompanied by flashing red lights. He shot to his feet. The wail of it echoed off of the walls. It shattered their doomed thoughts.

"Put us in lockdown!" He rushed to the door and looked down the hallways before turning back to the captain's screen. The door shut closed behind him as Reina opened up the report. He already knew what it said.

"There's been a breach," Reina breathed, her eyes wide and focused as she opened up her live schematics to find the source of the issue. "It's in the underbelly where we were hit," she sighed as if it were a relief.

Atlas tightened his fingers around the handle of his gun as he watched her. Even without a direct target, the twitch of wanting to pull the trigger strained his joints. The screen widened and glowed with red, indicating the problem area but there was nothing else there, which was to be expected as the creatures outside were invisible to all but the eyes.

The piercing noise came to a stop and Reina slumped into her chair. The abrupt quiet was louder than any noise that had come before. Strain permeated the bridge and built as each new tentacle thumped and slid across the window, demanding attention he no longer wanted to give.

The ship rolled to the side, stuck in a slowly swaying wave of goo.

The slap of Yesne's hand broke the silence as he grasped a metal rail to keep his balance.

Reina spoke up, saying the one thing no one wanted to say. "They're in the ship." She drew her thumb across her bottom lip. "We need a plan," repeating her earlier sentiment. Atlas kept his eyes on her as the time ticked away, every second bore them closer to an outcome that was inevitable. He walked over and buckled her into her seat as the ship continued to shift and jerk.

"I think they're sentient." Yesne, still enchanted by the amorphous, color-changing tendrils mumbled, unmoved and unworried by their situation. The ship moved again and the doctor stumbled until he found his balance. Atlas shifted his eyes back to his captain, who remained lost in thought, lost in the circuits of the ship. He could feel her flow through it and caress him like a feather before drifting away.

He realized he didn't know how to get them out of this; he was stuck in the same brooding state as Reina and the doctor. His nails bit into his palm as a feeling of uncertainty washed over him.

Atlas stormed to the barred door, placing his hands at the bottom and forcing the metal barrier back into the wall with the magnets in his palms. His fingers traced the gun on his hip in reassurance. Reina was at his side as he ducked under the grinding door.

She grabbed his arm. "Where are you going?" He strolled forward toward the passageways that led to the breach. Reina tugged on his arm, briefly stopping him, surprised by the strength in her arm. "You can't fight them off alone."

They reached the next door and he broke it the same way.

"I'm going to read my enemy. If it comes to bloodshed, it won't be me that starts it." They passed the lounge and eatery. Reina trailed behind him, half jogging to keep up with his gait. The ship shifted and he caught her before she hit the wall. "Reina, you need to go back to the bridge, the doors will shut again if you put them back into lockdown."

Her fingers tightened on his arm.

"I'm not leaving you," she hissed. "This is my ship and I'm the captain. You're going to need backup to repair the breach." The fingers on his arm pierced through his armored suit. "You can't stop me. There is nowhere on my ship that can keep me away from you. They could be dangerous. They could be fast."

Atlas took a step back as his captain let go of him and strolled forward. "They could also be nothing more than pretty blobs swimming through empty space." He couldn't help but smirk. She led them to the gear room and he lifted the door for her.

"I'm glad you've come to your senses," she murmured under her breath. They picked up space suits and tugged them on. The sirens flared back to life, screaming in their ears.

Atlas grabbed Reina and kissed her hard, taking, demanding, one more kiss from her before they put their helmets on. The warning lights made them glow a neon red. He sought her tongue and sucked on it. A bite of desperation fueled them. They parted just as quickly, just as painfully.

"You taste as good as the sex we're going to have when we survive this."

That taste remained at the forefront of his mind. They made their way to the hatch, guns at the ready.

• • • •

SHE COULDN'T STOP THE chilling shivers that rocked her body. Spots formed in her eyes from the bright red flashes, her hearing was nearly deafened from the wailing of the ship. But she could still hear the thunderous noise just beyond the last door. The flailing of heavy limbs and crashing, crushing machinery just beyond her sight.

Atlas shot her a look as he bent down to lift the door open. His face grim, his lips downcast, his hair wild, and his hands pressed against the metal. Reina checked her gun, the grenade on her belt, the long knife attached to her hip, and knelt next to him, nodding for him to continue.

Her self-assurance was fake; she wanted to run screaming back to the bridge and hide in a corner, pressed up into a closet and chant how she shouldn't be here. She had never trained for frontline battles.

But she was better than what her reflexes wanted: she was a goddamned captain, a Neoborg who faced off with Trentians, space pirates, and now monsters. Reina balanced on her knees and aimed forward.

The door lifted up with a screech as if upset for being disturbed, and forced to disobey the commands of the ship. The screech of metal on metal drowned out the heavy flopping on the other side.

A silvery, red-streaked tentacle flooded under the growing space, slapping Atlas's knees before shooting back into the room. Reina fired a shot that missed.

She winced and jerked back. Atlas gripped her forearm.

The rest of the slab slipped into the wall and Atlas hit the side, peering into the darkened room as the air from the ship vented out of the jagged rent in the hull.

Reina felt the buffeting atmosphere of the ship press her forward; she spread her legs and leaned against it. Something bright, elongated, and red sailed across the room. It disappeared into the darkened corners.

Whatever it was, it wasn't coming at them. It seemed content to stay in the destroyed underbelly.

Atlas nudged her, placing the barrel of his gun over his helmet in a hush.

Reina shifted to the side, hoping to catch a glimpse, only to be confronted by more darkness. The flash of green caught her attention just as a chemlight was thrown into the room.

The glow from the hallway, down farther now as the pressure was shattering the stripped lighting and being sucked into the dark room, was now fused with an oily green. Reina squinted, her attention brought to the opening, seeing nothing but a pearly glob about to burst through the seams.

Atlas motioned to the side.

She turned to look where his gun pointed and was met with the sight of two of the squirmers twitching in the corner, the subtle colors of their stringy limbs, still a gross yellow, was fading into their bodies, muting the glow. The longer she stared at them, the more they seized, the more their transparent skin solidified into a sickly, white form.

Atlas said something that she couldn't hear. Reina crept back slowly, away from the doorway and opened up her portable console, turning off the ship's screams.

She looked up just as her Cyborg entered the room, feeling her fear replace her hard-earned resolve and hurried to cover him.

"What are you doing?" she wheezed, entering the room, her eyes on squirmers. Tiny pieces of unhinged debris flew past them and into the unfilled cracks of the opening. "Atlas?" Reina shivered with every step closer, the ship rolled and shook with her. Her fingers clenched the handle of her gun like a lifeline.

"They're not attacking us." Atlas canted his head toward the two in the corner. "Don't let them touch you. We don't know what they can do to us. I can't read them. Still." His voice had a hard edge of annoyance to it. "But I can sense these three now, their biology is changing."

Reina stood up and made her way to the opposite corner from the two monsters already in the room.

"Changing?" She didn't try to read them. She wasn't sure how too, knowing her cybernetics were built more on emotion and feeling and a direct connection to her ship. Reina was afraid of how much control she had and how to use what she controlled. Atlas had far more wired inside him than just a single chip in his head and a heavy arm.

He shook his head, moving forward deliberately, a hunter on the prowl. Reina sucked in a breath, seeing him as the killing machine that he was.

All at once, she was glad that they were on the same side, knowing instinctively that she wouldn't stand a chance if he had tried to kill her after his revival.

The alien mass in the crack plopped forward, demanding her attention.

Tiny hairs released from the globe of its body, shifting in color, size, and length, slithering around as if feeling for something. Reina saw another squirmer take its place in the crack. She rounded the side of the newcomer and picked up a large metal rod, adjusting to the weight of it in her hand.

She was met with the sounds of thumping and the wet slip of slime. Atlas pointed his gun at the target in silent communication as she edged near the one writhing its way across the dank floor toward the others in the corner.

Reina shifted to make herself a smaller target and steadily pressed the rod forward until the blunt tip poked into the body of the mass. The tiny tentacles shot out and grabbed the metal, rolling around its length but it didn't tug it out of her hands. She pushed it harder into the thing and it slithered back, away from the probe. Streaks of yellow and a dead grey wormed its way through its body. Reina pulled the weapon back just as a tentacle shot up its length and swiped across her gloved hand. She jerked back. The thing slithered away.

Atlas lowered his gun and came toward her.

Dust and debris continued to flow through the room. He took the hand still holding the rod and looked at where it the thing touched her. There was a line of silvery mucus across her glove. Reina noticed that he didn't have the same streak over his knees.

All three squirmers were piled in the corner now. Atlas took the rod from her hand and shoved it into the creature wiggling its way through the crack. He slammed the end of it over and over until it was pushed back out into the bloated mass surrounding the ship.

He bent the metal and shoved it into the gap.

Atlas stopped abruptly and cupped the rod. "What the hell?"

Reina moved to his side and focused on where he looked. Flakes of metal peeled off and flew into the crack. It was deteriorating at an alarming rate.

"How is that possible?" she asked, eyeing the floor, finally noticing that the dust and debris that was being suctioned out came from her ship's floors and walls.

"They're corrosive, whatever they are." He stuck his arm through the gap and rubbed the outside, a feeler came through and swiped at him. When he pulled his arm back into the room he had a clump of metal in his hand.

Reina grabbed his arm and looked at the crumble of her ship's exterior plating, pieces of it began to vanish in thin air.

"They're destroying it!" Watching in horror as the clump turned to dust in his palm. She glanced at her glove It was still intact. *Only metal?* "Atlas—don't let them get under your skin."

"Shoot them if they move." He headed toward the exit. "I'll be right back." He left her in the room with the creatures before she could muster a response.

Reina eyed the squirmers in the corner, the green flare was all but a dull glow now, leaving only a muddy look to the destroyed landing mech. Long tentacles flooded through the opening, reaching in and exploring the walls and the bar that denied them entrance.

The crack was growing bigger.

The ship rolled abruptly, turning on its side, making her stumble and fall into the opposite wall. Something silky and strong slipped across her body, shielding her from direct impact. It was the one she had poked. It covered the other two, twitching creatures, shielding them as well.

Reina shifted away and the feeler let her go. It turned grey before her eyes and then to her horror, it cracked like brittle clay and fell off its body.

The jellyfish thing slumped into itself as she backed away, scooting across the wall.

"I'm sorry," she felt the need to tell it, whispering into her helmet. Her gun slid across the wall toward her, and she caught it before it flew past. With it in her hand, Reina shuffled her way to the exit, trying not to look at the fallen limb slowly being pulled to the crack.

She felt the need to get away from the yellow squirmers; they didn't make sense to her, a gleam of intelligence that shouldn't have been possible. She could have sworn the third one caught her and with that notion, her thoughts drifted to Yesne's sentiments. Reina stiffened. *They don't have eyes.*

Why do I care?

Reina ducked through the door, releasing a heavy breath. Atlas was storming down the passageway toward her with plates of metal in his arms. Their large size made him look awkward.

Concern clouded his features as he went to her. She shook her head, urging him to finish the job, communicating in silence. He stood over her, staring at her with eyes that pierced her soul, burrowing into her and taking the unease from her.

Everything came to a stop and each second lasted an agonizing eternity. There was so much she wanted to say just then, her mouth opening and closing but no words came out. He just continued to stab her with his steely gaze.

The ship rocked back into position, breaking the tortuous moment.

Atlas walked back into the room, followed shortly after by the sound of punching metal. Reina buried her head into her knees. *We still need a plan.*

A plan.

We're still stuck. What can we do? What can I do? A plan...a plan...

Three gunshots went off. Tears trickled down her cheeks. They gushed hot over her skin. Tiny streams of molten lava, burning her anew with each drip.

His shadow appeared over her again, the door shut closed with a grinding thump. The suction was gone, leaving nothing behind but dust motes in the air. Air capsules released and stabilized the ship's atmosphere.

The Trentians came to mind, her superiors, the lost souls that had never returned, and the dozens who had died from the cybernetic mutation. She thought of her regression and the loss of her freedom, the loss of the network, the digital channels, Taggert and the mysterious Larik and his stolen goods. She stumbled further inside herself, seeing Atlas as a hologram, hearing his voice the first time, seeing him come to life, choosing to break down some of her walls to let him in. She thought of Antix and the pirates... the pirates. Her ship.

And everything that had led to this.

"We have proof," he said with harsh reality.

Reina tugged off her helmet and wiped the sticky tears off her cheeks. Atlas kneeled before her, his helmet off as well, and kissed the remaining dew off her face. His velvety, hard mouth trailing over her, affectionately, cleansing her, worshipping her in silence.

She thought of the creatures outside and their colors–the dead, grey tentacle that had broken off after wrapping itself around her. She leaned into Atlas's kisses, her gloved hands rounding his head and gripping his unruly hair.

"I have a plan," Reina said as determination replaced the lingering sadness in her heart.

Chapter Twenty-Four:

· · · · ·

Reina sat at the helm and stared out at the jellyfish beyond the glass. The ship continued to sway and her nausea slowly vanished as her body became used to the rocking.

Once again she had to wait and hope. *Waiting* and *hoping* were two things that she had begun to hate.

The sirens began to shriek again, but she kept her fingers on the console to turn them off as soon as they started.

"I want to see them." Yesne broke the silence, now with a scientific note-screen in his hand. Atlas, hunched over with his elbows on his knees, twirled a flash grenade in his hand.

"No."

"I could learn more about them–"

"No." Atlas cut him off.

"They didn't attack you," Yesne continued to argue, "And you killed them anyway."

Reina tried to ignore them, watching the readings on her screen, waiting.

"If you ask one more time I'm going to stick you in the closet with this grenade." Atlas tweaked the weapon in his hand before clipping it back onto his belt. The sound distracted her. Yesne sighed and paced. Atlas shifted the screen his way, preventing her from monitoring the reports. "You're going to burn a hole through it if you keep staring at it like that."

Reina leaned back. "They should have received it by now." She heard a thumping noise, but dismissed it and looked at Atlas. "They're still within your reach?"

The sirens blared to life, she winced and shut them off. *One more time.*

"Yes."

"Quite an answer, Cyborg, since you're so keen on saying no," Yesne grumbled.

They both ignored him as he was unconcerned with their predicament. Yesne's lack of a self-preservation instinct was a magical quality to behold.

The sound of slimy, slithering thrashes grew in frequency, and Reina wondered if it was because her ship was literally disappearing around her. The bubble they had was quickly vanishing, and she didn't want to leave this world huddled in the center of her ship, waiting for her own asphyxiation.

Her only source of comfort was that the window, the reinforced glass, was unaffected. Just as much as Yesne was.

"They're getting closer," Atlas interjected.

"I know." She eyed the squirmers.

"I meant the pirate fleet."

Reina could scream with joy. "We don't have much time! They're picking up our distress call." She shot forward with excitement and hugged Atlas. "We need to get them close enough."

"Oh they'll get close, sweetheart. We have the best bargaining chip."

She was almost giddy with haphazard hope.

"We need to be ready. If this works, we may only have a small gap of time to get free."

"And that's only if they don't destroy the exterior," Atlas added with a laugh, all while confirming the path back to port. The sector system hologram filled the room, showing their previous course, and now the incoming ships that wanted them. "They'll suspect it's a trap."

"Of course they will, because it is," Yesne huffed. "We don't suffer idiots, ignorants, or fools in this age."

"It won't matter." Reina just wanted things to come to a head, impatient to be away from the jellyfish that surrounded them. "They just need to get close enough." She released her hair and re-tied her bun, wanting to burst from her skin.

Wanting to find the temporary bliss she had had in Atlas's arms again. Wanting to either move forward in time or go back to the stolen moments that they had already had together.

Reina looked over at him.

He was watching her as if he knew what she was thinking and what she wanted from him. His large hands clutched his knees and as they continued to look at each other, his pants bulged between his spread legs, she responded in turn. Her body attuned to his as a tingling, empty pressure opened up, wanting to be filled.

It was unreasonable, but the adrenaline was pumping through her veins, the risk was near, and all she wanted was to straddle his lap and ride him as if death itself was breathing down their necks.

Something hissed and wheezed nearby. Larger flakes of her ship were breaking off and being caught in the bodies of the creatures outside. The mass was a rainbow of colors as they swallowed up the pieces but the majority of them were still flashing yellow.

A strange smell permeated the air. Atlas stood up just as she wrinkled her nose.

It took her a moment to discern it.

Citrus. Sour, pungent citrus.

With a quick glance back at the creatures outside, Atlas made his way toward the door that was now back in place. Reina and the doctor followed him curiously until a pained cough, an inhuman cry, like the ones she had heard just minutes ago stopped her. But they were much closer.

"Stay back," Atlas warned.

"It can't be. You killed them." The acidic smell filled her nostrils, overwhelming her. Yesne gagged next to her.

"I did. They were already dying before the shot." He felt around the door. "I left them unmoving, unreadable," Atlas hesitated when the sound of cracking cut him off. "The density of the door..." A gap appeared before he finished his sentence. Atlas had a gun in his hand.

"The smell, oh hell," Yesne sputtered, his hand clamped over his nose as his eyes watered.

The waves of reeking fruit filled the room were now mixed with the stench of sulfur.

Something pale and grey flashed across the hole, and what looked like long, slender fingers threaded through.

Atlas shot his entire clip. The sound stopped and the elongated, ghoulish fingers fell away.

The bottom of the door broke to pieces, revealing the twitching body of a human male covered in greasy tentacles sprouting from his body, and dulled, dead-looking blood bubbling up and pouring from his wounds. It trailed down the passageway behind him...*it*. Reina cried out and stepped back in horror.

Yesne clutched his stomach and vomited, turning away. The bridge went crimson as the squirmers outside the window switched from yellow to a ruby-red.

The wounds on the creature closed up, replaced by stiffer, grey skin. Atlas stepped forward, blocking her and Yesne from the door and she wasn't sure if it was a relief to be shielded or a shock at the sight of the suffering creature bawling on the ground.

The metal began to splinter beneath it.

Sirens flared back to life, drowning out the hoarse sounds of the amalgamation, as its brethren outside began to attack the ship.

"We're out of time." Atlas stared down at the thing creeping its way into the room.

* * * *

ATLAS EYED THE HALF-living mess on the floor at his feet, a humanoid hand slothed forward and touched his boot. The pinch of fingers straining at the buckle on his waist, tugging him away, could not make him move. Without glancing back at Reina–keeping his eyes on the target that appeared immune to bullets–he finally took a breath.

The stench didn't bother him, he had smelled worse than this creature when he had awoken from the dead. Dead things never smelled good, it was a universally understood truth.

"Atlas, we need to contain him." Reina gave the squirmer a gender. She tried to move to his side but he blocked her.

His head snapped up. "Captain, fire up the ship." Atlas stepped away and the hand slipped off his foot with a harried cry. He took her arm and led her away. "Power up the cannons."

"It won't work, we tried. Twice."

"We're going to try again."

They shared a look before she strapped into her seat, bringing the console to life. The energy began to flow. Sparks shot through his system, Atlas ate it all up.

"Yesne, guard the creature," he ordered. The doctor took a blanket and covered it up; it slumped to the floor like a deflated balloon. The others at the window thrashed against the glass as the cannons initiated.

Atlas hovered his finger over the trigger.

"Captain, Atlas, there's another one crawling down the hallway."

His hand twitched, waiting for the right moment. He could hear the other slither closer but he was waiting for something else. Reina watched him, her eyes narrowed with curiosity.

Come on. COME ON!

The beasts outside shattered entire plates of metal, they streaked across the window and into the horde before they vanished. Atlas could feel their shell breaking apart around them, shredding like gossamer.

He couldn't imagine what Reina was feeling, he couldn't find her within the channels, knowing as well as she did that if she connected it would feel like her skin was being sliced off.

His fingers spread out, his thumb hovered. Yesne made a sound of distress behind him.

The comm dinged and he hit the trigger.

A plasma blast that made the swaying ship shudder and creak like old wood. It blasted out into the crimson monsters, lighting them up like beacons but went nowhere, absorbed by the creatures.

"Fly!"

Reina shot the thrusters with all their remaining power just as a minuscule opening appeared in the bubble. Beyond lay a dozen ships, arranged in a spherical grid to enclose them from every side, now visible through the swarm.

His captain let loose a sound between a cry and a shriek, a harpy of adrenaline. Atlas felt it too, seeing the ships.

The ship tilted and shook, fighting with everything it had to break through. Atlas gripped the armrests of his seat and crushed them as he surged into the systems.

The heavy contraption in his chest went ablaze, burning him from the inside-out. He couldn't bring himself to care, nothing mattered when he subdued his humanity and gave himself over to his Cyborg side. Nothing but his goal.

Reina cried out somewhere in the distance. The ship was cracking like an egg.

Atlas was vaguely aware that she had answered the pirate's call. The flyer burned up around them, the sad weeping of the squirmers overlaid the crushing destruction.

Even if we get away...we might never make it back.

"Atlas! Where is Larik? They won't help us without something now!"

He spoke without thinking, "Not on Taggert."

"That's not good enough, *Robot*." An unknown voice filled the bridge.

"He's alive."

"More!"

"Please," Reina begged, "Our ship is breaking apart. We'll tell you everything once we're safely retrieved." Atlas would have commended her for her lies, if he cared enough to process them.

"We'll move no closer until you tell us where he is," the man answered.

Atlas could feel Reina's eyes on him. A pressure that added little to their situation.

"Urbà," he said. "You'll get no more from us, shoot us down, save us, or go away."

The ship shot forward half a league. Everything felt on fire around them. Sirens kept wailing only to be shut off and overridden afterward. The man on the other line didn't respond. *Probably looking up the classified planet. He'll get no more.* Atlas could practically feel the rage on the other end. Someone always had to concede in a standoff.

One of the ships sailed toward them, every league set off in internal radar.

"What the fuck is around your ship?" The voice yelled, then called out, "It's not a shield! Fire at the lights, Axel!"

Blasts could be heard in the background, Atlas sucked the energy generated between the ships, feasting on it and giving it back to his ship. Their vessel broke through the balloon, only to run into a riotous spray of gunfire of every kind. The swarm might have popped but now they faced immediate annihilation. Reina flew up and into a cluster of flashing squirmers.

Atlas tore out of his seat and rushed to the window. His hands hit the glass as he sourced out any nearby ferromagnetic material.

The comm shut off on a screamed order to subdue them.

He shielded what he could of all incoming firepower, holding it outside the ship, keeping it and building a secondary wall around them to waylay the creatures. The ones that clung on began to fall off the ship, and every microsecond they gained a little more speed.

Reina pushed them hard, he could feel her need to create as much space as possible between them and the globule regardless of what cost the ship may have to pay.

Come on. Come on. Come on, Atlas chanted.

His fingers spread as electric pressure flowed through him, his muscles strained as he focused his magnetic antennas toward each target, capturing them in a net of his own power. Hurling pieces away into any creatures that tried to attach themselves to the exterior, knowing without knowing that they chased after them. Knowing that there could be millions more that awaited invisible, hiding amongst the stars.

But they continued to gain speed and he could smell the sweat trickle down Reina's brow. They flew up and up and as they did so, other ships, ones that had not gotten caught flew outward and away.

Reina shut off their distress call.

He could practically hear the pirates scream 'HELP US' from countless leagues away and gaining.

Atlas shifted their coordinates and, releasing his breath, he saw his eyes flash red in the glare of the window. He had overclocked himself. Striations of muscle grew up from his fingers like vines to his neck. The blood vessels in his eyes framed his pupils, clawed over, revealing burned wiring. He smelled smoke and burnt flesh, sour citrus and death, sweat and soft oatmeal hair.

Atlas shuddered as he lifted his hands from the window, leaving infinitesimal cracks. His brow hit his sleeve.

"Follow my route," he rasped. Reina was already making her way toward it but he had to say it anyway.

His hands lifted back to the walls of the ship now to keep the exterior from continuing to fall away.

They had escaped. Atlas turned himself off and became part of the ship.

Chapter Twenty-Five:

• • • • •

It took them several weeks to make it back to Port Antix. The first time they had traversed this distance, it only took three days.

The ship was dead around them, only being held together by the sheer willpower of Atlas. Everything was broken. The sanitation systems, the landing tech, they couldn't even power down the cannons, as they were stuck in target lock and partially destroyed.

They slowly ate their way through any pre-processed food, even resorting to swallowing the powder stored in the replicators. Reina washed the tasteless sand down with a water ration.

But they had survived. And they hadn't encountered anyone or anything since. She reached up to retie her hair only to have her hairband snap over her fingers.

She sat there, in the lounge alone, half-dead from lack of sleep, and stared at the elastic string in her hand.

Reina took a shaky breath and pocketed the band. She gargled the rest of her water and headed toward the bridge. Atlas was still standing sentinel at the helm. He hadn't moved nor responded to her or Yesne since their escape.

She missed him. She missed his presence in her periphery. *He was always at the edges.*

Yesne was at his side, checking his vitals. "Any change?"

"No. Has he contacted you in the channels?"

"No." Reina turned away and grabbed a cleansing cloth and began to wipe it over Atlas' skin. They had cut off his clothes weeks prior when they realized he wasn't going to awaken. It broke her heart. Yesne stepped away to give her privacy as she untied the sheet around his waist. "I'll take over now. We're do to arrive soon. Whatever that means for us," she took a deep breath and glided the cloth over his wrists and under his arms. "We'll face it like we've faced everything else." There was no way they could survive a warp.

Yesne's footsteps stopped at the other end of the bridge where the entire back section had been divided off, medical supplies and beds from the empty crew's quarters lined the walls, between unused chairs and consoles. Reina bent down and rubbed Atlas's thighs while looking back at their new additions.

She still thought of them as squirmers but they resembled nothing of the sort now. One of them, the female, stared back at her. Reina broke eye contact and folded up the cloth and located her moisturizer, massaging the shea butter into Atlas's skin, having hoped that her scent might bring him comfort, or better yet, wake him up.

Reina stretched up and kissed the back of his neck. "I miss you."

She re-tied the cloth around his hips. When she looked back across the room the female 'it' was still watching her. She tried not to let it bother her. The eyes of the female were white with tiny black pupils in the center. There was no irises, no color at all.

Yesne placed the hand of the male next to her into a bowl of water. "Water," he said. "This is water. Water." The man's fingers wiggled in the liquid, he was sitting up, and there was a look of awe on his face.

"Wha. Wha." It was a weak whisper.

It's better than their crying. At least they no longer cry. Reina snaked her arms around Atlas's stomach and leaned into his side.

"Water," Yesne repeated.

"Whaaner."

"Yes! Water, keep trying." Yesne swirled the bowl from side to side, some of the liquid sloshed to the ground.

"Whater." The male tried again. The doctor preened with encouragement.

Reina glanced at the female before quickly looking back at the doctor, only to move on the third creature. Another male, one they had extricated from the underbelly, he lay on his cot with a blank stare, only moving when his companions touched him. And they did that a lot, Reina and Yesne often had to separate the three from whatever bed they piled up on together.

"How are they?" she called out.

Yesne didn't look up, his focus on his new project. "Quite great. Growing."

"Growing?"

"They're growing nails now. It's amazing. They all have teeth coming in. Water, try again. Water," Yesne emphasized.

"Waiter." The male responded absently, taking his hand out of his bowl and dripping it across the skin of his arm. "Water," he said perfectly soon after.

"Yes!" Yesne sat back, placing the bowl on the male's lap. "Every day, progress." He looked over at her. "They're miraculous."

"They're not human."

"They will be soon," he responded with a pleased laugh. "They could be the solution to everything."

Reina looked back at the female, who had yet to look away from her or move, and shivered. She tightened her hold around Atlas's waist, breathing him in, and wanting him to be there next to her like he had promised.

The doctor continued while changing out the IVs attached to the 'new' humans. "They're sentient–"

"Sentaent," the male from before mumbled.

Yesne kept going, "They can learn. They are becoming more like us every day. Soon they may even grow hair."

"If they're becoming human, they're becoming more dangerous."

"Dang. Dangrous," the male was repeating words that she was uncomfortable with. Or at least trying to. "Dangerous."

Reina felt a chill sweep up her spine.

"Very good!" Yesne gave the male a sweet candy.

She looked away and buried her face into Atlas's back, stealing his heat, and taking whatever comfort she could from his statuesque form.

Reina didn't want to admit it, not even to herself. She was afraid–afraid that they would make it to Port Antix and find an ambush waiting for them or that it would be abandoned with nothing left but the stink of corpses. She was afraid of the three squirmers on the other side of the room, and what they could do. She was also afraid of what would happen to them once the Earthian Council took them away.

Will they send ships out to the fake star-fields and capture more?

She closed her eyes. *Please come back to me.*

Reina had tried to go into the channels of the ship but was thrown out by the chaos and the pain. The ship was still her, and that part of herself was broken inside and out. It had left her shaking on the cold floor of her quarters in shock.

When she had recovered, she tried again. Each time it filled her with agony. Her skin felt like it was being fried. Reina knew that she didn't want to continue her life without Atlas in it. And her biggest fear of all was that they would be split apart by those they worked for.

Her fingers gripped his side, digging into the strained muscle and bunched up cloth. Reina's ear twitched as the heady rush of a familiar voice washed over her.

"We can see the universe, we can sail through galaxies, explore uncharted planets, and name the stars. Just the two of us until we reach the end. We can disappear," Atlas said softly. Reina felt her eyelashes dampening as she tried to hold back her tears. "Like so many others before us."

His hand slid down the panoramic glass shield, leaving a sweaty streak behind before lifting away and cocooning her under his arm.

"You're back," she gasped into his side.

"Don't cry, sweetheart. I was never gone." The ship shuddered as it lost Atlas's protection. Their speed slowly dropped until they were merely shucking along, no longer traveling by light measurements. "I knew you were there." His other arm shook and lifted from the glass. "I would never leave you willingly."

They stood there holding each other, both willing time to stop, so this moment could last for all eternity. Reina couldn't bear the thought of ever letting him go again.

Her eyes opened as she realized, for the first time, that she was stronger with Atlas by her side. That she could feel relief in letting someone behind her walls. That life wasn't as hard as it had to be when you had the right person by your side.

"I love you, Atlas." Reina lifted her head and found his eyes. They were bloodshot and beady.

"I love you too, Captain."

She blinked away her tears and they shared a smile.

"Oh good, you turned yourself back on," Yesne gleefully, once again, broke the moment. "How do you feel? How is your recovery?"

Atlas shifted to face him, turning away from the window. "I've felt worse." He left it at that, releasing her to wipe a trickle of blood coming out of his nostril and rip the IV that fed him from his arm. "I see we have new additions."

With her hand firmly restrained in his, he led them over to the creatures. The two males stood up as he came close and closed ranks. Streaks of yellow glowed under their skin. Yesne practically fell, rummaging around for his note-screen.

Atlas stopped short, his muscles strained, the hard edges and planes of his chest stood out as he eyed the males before him. They were taller in stature and slight in nature but the warning in their eyes could only be learned by humans. Reina could physically feel the tension between them.

"Are they not miraculous? You and Captain Reina did it, now we can bring them home to Earth. They could be the answer to everything."

"Where's my gun?" Atlas asked without taking his eyes off them.

Reina felt her heart skip a beat. Yesne choked in response. The males they faced didn't move. She slipped her hand from his and located his gun.

But she didn't hand it over.

Yesne was between Atlas and the males, arguing up a storm. "You can't kill them! They're our only proof of what's out there! The images show nothing except the occasional flash of light and the pirates. Without them, they'll believe it's a trap and they'll send more ships out there to apprehend the perceived threat. More will die. A lot more."

Atlas didn't answer.

His eyes were charged in crimson and blood continued to leak from his nose to drip onto his chest. Gone were the days where he was airy and blue, and minuscule numbers flowed over his projected skin. Reina wasn't sure if she would miss that phantom side of him, all she knew was that she wanted him in her life as a Cyborg with blazing eyes, but would take what she could get and what he would give her.

311

"What do you sense?" she asked.

"They're trying to imitate being human. That what you see on the outside is not the same as what should be on the inside. Their cells are constantly growing and mutating but not like a Cyborg's. As we speak, these two are adapting to be more like me. I don't trust it. I don't trust the implications."

"Why?" Reina looked behind the males and at the female huddled on the bed behind them, her long arms hugging her knees to her chest, her body shapeless under a large undershirt.

"If they can become human, they could become anything," Atlas answered.

One of the males stepped forward, his slacks hanging loosely around his hips. She couldn't help but wonder what was just beneath the clothing.

When Yesne and I dressed them, they didn't have sexual organs. Reina had a gut feeling that they probably did now.

"Do you think they could terraform? They can transform. I wish we had use of the medical bay," Yesne asked, intrigued.

"Possibly."

Reina asked, quickly, quietly, "Do you think they could breed with us?" She still hadn't handed him his gun. Atlas looked at her knowingly, and for a frightening moment, with the trails of blood over his face and chest, made him look more like a monster than a man. Her feet twitched to jump back.

"Pussibley," the same male said. The yellowish lights on their bodies became a brilliant gold before the color faded completely from their skin. The ship rocked and groaned, an entity in itself all around them.

Reina hugged her arms around herself, caressing her bionic appendage in comfort. She closed her eyes tight and cooed at the ship.

I'm sorry you're hurting. I'm sorry you got stuck paired with me but I'm going to fix you, and Atlas is going to fix you.

When she turned back the male from before was shuffling toward Atlas, his hand out in supplication, his fingers abnormally long. They grew out like tiny little snakes, and what she could have sworn had been joints before when his hand was in the bowl of water, was nothing more than fluid ripples.

She interjected quickly, "We have to talk about what we're going to do. We're almost to Antix."

Atlas wiped the blood off his face with force and it sprayed across the room. He reached forward and grabbed the squirmer's wrist then let go. Atlas turned to her as if their interaction had never happened. The charged, almost violent, moment gone.

Reina could see in Atlas's eyes, behind the crimson veil, that everything was about to change.

Chapter Twenty-Six:

. . . .

"WE HAVE NO CHOICE," Reina argued. "Antix is the only base within reach, the ship can't warp, it can't hold out much longer. *I* can't hold out much longer and you, you need help."

Atlas and she had left the bridge, leaving Yesne with the aliens.

"I know. But if we go back we'll be delivering the metal-eaters right into their hands. Reina, this could start a war."

She pulled at her hair, wanting to deny his words, but it was the fear that she had been harboring inside herself. The thing she didn't want to admit, nor to voice. "I won't kill them."

"You wouldn't. I would." *Thousands.*

Atlas took his sheet off and wiped himself down, gulping a water canister simultaneously.

"Did you feel something? When you grabbed the male?"

"Confusion, fear, want."

"Want? You felt want? What did he want?" Reina asked.

Atlas dropped the dirty sheet. "It wanted to understand. It wanted to be me, I think. And right now, as we speak, its biology is changing. It's going to have a hell of a time trying to replicate my metal frame," he muttered.

"Yesne thinks they could be the cure."

"Enslavement, death, the Trentians...can you handle that?"

"It won't come to that, you know it won't. We can't fight another war, neither could the Trentians. The pirates could have escaped, they could know what we know. If it's not us, it could be them."

Reina found herself locked in his embrace.

"But can you handle it?" Atlas tilted her chin up and asked.

"Yes." *I can handle it. Someone has too. I trust myself.*

"Then we'll handle it together, Captain."

She ran her hands up his back until she cupped his neck and pulled him down to meet her lips. Atlas sucked her tongue into his mouth and the taste of metal consumed her. She bit his lip as his rough fingers threaded through her loose hair, he gripped her head, pulling at the curling brown strands and sucked the life-force out of her.

His hold was painful and desperate. Her nails clutched his shoulder blades, scratching at his skin.

Atlas released her head and she felt the pressure of her space suit press up against her breasts, followed by the sound of shredding behind her. Cool air touched her spine as he palmed his way up to the shredded material at her shoulders and tore it off.

Reina contorted her body until the cloth fell in waves at her feet.

"I missed you," he groaned, picking her up and carrying her into the lounge, setting her on the table.

"I missed you too."

Atlas grabbed her feet and pulled her legs apart until she was spread breathlessly before him. He pushed between her and snapped her panties off. His hands ran up and down her sides.

Reina moaned, arching her body off the table, and feeling her body tingle and drip with want.

She straddled his hips. He ran his heavy cock over her pussy, dry humping, with their bodies writhing against each other.

Atlas appeared over her, grunting with each teasing thrust, sliding his hands up to tug down her bra and expose her tits. The cool air of the ship made them painfully taut until his fingers pinch them softly. Teasing them like his cock teased her clit, bumping it in rhythm with his hands.

"The prettiest sight I've ever seen," he rasped over her ear, sending goosebumps down her body, "is watching you come undone under me."

The ship croaked and guttered around them. The clang of something crashing to the floor was ignored. Reina arched up in response as Atlas lifted away from her, retaking the heels of her feet in his hands and bending her knees to her chest.

They shared a heated look. She drowned in the red, possessive, uncontrolled look in his eyes.

I wonder what he sees in mine.

With him bearing down on her, her legs spread, pinned completely to the tabletop, Reina clawed at the edge for leverage as Atlas pushed into her. Her hips came off the table as he stretched her open and took her recklessly, sinking into her again and again.

The smell of sweat and sex perfumed the air, creating a euphoric haze. The loud banging of the table and thumps of her hips hitting the metal top with each thrust filled her ears.

Reina arched up as if possessed, an electric shock coursing through every fiber of her being as Atlas

316

came deep inside her, burning her, branding her, shocking her as he released himself again and again, thick and vibrating.

She strained her head from side to side, needing to fall off the edge with him. His hips pivoted upward until the thick, mushroom head of his Cyborg cock hit her g-spot, buzzing against it with short and shallow thrusts.

Her fingers crushed the metal edge of the table as her body shook with relief, an orgasm ripping from her pussy, stolen by Atlas, and flooding her head as her screams echoed off the walls.

"Yes," was the only thing she heard, growling above her.

Reina pushed him away feeling oversensitive all over but her muscles had lost all their pent-up strain. Without breaking their strangling, wet connection, Atlas lifted her in his arms and sat them on a nearby chair.

"The *Reincarnation*."

"What?" Reina asked sleepily, her throat hoarse.

"Should be the name of our ship."

Reina smiled. "I like it."

"I like it too."

And with a sated breath, she found the beautiful oblivion of sleep in Atlas's marvellously real arms.

* * * *

ATLAS REJOINED WITH the ship sooner than she would have liked and within hours they received a hail from the Earthian Council. A company of battlecruisers and freighters surrounded the airspace of Port Antix; they intercepted them and hauled them planetside.

It was a relief that they weren't met by pirates.

It seemed that they had a little luck on their side. Reina stood to attention, having donned her military uniform, and was escorted off her ship by several guards.

Atlas had stayed behind with the metal-eater-squirmer-mermaid-shifters. They had a lot of names now. No one knew quite what to call them. Atlas demanded they waited to make any official reports on that matter until their cognizance developed enough so that they could name themselves, as was the Cyborg's way.

She was interrogated for days by a multitude of people, about Antix, the pirates, the decision to abandon the setup of the relays, and the damage to the ship until a man in a dark grey suit sat her down and asked her the harder, more dangerous questions.

Those of Atlas's resurrection and the creatures they had taken on board. The images were taken, all of them, and then deleted off her ship's personal databases.

"Your name will not be released."

"I don't understand?" she asked, putting down her coffee.

"We need to know that you will never speak of the events of this mission to anyone, ever again."

"I can't promise you that," Reina sat up. "I need to know my crew is okay, that Atlas will remain my navigator, and that the...the..."

"Aliens?"

"Yes. That they will be okay." She reached across the interrogation table, one that was an exact replica from her last interrogation and grabbed the suit's wrist. "We came back. You owe me some answers."

The suit pinned her with a stare before shaking off her hand. He was older, but not by much, his hair dark and peppered with grey and slicked close to his head. His skin as dark as ebony and his eyes were brown. Although he retained a cooled attitude toward her, she couldn't miss the laugh lines on his face nor the flash of sympathy in his eyes.

He looked at something behind her, a glimpse, before he returned his attention to her.

Reina kept her face stone, but it was harder for her now, she felt so much these days. Emotions pooled from her when she found herself alone, screaming into her pillow during the rest cycles.

If we had vanished–if we had disappeared–we could have stayed together.

She missed her makeshift family and would do whatever she could to ensure their safety. Even that of the creatures. The female had seemed like she wanted to approach her, like the alpha male of the group approached Atlas.

When they had returned to the bridge, the male that had touched Atlas had begun to morph rapidly into a different shape, one that resembled a Cyborg. She wondered if the female wanted to mimic her form.

It was an odd thought.

"Dr. Yesne will be tried for treason, but he will remain with the aliens until his trial as head scientist."

"Will he be found guilty? I'll testify on his behalf."

"He will be found, what the jury finds him," he answered cryptically. *He'll be okay.*

"And the aliens? I assume they won't be killed if the doctor is staying with them?" she asked.

"They are no longer even in this galaxy."

Reina sat back and stared bullets at the man, feeling a loss she couldn't explain, having never discovered which one had caught her fall and saved her life.

The suit continued, "Atlas will also be tried for treason."

"What for? For reclaiming his body? The Earthian Council forced him to take this mission and used his body for insurance. Without his resurrection, this mission would have never been a success."

"And your arguments will be taken into account, Captain."

Her anger grew into something she could psychically hold.

"I won't be able to see him, I'm assuming? What will happen to me? Will I be tried for treason as well? I am the captain of the *Reincarnation* as it stands."

"We commend you for your service to the Earthian Council and to the human race, Captain." He responded, unfazed.

"So that's it." Her nails bit into her palms.

He pushed a document toward her across the table, "That's it until you sign for your silence."

She took the stylus from him and signed her life away. She would do what she needed to, to protect those she cared about.

"Now, Captain, do you know that Commander Anders has gone missing? I have some questions about your relationship with him."

Epilogue:

· · · ·

Atlas sat at the bench before a number of his peers, including Jack and Yuric–other Cyborgs like himself–as they stood up and walked out of the room. It had been months since he had last been free, and since his return to civilization, he went clad in reinforced chains with a guard of twenty trained soldiers to accompany him wherever he needed to go.

They should have assigned me fifty. He was offended by the lack of guard. If he had wanted to escape, he could have. But he didn't, he knew the protocol and the corruption of the council. They would need to find him not guilty, on the official record, to be able to reinstate him to his post.

I wonder who they bought.

I wonder what the price was to have two Cyborgs on the jury.

The thing about Cyborgs was that they worked well together, built for teamwork, but they were also built as alphas. Warriors.

Though he had served at the sides of his brethren for years, when the war had ended, most of them had gone their separate ways. After the command structure had fallen and their freedom had been won, they realized they couldn't exert authority over one another, as not one of them could bear *not* being the leader.

Cyborgs worked better alone when they were free.

Like magnets. Atlas signed internally. If war was on the horizon, he was ready for it, guns blazing and magnets at the ready. His fingers twitched.

The jury walked back in, the silence broken by footsteps. Atlas stared hard at the judge as the men and women took their seats.

The courtroom smelled musty and old but it didn't detract from the reek of his appointed attorney. He had stopped going to sleep at night as the smell of drug-store-bought body spray haunted him. The Earthian Council still had a firm hold on every part of his life, even his nose.

And no one would tell him about Reina. Not even his Cyborg brethren on the jury, when he had reached out and tried to connect with them. Their firewalls were up.

They were strong. Atlas envied their updated systems.

"Will the jury foreperson please stand? Has the jury reached a unanimous verdict?"

An older woman stood up. "Yes, your honor." The clerk stepped forward and took the verdict from the woman, in turn handing it to the judge.

Atlas strained against his chains without making a sound. He trusted no one. No one but his captain.

Silently, the judge handed the verdict back to the clerk.

"On the count of treason against the people of Earth and the sole count of the indictment, the jury finds the defendant not guilty."

The judge glanced his way before turning to the jury and the two Cyborgs sitting amongst them.

"The jury is thanked and excused. The court is adjourned."

The heavy footsteps of the few people in the room faded as they trickled out of the room. One of his guards unlocked the chains around his wrists before they, too, vanished into the gloom outside the double doors. There was no one to congratulate him.

Reina was starkly missing.

Months had gone by with him in isolation, only to be visited by military personnel and Dr. Estond. The doctor wasn't thrilled at his makeshift heart but he had been impressed by Dr. Yesne's resourcefulness. Not to mention, he had undergone drug questioning, after he divulged that the methamphetamine was created by him–and not by Captain Reina or Dr. Yesne.

Atlas rubbed the chafed skin of his wrists. He had a hard time admitting it to himself, but he missed Reina, she was life to him. Even the hollow victory of his freedom was tarnished without her presence.

His lawyer clicked shut his briefcase and offered his hand in farewell before he too left the room.

Atlas looked around the room and took a deep breath, flexing his muscles, and finding a modicum of joy in being able to lift his arms. He headed for the door, already knowing who waited for him on the other side.

Lieutenant General Wasson stood with stiff ease as Atlas approached him.

"Are you ready to get back to work?" Wasson asked.

"Never a day off with you, General. I'm surprised you weren't the one interrogating me these last few months."

They walked companionably outside the courthouse, through a series of metal brigades and out into the rain.

"I was too close to you."

"I suppose you were," Atlas said. "So what happens now?" He lifted his face to the rain, finding a soft bliss in the feel of the droplets trickling down his face and the cool breeze that enveloped him. "You don't own me anymore."

"We never owned you, Commander. Your body owned you."

Atlas laughed. It slithered up with disbelief until it turned into something sinister and hard. The lieutenant general stared at him as his chuckles slowed down and his body started to ache from the intensity.

"You have some nerve, Wasson. For years, all I wanted was to be revived, to live again. And to kill everyone who kept me trapped. Including you, especially you." *I still plan to.*

They stepped into a waiting hover-car as he brooded in silence.

"We have a new assignment for you," the general said eventually. "If you wish to take it." Choosing to ignore the threat Atlas presented.

"What is it?"

"We have a new captain joining our fleet, just promoted to senior, who requested you as her navigator. That is if you can take orders from someone ranked below you. She's stubborn."

Atlas leaned back and uttered a soft curse, a smile tugging at his lips.

• • • •

THE TRANSPORT FLEW into the space battle station hangar outside Earth's atmosphere. The *Reincarnation* came into view, lifted up on giant supports extended from the ceiling. Atlas could feel the specialized electronic channels; he could feel Reina for the first time since Antix.

He shielded himself, wanting to surprise her, although resisting the urge to shoot up her bionic arm was difficult. The second the transport settled onto the supports, he was out the doors, ripping them open and leaving a furious pilot behind.

Somewhere in the room, something smelled of oatmeal and shea butter.

Atlas stopped as his feet grew heavy. The ship rose before him, with a crew of mechanics and engineers surrounding it, sparks flew like fireworks underneath the ship. Bright white lights pierced the steely, austere heaviness of the room.

Somewhere in the distance, heavy rock played on a loudspeaker.

And then he saw her, bent over with a metal cutter in her hand, wearing slacks and a white tank-top, wet with sweat. For the first time in all his long years, he wasn't sure what to do.

So he just stood quietly and watched her work. His fingers twitched to take down her pulled back hair.

Time passed.

Eventually the workers began to retire for the rest cycle, and new men and women came out to replace them. His captain continued to work.

He knew he couldn't stand there forever. He knew that she would eventually retire for the day.

Atlas also knew that he had garnered some attention and that his presence wouldn't be a surprise for much longer.

Reina tore of her gloves and wiped her hands on her slacks. Her arms lifted up in a stretch before she pulled off her goggles. They left a red outline around her eyes.

Enchanting. His mouth dried up.

Atlas stepped forward as her hands ran through her hair and tugged out her hairband.

He brought down his shields and channeled her arm. She stopped, dropping her hands. Her hair fell in cinched waves just past her shoulders.

Atlas made his way toward her, drawn to her, drawn to her in such a way that had nothing to do with his tech until he stood just behind. He lifted a small handheld projector from his pocket.

A beautiful array of flowers from all over the universe filled the space before them. Blue and airy, just like how he use to be.

Reina stopped her breathing, reaching out to ghost her hand through the petals falling from the sky. Atlas waited until she turned around. He could smell the tears on her cheeks.

He could see his reflection in her glistening eyes.

"You requested me, Captain. I'm here reporting for duty."

"Atlas," she said softly.

"Reina." He cupped her face and kissed her tears away. "Don't cry."

"They wouldn't let me see you. Wouldn't let me testify."

"It was rigged."

"That doesn't matter. I should have been there." She sagged into his arms. "I missed you. I missed you so much," Reina sighed into his chest.

"I'm never going to leave you again, Captain. You'll never have to miss me again."

Atlas held her tightly to him and breathed her in. There was no better reason to come back from the dead. And like every moment when they were together, he wanted to make it last for an eternity.

So he did.

Author's note:

. . . .

T hank you for reading Star Navigator, if you liked the story or had a comment please leave me a review! I'm always trying to improve and appreciate the feedback.

I never thought I would find a creative outlet better than drawing and painting. I even went to college for art and graduated with a degree in illustration and a degree in art conservation. It wasn't until last summer, after a particularly long week at work, that I decided to write a story.

Now I have a small library of books on writing, a stack of blank notebooks, and more notes than I can keep up with. I can't wait to bring my stories to life. I only wish I could write faster so I can get them out of my head.

If you love cyborgs, aliens, anti-heroes, and adventure, follow me on facebook or through my blog online for information on new releases and updates.

Join my newsletter for the same information.

Keep an eye out for my fourth book: a reclusive Cyborg hunter who is forced to take an assistant. Monsters, beasts, and aliens oh my!

Naomi Lucas

Made in the USA
Las Vegas, NV
31 March 2022